SOLOMON'S FREEDOM

SOLOMON'S FREEDOM

DENNIS MEREDITH

Glyphus

For information about this title or to order other books and/or electronic media, contact the publisher:

Glyphus LLC
4159 Summit Rd., Purlear, NC 28665
www.glyphus.com
editor@glyphus.com

Library of Congress Control Number: 2012950634

ISBN: 978-1-939118-09-7

Printed in the United States of America

Cover and Interior design: 1106 Design

ACKNOWLEDGEMENTS

My deepest thanks to psychologist Sally Boysen, who generously gave of her time and expertise and offered me the profoundly moving experience of spending time with her extraordinary chimpanzees: Bobby, Darrell, Emma, Harper, Ivy, Keeli, Kermit, Sarah, and Abby. Her laboratory was closed by The Ohio State University in 2006. Sadly, Bobby, Kermit and Darrell died after this book was written.

Special thanks to our eagle-eyed first readers of the manuscript: Mike Bratcher, Vicki Duckworth, Chris Evans, and Wendy Hunter. They helped make the book as perfect as it could be, although any errors are solely the fault of the author.

Also, much gratitude to legal scholar Steven M. Wise for his advice and for his deeply insightful writings on legal rights for animals.

For further information on this novel, go to www.Solomons Freedom.com.

ALSO BY DENNIS MEREDITH

Fiction

The Rainbow Virus (RainbowVirus.com)

Wormholes: A Novel (WormholesaNovel.com)

Non-fiction

Explaining Research: How to Reach Key Audiences to Advance Your Work (ExplainingResearch.com)

To Louette and Mike

CHAPTER 1

Monday morning

Solomon knuckle-walked his hulking body back and forth across the cage, the chimpanzee's coarse black hair raised with anxiety. This was the day it would happen, he was certain. Abby had explained everything and told him it would be all right, but this morning the dread still haunted him. To shake it off, he stretched and yawned, peeling back lips to reveal the formidable ivory canines that helped make him the group's alpha male. His middle-aged joints ached with the usual collection of twinges, and his muscles suffered their usual morning kinks. His great skull throbbed with its usual leaden headache from hard slumber. But all these would recede with the day; they weren't the cause of his unease.

With his body hair puffed out, Solomon presented a formidable sight, but he was an imposing animal even when relaxed, hair flat. His broad, mature face, with its sparse, gray stubble, marked him as beyond youth. But his knowing amber eyes, set beneath a prominent brow, glistened with an intelligence that had taken advantage of those years to achieve both wisdom and shrewdness. Although his body had grown distinctly rotund, his thick arms and legs were packed with muscle capable of hefting his weight with practiced agility.

In their sleeping cages, the others went about their morning routines with just a little more grunting and activity than usual, sensing the tension emanating from their leader. Occasionally, they stole furtive glances through the cage mesh at the pacing Solomon. They also warily watched Jonathan for any clues about the status of the ongoing power struggle between the two big males.

The younger muscular Jonathan gave no hint of his plans for the day. He sat stolidly in the corner of his cage, placidly nibbling with prehensile lips on the yam that was part of the chimpanzees' usual breakfast. He stuck out his legs and stretched easily, grasping the cage mesh with his feet, giving no sign that, only days earlier, for the first time, he had overtly challenged Solomon's authority in the yard. Abruptly, he had refused to pay the normal obeisance—grunting softly, hair flat, bowing down and covering his head so Solomon could tower over him, hair erect, as an alpha ape should. Instead, Jonathan had stalked up near to Solomon, stiff-legged, his own hair on end, notching up his challenge to Solomon's leadership.

As Solomon sat in the corner of his own cage, forearms on knees, he contemplated the ongoing struggle with Jonathan—one reason Abby had given for his departure. He examined the healing slash on his hand, inflected by Jonathan's impressive canines during the fight that had resulted from the young ape's challenge. Despite the wound, Solomon had clearly won by enlisting his ally, the fierce Bruno, to eventually chase Jonathan away.

Surely, the volatile Jonathan plotted to challenge him again today when they met in the dusty open compound. Perhaps he'd give Solomon a bump or an insolent stare, or issue a defiant pant-hooting. And just as surely, there would be more fights, perhaps even bloody ones.

Solomon grasped the heavy steel mesh of the cage wall with thick, leathery coal-black fingers. He hauled his mass adroitly up the side, nimbly swinging across the ceiling mesh into the high transfer tunnel connecting all the cages. The sliding door to the next sleeping cage remained shut, separating him from the others as the keepers arranged the night before. Today was surely the day he would leave, but there was no sound, no movement where the people stayed.

He crouched in the wire tunnel, grunting uneasily to himself, peering into the other cages at the animals moving sleepily about. Besides Jonathan and Bruno, the group included young Earle, the handsome female Sandy, old Caliban, and the young mother Wendy and her infant Wombat.

He could see Sandy best, which was good, because he found her deeply attractive. She turned so he could see her face, with her wide eyes and softly contoured jaw. He remembered their last coupling in the yard during her estrous. Despite their appeal to one another, though, they'd had their quarrels—as had happened yesterday when he had crankily meted out a slap at her. But later they'd made peace; he'd offered a hand as a peace gesture, which she took in her mouth as acceptance, and they'd shared a make-up kiss.

A metallic click interrupted Solomon's reverie. He instantly recognized the sound of the door to their wing unlocking, and he swung out of the tunnel and over to the cage front. He clutched the wire and pressed his large face against the thick mesh trying to peer down the row of cages to the open door. A low babble of unfamiliar human voices filtered through the open door. Solomon sensed that the whispered commands contained an urgency, a tension. The others began to grunt in jittery curiosity at the strangers invading their home. Jonathan, trying to advance his status as alpha male, began a low pant-hooting that grew into a furious scream, slamming his body with a massive boom into the metal door to the outside. The others leaped and swung about their cages in anxious reaction to the visitors.

But Solomon remained quiet, focusing his senses. Now was the time, he knew. He stared suspiciously at a shadowy figure in the doorway. It was joined by another, and perhaps a third. At first he wasn't sure, but one of them appeared to be Abby striding toward him down the row.

It *was* Abby! Their leader, their protector, the most trusted human in their lives. The apes danced and swung about with gleeful hoots of greeting or raucous lip-razzes to attract her cherished attention. But she merely greeted the others in passing, stopping in front of his cage. Solomon pressed himself as close to the mesh as he could, studying her face for clues to the decision he still did not understand. The slump of her shoulders told him it bothered her. He wanted to communicate with her, to go to the machine room to make more talking with the touch screen.

But the hypodermic needle she brought up meant there would be no more talking about this. Now would come the needle-sleep. The others saw the needle, and their raucous hooting and screaming rose in volume to thicken the atmosphere with fear.

She slid a plastic pipe through an opening in the cage mesh—the pipe with the cutout used for taking blood and giving shots. Without being asked, he slid his arm into the pipe, exposing his arm to her, looking into her eyes.

"Okay, Solly, we've got to give you a shot," said Abby. "Just put you to sleep for a while. Got to give you a physical and check that wound. And then. . ." Her voice trailed off. Solomon detected a strain in her voice, not a difficult task after decades of paying rapt attention to her every mood. She didn't want to finish the sentence. Then she said more emphatically, "Here goes, Solly."

He hooted softly, in a question. Why was she so nervous? From beyond the door, the strangers' voices rose again, one calling, "We need to get this operation underway, Dr. Philips."

Solomon gave a small whimper as the needle entered his arm, as Abby pushed the plunger. He'd had many such shots before, but this was different. Abby was trembling.

A wisp of sleep fog began to curl through his brain. His vision blurring, he turned to see the strangers walking along the row, their appearance producing a new round of raucous eruptions from the others. Jonathan pant-hooted his way up to another piercing scream, and Bruno let loose an alarm whoop, as Earle skittered about in panic, hair raised. Others cowered, barked or slammed themselves against the wall with clattering crashes.

But for Solomon, the sounds faded as the fog thickened and brought darkness. The last thing he heard was Abby saying in the distance of receding consciousness, "It's okay, Solly. We just have to do this."

CHAPTER 2

Tuesday morning

"So, sir, you claim you shot the victim in self-defense?" asked the prosecutor, glancing dubiously back and forth between the witness and the jury. The prosecutor, with his darting movements, prominent nose and receding chin, looked like a hawk trying to figure out which rabbit to go after first.

"Yeah . . . self-defense," muttered Johnny "Eyes" Califano, shifting his perspiring bulk in the witness chair. He shrugged and opened his pudgy hands to show the sincere unhappiness he felt that such a terrible thing had happened to Rufio Gonzalez. The fleshy folds of his jowls nearly engulfed the knot of his thin black tie, and the tie draped down over his ample front in a futile sartorial attempt, reaching down to the general vicinity of his belt, which the overhang of his belly also concealed.

Califano directed his small, close-set eyes as beseechingly as he could toward the jury members, who studiously avoided his gaze.

Then he similarly scanned the large wood-paneled courtroom and its capacity crowd. He especially concentrated on the gathered reporters typing his answers on their laptops and the courtroom artist sketching his portrait for the evening news. However, he avoided looking at his victim, Rufio Gonzalez, who sat in the front row, fidgeting at being in a courtroom, even though he wasn't the defendant this time.

The prosecutor rolled his eyes and paced the floor. "Six times you shot at him in self-defense," he said, his voice soaked in sarcasm. "*Six times,* Mr. Califano. Twice you got him: once in the shoulder, once in the leg. Seriously? Self-defense?"

"Yeah, well, he was still up, still threatenin' me. I feared for my life."

"Mr. Califano, he was still up because one of your nine-millimeter bullets threw him back against the wall!"

"Yeah, well, I couldn't see—

"I have no further questions," the prosecutor interrupted, waving dismissively and sitting down, making sure the jury got a good look at the disdainful expression on his face.

"Well, I can see from the defense counsel's posture that he wishes to spring to redirect," quipped the judge, a balding portly man, who slouched easily in a chair he'd occupied for twenty-three years, watching the pyrotechnics of fireball lawyers like the one who was about to take the floor.

"Indeed, Your Honor, I certainly do," announced defense lawyer R. William Colter, coming confidently to his feet behind the defense table. He paused to let a silence settle on the courtroom, all the better to dramatize his presentation. He stepped smoothly from behind the defense table, adjusting his wine-red tie and buttoning the jacket of his tailored dark blue suit, which draped elegantly on his slim, athletic frame. Although a compact man of medium height, the confidence of his easy animal grace gave him more presence than his size would normally command.

He was also only conventionally handsome, with a small straight nose, an expressive mouth that grinned readily to reveal white, even teeth, and a finely sculpted jaw. But the face was rendered more remarkable by piercing gray eyes that made it magnetic to women and uncomfortable to men.

His jaw set, his expression serious, eyes riveted on his client, Robert William Colter took one step forward, preparing to lead the jury to the golden light of Truth.

"Mr. Califano, how is your vision?"

"Not good." Califano shifted forward in his chair, his prodigious jowls now devouring the tie knot entirely.

"How bad? Twenty/thirty? Twenty/forty?" With each question, Colter took a step closer to his client, bringing the jury closer and closer to the defendant's answers. Closer and closer to Colter's truth.

"Don't know; just not real good."

"Well, let's just find out," said Colter, stepping back, clasping his hands together and smiling benignly. "Your Honor, I would like to ask Mr. Califano to step down while I call his ophthalmologist." The judge agreed, and the ophthalmologist made his way forward, slight, balding, and with stylishly gold-rimmed glasses. He precisely testified to Califano's visual defects, as the prosecutor tried his best to maintain his composure, feeling the first inkling that the momentum and the jury might be slipping away.

Next, Califano resumed his place on the stand, arranging his bulk in the creaking chair.

"So, your ophthalmologist has testified that you have twenty/two hundred eyesight, Mr. Califano. Does that surprise you?" Colter stood near the jury, so that his client would face them in answering questions, the better to establish rapport.

"Well, no, it don't. I ain't never seen that good."

"Did you wear your glasses the day of the shooting?"

"Nah. They was broke. Took them to the glasses place to be fixed. Garry, he drove me to Rufio's and waited in the car."

"So when you walked into that dark garage out of the sunlight without your glasses on, you couldn't tell what Mr. Gonzalez was picking up?"

"Looked like a gun."

"So, you shot him." Now Colter moved away down the jury railing, bringing the jury into the questioning, into his truth.

"Had to."

"Mr. Califano, could you put your glasses on now?"

"Yeah, sure." The defendant fumbled in several pockets before producing a pair of thick-lensed glasses, placing them on his large face. The glasses magnified his eyes to large, limpid globes.

"Okay," said Colter smiling. "Now I understand why they call you 'eyes.'" Several jurors smiled, and one laughed.

The prosecutor leaped up. "Objection. This is grandstanding . . . a piece of theater."

"Overruled," said the judge. "The defendant can put on his glasses if he's asked to."

"And you shot at him six times?" asked Colter, his hand hovering above the railing of the jury box, not touching it, which would be a breach of court etiquette, but seeming to reach out to the jury.

"Yeah, six."

"Mr. Califano, are you a good shot?"

"Damn good shot."

"How do you know?"

"I won the marksmanship trophy at my shootin' club six times. Gardena Gun and Social Club."

"Objection, Your Honor." Once more the prosecutor rose. "This is leading nowhere. So what if the defendant was a good shot?"

Colter raised his eyebrows. "Your Honor, I intend to show relevance." He retained a tolerant smile as the judge overruled the objection.

"Mr. Califano, you're a good enough shot to have killed Mr. Gonzalez, are you not?"

"Yeah. I coulda pumped all six into the little spi. . . into Mr. Gonzalez."

"But you did shoot six times. And you hit him only twice, only wounding him. Was it because you couldn't see?"

"Yeah . . . sure . . . if I coulda seen him, I woulda iced him."

"So, again, why did you shoot him?"

"Yeah, I feared for my life. And I couldn't see the . . . uh, Mr. Gonzalez."

Colter scanned the jury, as if making sure that each member understood the import of what his client had said. "No further questions, Your Honor," he said, sitting down.

The prosecutor regarded Colter with a stony expression, jaw clenched, but, as an idea formed, his jaw unclenched. He signaled that he had another question and then rose, a faint, smug smile on his face.

"Mr. Califano, if you really can't see, why haven't you worn your glasses in court?" asked the prosecutor, inclining his head and raising his eyebrows expectantly.

"He said I looked better without them. Y'know, big lenses and all."

"Who told you that?"

"My lawyer."

The prosecutor shook his head and smiled knowingly at the clever lawyer's trick he just knew would not sway the jury from the absolutely correct verdict of guilty.

But Colter was ready with the finale in his carefully crafted legal theater. Science would rescue his client. Califano was excused and the ophthalmologist recalled, sitting with the primly erect posture of one who provided only scientific fact.

"Sir, my apologies, but I forgot to ask you about this earlier." Colter shrugged and smiled at the jury, his humility on display. "You have prepared a slide that compares normal visual acuity with that of my client?" asked Colter.

"Yes, I have," answered the ophthalmologist. The digital projector and screen were set up, and the image appeared. The left side of its split scenes showed a clear view of a man holding a wrench; the right, a blurry image of perhaps the same figure, perhaps the same object.

"Sir, when you see the image my client might have seen, can you make out what the object is being held?"

"Oh, no," answered the ophthalmologist. "I can barely make out that it's a man."

"And what would you conclude from this slide?"

"Well, I certainly wouldn't go near your client when he didn't have his glasses."

Again, someone in the jury giggled, and a few smiled. Colter allowed himself a quick, triumphant glance at the prosecutor.

•　•　•

The golden sunlight that washed the southern California day shone especially for R. William Colter, triumphant attorney. The traffic along the broad, straight avenue through downtown Los Angeles had been cleared solely for his benefit. The crowds of people—from intent corporate types to the tourists strolling the sidewalks—had come out to pay tribute to him in his victory parade.

As he drove toward his office, full of lunch and of himself, Colter just knew that his inevitable win had given him rightful title to this glorious day. After all, he'd masterfully insinuated reasonable doubt into the mind of every jury member. The defeated prosecutor had immediately requested a recess so he could figure a riposte to Colter's thrust. Colter had left his law associate, Darrell Beckman, to wait for any plea-bargain offers. He drove himself in a one-car parade down Wilshire Boulevard in the silver Mercedes sedan, his meant-to-impress "court" car, spending the time at the stop lights grandly surveying his domain.

But still, he needed something more. At a stop light, he spoke a number into the car's phone system and waited for an answer over the speaker. He decided that the entire cell phone system was waiting to serve him, too.

Cindy's bright feminine voice answered.

"Hi, sweetheart," said Colter. "Where are you?"

"New York," answered the voice. "Where are you?"

"Here in LA. How long'll you be there? You back tonight?"

"Nope. A week. Magazine shoot."

"Damn. I wanted to celebrate."

"You got that scum off?"

"Cindy, he's not scum; he's an innocent-until-proven-guilty client."

"Sure, Bobby, and my hairdresser likes girls. Gotta go. Call on the set."

"Okay, so call me when you get back. Miss you."

"Miss you, too."

He disconnected, drove for a block thinking, and at the next red light activated the BlackBook app on his smartphone. Thinking for a moment, he specified a geographic area, body type, and a history of successful and satisfying sexual encounters. Several listings appeared, and he scanned the photos, chose one and touched the screen to dial the number. Another bright feminine voice answered.

"Rachael, sweetheart, you up for a ridiculously extravagant celebration?"

Rachael laughed, which he took as a yes, so he picked a restaurant, Providence on Melrose, a top bistro that was a good place to see, and be seen by, prospective clients. He called his legal secretary, Sheba Sinclair, to make reservations for him and Rachael.

But Sheba had other ideas. "Bobby, you might have to put your date off," she said. "You've got a visitor. I put her in your office."

"Her?"

"Not your favorite kind of 'her.' An old lady."

"Who?"

"First, tell me. You won the case?"

"Sheba, I *buried* that case under reasonable doubt." Colter dove past the massive stone LA County Art Museum, only a few miles from his office now.

"And you're not going to thank me?" Sheba asked. Colter knew that if he had actually been standing there in Sheba's office, she would have been looking reprovingly at him over her half-glasses.

"Why should I thank you? I thought of the vision thing."

"And who thought of presenting the vision comparison? Who did, Bobby?"

"Who is the old lady?"

"I should get a day off for that. My baby's got some important games I gotta go watch."

"Your baby is six foot two and can swish three pointers all day without you."

Sheba assumed she'd won a day off of her choosing. "Yeah, well, he still needs his mama in the stands. Name on her card is Sarah Huntington."

Colter sat up straighter. "You mean like Huntington Gardens?" He'd attended receptions at the vast public garden estate in San Marino donated by the old California family. Even a distant relationship would be really something.

"Don't know. But it's a fancy card. She's dressed like money. Designer dress. Has an assistant with her."

"Yeah, well, Cindy says there are lots of designer knockoffs. Google her, check the credit bureaus; see what you can find out." He started to hang up and then stopped himself. "And call Digger. Ask him to give you what's in his head about her." His private investigator, Digger Murray, had juicy information stored within his grizzled old cop noggin that would never show up in any database, which was why Colter depended on him so heavily as an information source. That, and the fact that Digger had been his father's partner on the force for twenty years and was Colter's godfather.

Ten minutes later, Colter guided the Mercedes into the shade of the underground garage. He flipped off his sunglasses and deftly swerved into the space beside his white 2010 Porsche. It needed washing, he reminded himself. Tomorrow he'd drive the 2011 BMW or the 2009 Corvette. Or, maybe he'd finally spring for that gorgeous red Viper as his reward for the latest case. Johnny Califano's employers were quite willing to pay handsomely to defend him.

He nodded at the guard and took the elevator to his fifth-floor office, high enough to be prestigious, but not so high as to be ostentatious. He didn't want clients to think he overcharged because of lavish office perks, especially clients whose mistrust could lead to an abrupt drastic deterioration in his health.

Nevertheless, several local fine arts dealers had profited handsomely when Colter and Associates decorated its offices. The walnut-paneled walls held a Turner lithograph of a Parisian city scene, several handsome Nathan Lowe landscapes and a minor Degas sketch. And the oak floors were covered with matching Chinese Aubusson carpets of wine and gold. All the furnishings were designed to inspire confidence in the venerable, established firm, which had opened its offices five years ago.

Sheba's desktop was almost clear as always, except for two neat piles of papers and files. The amply built woman with the rich caramel skin sat with her usual stern authority behind the desk, wearing the ubiquitous telephone headset. The headset allowed her free range to gesture, which she sometimes did emphatically when berating a foolish court clerk or a lawyer unfortunate enough to get crosswise with her. Clenched between her teeth was a ball-point pen, a habit from when she'd quit smoking. As he'd expected, she did indeed look reprovingly at him over the top of her half-glasses.

"Well?" he asked.

She shifted the mouthpiece of her phone headset out of the way. "Digger's out in Palm Springs. His cell went to voice mail. But I did get some newspaper stuff. *LA Times* mainly." She tapped a few computer keys with elegantly manicured fingernails, launching a list of headlines scrolling down the screen. Colter leaned over and guided the mouse, clicking on the headlines to bring up the articles. Some were from the society pages, some from the business section, and a few from the news section. As he read, he furrowed his brow and scratched his cheek.

"Whuff!" he exclaimed finally. "Interesting lady. I'll see her, all right."

Chapter 3

Tuesday afternoon

Colter strode into his office wearing a fully deployed smile, adding a friendly gleam to his eyes. An older woman sat in one of the sumptuous leather armchairs that flanked his leather sofa, a younger woman on the sofa itself.

The older woman regarded him with the appraising straight-on scrutiny one might apply to a painting by an artist one does not quite approve of. The spare, thin-faced woman, perhaps in her seventies, seemed to occupy by force of personality the entirety of the large leather chair. Her small, wrinkled hands rested lightly on its arms, her legs crossed at the ankles, her posture erect and non-negotiable with regard to any infirmities of age. She wore a wedding ring whose diamond would have easily bought Colter several Vipers. Her straight gray hair was styled to a length that could be held back with a scarf for tennis or an afternoon on a yacht. She wore a conservative dark-blue wool pants suit with a blue-and-white striped Egyptian cotton blouse, open at the neck. Colter recognized the ensemble as either Armani or Marie Gray, and not off the rack, but hand-tailored. He'd made Cindy teach him about women's clothes. In his line of work, any bit of information about a client or an adversary could make the difference.

The woman on the sofa smiled shyly—young and round-faced, with short, mousy-brown hair and efficiently dressed in a simple dark brown skirt and pale yellow silk blouse, both likely Ann Taylor designs. She held in her lap a leather-covered iPad. A laptop sat in front of her on the coffee table, its screen filled with text, and a smartphone sat beside it.

"My apologies," said Colter. "My secretary said you've been waiting. I haven't had the pleasure. I'm Bobby Colter."

She took his offered hand without rising. "I know who you are. This is my assistant, Emma Welch."

He shook hands with Emma and sat down in the other armchair, offering them coffee, tea or soft drinks, all of which Sarah Huntington refused.

"Have we met?" he asked. "Perhaps at the Norton Simon opening of the Mondrian exhibit last month."

"No, but my advisors tell me you have a reputation for being a clever son-of-a-bitch."

Colter startled a bit and chuckled. "I have been called those things, both together and separately."

"In fact, some of my advisors warned me not to engage you because of that reputation. But I've decided, in fact, to give you the case."

"Give me the case?" He wrinkled his brow in puzzlement, maintaining the smile. "Well, I would need to understand what kind of case we're talking about. I'm a criminal defense attorney, you know, and I—"

"Of course, I know. We'll talk on the way. The reason I came in without an appointment is that this is an emergency. You need to start the process of getting him out. I don't know how long he has to live."

"Get who out?"

"Solomon."

"And he is where?"

"He's being held against his will." Her voice tightened with a twinge of anger, perhaps even paranoia, alerting him. The last time a client had adopted that tone, he'd had to hire a bodyguard for two months.

"Mrs. Huntington—"

"Call me Sarah." The instruction was not so much an invitation to familiarity as a means to more efficient communication.

"Okay, call me Bobby."

"I'll call you Mr. Colter." It was not so much a snub as a means to remind him that they were not friends; he was an employee whom she would decide how to address.

"Sarah, to be honest, I've got a rather pressing engagement, so perhaps we could schedule a later meeting to fully explore your problem."

"Maybe this will encourage you to consider immediate action." She nodded to the assistant, who handed a check to Colter.

After looking at the amount, Colter tried his best to hold his expression to one of merely mild surprise. "Fifty thousand dollars. This is a retainer?"

"That is a signing bonus for taking the case. I'll pay whatever retainer and other fees you require."

The check firmly in his hand, Colter got up and pressed the button on his intercom, asking Sheba to step in. "Well, we can certainly begin to explore your case now, particularly since it is pressing. Shall we—"

"You need to *see* what's going on," said Sarah, rising from her chair and starting out the door, nearly colliding with Sheba. Emma efficiently gathered up her electronics and stood to follow her employer.

"Well, you understand it's extremely unusual for me to make a site visit this early in a case," he said, handing Sheba the check, watching the secretary's eyes widen in surprise. "I have a very reliable investigator who can determine whether—"

"Mr. Colter, understand my position." Sarah Huntington smiled tolerantly at him, as she had no doubt smiled at many other recalcitrant men who ended up doing exactly as she wished. "I have already said I would pay whatever fees you require. I also have many friends. They can be your friends, too. Or, they need not be."

Two seconds went by, and then Colter announced "We're going out," smoothly to Sheba. "Please have Mr. Murray call me at his earliest convenience. And cancel my dinner engagement." Sheba nodded, knowing the drill. She would track down Digger Murray on whatever low-life investigative job he'd gotten for himself. And she would retrieve Rachael's gift history from her database and would call the shopping service to select a trinket at an appropriate level to cushion the blow of the broken date. Sheba could also forge a note of apology that would leave him fully eligible for future dates.

Colter opened the office door for Sarah Huntington, and they walked to the elevator, followed by Emma. In the elevator car, as the floor numbers counted down on the lighted display, he tried his best diplomatic cross-examination tactics to get information on the case. Was this Solomon a political prisoner? Held by a government agency? The police?

But Sarah Huntington repeated only that Solomon was being held against his will and that her advisors had recommended a good courtroom attorney.

"My car is in the garage," he said as they emerged on the ground floor.

"Mine's out front," she said, marching toward the front door, slowing for Emma to open the door for her. They emerged into the sunlight to see a waiting ivory-colored limousine with a trim middle-aged man in a chauffeur's uniform standing beside it. He opened the door and Emma climbed in, stowed her portable office, and sat primly. Sarah followed, but Colter hesitated at the door, performing a complex accounting that balanced Sarah's eccentricity and her strange urgency against fifty thousand dollars and the golden promise of new contacts. Money and power won.

"Well, Mr. Colter? Do I get myself another lawyer?"

Colter checked his customary three cell phones before crawling into the limousine. He patted the two obvious phones in his jacket pockets, and, as inconspicuously as he could, checked the tiny disposable phone nestled in a hidden pocket in an intimate region of his pants. His practice of equipping himself with multiple phones had begun when a dead phone put him in some danger from a pissed-off client. Now, though, having all his phones would allow him to avoid any possibility of being incommunicado if Sarah Huntington had somehow gone batty.

As the limousine accelerated ponderously onto the Ventura Freeway headed west, Colter tried again with his questions.

"At least tell me something about this Solomon."

"He's very bright," she answered curtly. "And he doesn't deserve to die."

CHAPTER 4

Tuesday afternoon

"You will understand the situation when we arrive," said Sarah Huntington dismissively, turning to occupy herself with more important concerns than explanations to her hired lawyer. The expensive beach houses slid past on the trip along the freeway toward Santa Barbara, as Sarah went over plans for an ASPCA charity benefit with her assistant, who dutifully used the touch-screen iPad to move names around on a seating chart and type notes into the database on her laptop.

Colter eavesdropped on the process, gazing out the tinted window at the passing cars whose rubbernecking occupants tried to see through the limousine's deeply tinted glass to spot the movie star who might be inside. As Sarah Huntington reeled off guests' names, he noted at least four people who might eventually use his services to get acquitted of one white-collar crime or another.

The limousine exited the freeway into Montecito, an exclusive enclave just beyond the Spanish Mission buildings of downtown Santa Barbara. The car wound its way up a mountain road whose sides grew thick with eucalyptus, punctuated by the occasional gated entrance to an estate. Finally, the car eased to a stop at a black iron gate that looked massive enough to stop a tank. The gate was fronted by a raised steel barrier that certainly could. Beside the gate stood a small granite guardhouse, from which emerged a khaki-uniformed guard, his wide black leather belt supporting a holstered pistol, mace can, cuffs, and a billy club. A wire emerged from his collar, attached to an earpiece/microphone in his ear. Unsmiling, he adjusted his sunglasses and donned a military-style cap sporting an American flag and script initials WD.

The limousine's driver lowered his window and announced Mrs. Huntington, and the guard spoke into his earpiece microphone. After a moment, he shook his head decisively at the driver, who looked into the mirror at Sarah for instructions.

She lowered the window and stared at the guard, who shifted uncomfortably, even though he had the advantage of a pistol and eyes hidden behind sunglasses. "Tell him he'd damned well better let me in," she snapped. "I have come with a lawyer, and I can arrange pickets, publicity, and a great deal of trouble. Also, ask him if he'd wish the story to get out about that recent Bangkok business. I'd be pleased to call my friend at the *Times*."

Again the guard mumbled into the earpiece. Sarah raised the window and, staring straight ahead, said, "You never heard me mention Bangkok."

"Attorney-client privilege," answered Colter.

After several minutes, the guard bent his head, listening to a message in his earpiece. The message he received sent him back into his guardhouse. The steel barrier lowered into the pavement, and the huge gate began to slide ponderously open.

The limousine eased forward along a tree-lined drive, emerging finally onto a sprawling mountaintop estate whose vast green lawns looked out over the flat, gray-green Pacific gleaming in the lowering sun.

The three-story mansion sat like a carved stone outcropping at the top of the lawn, its elaborately ornate front marking it as a French Renaissance-style chateau. In front of the mansion, a huge American flag billowed in the afternoon breeze atop a white flagpole. The car turned into a circular driveway leading beneath a large portico of the mansion's central wing and eased to a stop. Colter, Sarah and Emma emerged into the cool dry shade, and Colter started for the front door.

"Not that way. This way," Sarah instructed Colter, marching off along a brick sidewalk that led around the side of the mansion. "You stay," she said to Emma, who settled back into the limousine. Colter followed Sarah past a life-sized bronze statue of a cowboy on horseback and around to a side rose garden surrounding a broad patio with a sweeping view of the ocean. Still, Sarah marched resolutely on, finally reaching the back of the mansion and another garden richly planted with flowers and ferns shaded by giant ficus and oak trees. Amidst the grove rose a huge-roofed steel-mesh cage, almost as high as the mansion, covering perhaps an acre. It consisted of two nested enclosures, with a narrow walking path between the cage walls.

Sarah and Colter wound along a brick walk past the flower beds and toward the side of the cage nearest the back entrance to the mansion, which had an expansive fieldstone patio and sets of French doors leading into the house. They came up under a roofed lanai beside the cage. It appeared to be a viewing area, with long oak benches sitting across from a section of the cage in which the mesh was covered by thick Lexan plastic smudged by several large blotches. Colter stood close to the clear plastic wall, to get a good look at the cage's interior. The grassy floor of the cage was inset with three large artificial boulders and strewn with several red and blue plastic barrels. From one side jutted a large, leafless artificial climbing tree, and dominating the cage center was a two-story steel-pipe framework hung with thick ropes, a tire swing and a wooden-stepped rope ladder. Across the cage on the outside stood a small gray stucco building that ran its full length, with a dark window, a steel door for keepers to service the cage, and a low sliding-door exit into the building. But the cage seemed empty of any animal occupant.

Still standing next to the wall, Colter turned to his client. "Now, Mrs. Huntington—"

"Sarah."

"All right, Sarah. I've been patient so far, but now I need explanations. This is a cage for animals. Is this where we're supposed to see my client?"

Before Sarah could answer, out of the corner of his eye Colter glimpsed a large, dark shape emerge from behind a boulder, and a low animal grunting began, rising to a succession of noisy inhaled pants followed by loud hoots. As he turned, the dark mass erupted toward him, filling his vision with screaming animal fury, slamming into the clear wall with a skull-rattling crash. The assault drove Colter stumbling backward tripping on a bench, nearly flipping over its back. He recovered and pulled himself up to see Sarah standing calmly before a furious chimpanzee that bared its teeth and screamed with a ferocity that would send most people running in terror.

"What the hell is that?" asked Colter, gauging whether even two rows of steel mesh could hold such a huge, vicious creature.

The menacing animal stalked away from them, its hair on end, still screaming. It flung a plastic barrel into the air, climbed a rope, swung back down and turned, beginning to pant-hoot, gathering itself for another run at the humans. It launched its body once more, and this time Colter stood well back as it slammed against the plastic, bounced off it some ten feet, landing at a powerful gallop. The animal, seemingly satisfied that it had fully expressed its hatred for the humans, shambled away onto a rock and sat down, arms on its knees, glaring at the intruders from beneath thick brows.

"That's Solomon," said Sarah. "That's your client."

"A monkey?"

"It's an ape. Monkeys have tails. More specifically, he's a chimpanzee."

"Chimpanzees are little and cute. That thing would never qualify as cute."

"He's grown. Males like him reach a hundred and fifty pounds, but his size is irrelevant, counselor. Cute or not, he's the one I want you to free."

"Jesus, you're kidding," said Colter. "An *ape*?" The chimpanzee climbed down off the rock, perhaps contemplating another assault, so Colter moved away from under the lanai. "I take it you want me to free this ape from the owner of this house." As he turned toward the mansion, he saw a person peering down from a second-story window. The shadow of the house interior made the pale, puffy face seem to float like a spectral presence. The face stared down at the cage for a moment and then at Colter, and then it slid away, out of sight.

CHAPTER 5

Tuesday afternoon

During the hike with Sarah back around the mansion through the elaborate gardens and to the front portico, a slight shift of draperies and the flashes of movement behind the windows told Colter someone was watching them from within. When they arrived at the front, Emma waited at the top of the brown granite steps before a massive, ornate steel door, which stood partly open. Blocking the door was a large-chested, middle-aged man in a dark blue blazer with an American flag lapel pin. His steel-gray hair, brushed back in a short pompadour, revealed a hairline that had refused to retreat. His jutting chin showed a deep scar that told of past battles, perhaps in the boxing ring, perhaps in combat. Sarah determinedly started up the steps, followed by Colter.

"Mrs. Huntington, he wants to know why you're here," said the man, still blocking the door. He crisply announced into his earpiece microphone, "Hold positions."

"He *knows* why I'm here," said Sarah, peering defiantly up at the large man.

"Mrs. Huntington, please—"

"Fred, I'd like you to meet my lawyer, R. William Colter. Mr. Colter, Fred Lunt. Takes care of security here. Very able man. Very reasonable."

Colter stuck out his hand, and Lunt's enveloped it in a grip that told of power carefully disciplined.

"Fred, my lawyer needs to understand what's going on here."

Colter decided not to argue with her about being her lawyer. His dad, a shrewd cop in his day, taught that keeping quiet at the right time could mean the difference between success and failure, even life and death.

"Mrs. Huntington, do you really need to see him? His health is—"

"Move, Fred."

Lunt hesitated for an instant, then stepped aside, and they entered a three-story atrium illuminated by light filtering down from a stained glass dome onto a small, lush garden of tree ferns, palms and fragrant orchids. They skirted the circular garden, the click of their footsteps on the marble floor echoing in the museum-like quiet. Behind the garden lay a great hall hung with a gigantic wrought-iron chandelier. Blue and gold Renaissance tapestries covered the walls, and a Persian rug the size of a racquetball court lay on the floor. On either side of the hall, curving stone staircases with wrought-iron banisters wound gracefully upward.

Following Sarah through the hall, Lunt tried again. "Mrs. Huntington, I'd be happy to pass on whatever message or information you wish."

"Where is he?"

"The flag room, last time I was up there."

"Then go on, and tell him I'm coming." Lunt bowed slightly and trotted briskly up the stairs on the right.

"Be patient, Mr. Colter. I know you lawyers want all the facts, but the good ones also want to know all the emotions involved. God knows, I've dealt with enough lawyers. I didn't think you could really appreciate this case without seeing all this."

"Well, Sarah, you understand I still haven't taken it. Especially since I think there's more to this. But I'll give you your money's worth for your. . . uh. . . signing bonus."

"Damned right, you will," said Sarah. She turned to Emma. "We'll be an hour at the most. Call the Chandlers and tell them our dinner will be half-an-hour late." She began to climb the curving staircase, and Colter followed.

On the second floor, the stairs opened onto a long walnut-paneled hallway lined with nineteenth-century paintings of western scenes, including several by Frederic Remington, Colter noted. He and Sarah walked past Indian raids, buffalo hunts, wranglers roping steers, and cowboys diverting stampedes. At the end of the long hall, they entered a high-ceilinged room that ran the entire width of the main wing. Floor-to-ceiling picture windows looked out over the green gardens below where lay the huge cage and, beyond them, to the tan southern California mountains in the distance. The walls were hung with dozens of American flags, large and small, each sealed in its own glass case. Flanking a massive marble fireplace were large leather sofas trimmed with carved wood leaves. The sofas were flanked by massive end tables, whose carvings matched the sofas'. Overstuffed leather easy chairs sat across from the fireplace. The room's center was taken up by three long glass-topped cases, each containing an array of small flags, jeweled pins, gold medallions, sabers and daggers.

A large door next to the fireplace opened, and Lunt pushed in a wheelchair bearing a frail, sallow-faced man, his sagging body bearing the remnants of a muscular build. His sparse graying hair still showed faint hints of black but giving way to liver-spotted scalp. His short, white beard circled his jaw, the lack of a mustache making him resemble an old mariner but one whose seaman's heartiness had been eroded by illness. He seemed to struggle to hold his head up, his heavy-lidded brown eyes surrounded by the wrinkled topography of suffering.

Behind Lunt walked a slim, handsome young woman with a model's high cheekbones, full lips and wide-set eyes. She wore a model's precisely applied, understated makeup, a simple white silk blouse and gray skirt and low-heeled shoes. The woman sat down on a sofa, crossing her long legs demurely and arranging herself decorously. Lunt rolled the wheelchair to a stop beside her, locking its wheels, and the man crankily regarded Sarah as one might an annoying salesman.

"Hello, Walter," said Sarah. The name sparked a shock of recognition in Colter. Jesus, he thought, this is Walter Drake! He should have known! But this frail man was not the Drake he had seen in so many news stories. That Drake had fiercely relished leading his media companies into any battle that came his way, from libel suits to presidential campaigns. But this man seemed a pale ghost of that earlier incarnation.

"Hello, Mother," said Drake in a weak, breathy voice.

Mother? Colter, stunned a second time, looked from mother to son, trying to use his lawyer's acumen to sort out the relationship. As they faced one another with grim expressions, the space between them seemed to harbor an almost palpable mix of contradictory emotions—venomous love, warm hatred, repulsive attraction, endearing estrangement.

Like any lawyer, Colter hated surprises, and he'd just suffered two huge ones. For one, his well-heeled client was mother to a very well-known heel—the dangerously eccentric Walter Drake, multibillionaire owner of web sites, television stations, radio networks, newspapers, paper mills, magazines, a baseball team and entire blocks of urban real estate. The other nasty surprise was that this powerful, vengeful man was apparently his opponent.

"You know why I'm here," said Sarah. "After I found out your plans, I retained R. William Colter here. He's a criminal lawyer, because what you are doing is criminal. I wanted to show him first-hand this crime that you are about to commit."

Drake did not acknowledge Colter, his tired eyes still determinedly fixed on his mother. Colter was an afterthought in this confrontation. "This *crime*, as you call it, is to save my life," he whispered.

Sarah turned to Colter. "Mr. Colter, my son has obtained Solomon under false pretenses. He made a large donation to the Primate Language Laboratory at California Technical University and asked for legal ownership of Solomon. He told them he wanted to own the animal as a sign of his commitment to preservation and research. But he didn't want to buy the chimpanzee. He wanted to buy its heart."

Her assertion took a moment for Colter to understand. "Heart? You mean as in heart transplant?" Trying to absorb the concept, he moved to the large window overlooking the cage to see Solomon's dark form cross the grassy expanse and climb onto the rock, settling himself down to eat an apple.

"What's it called, Walter?" asked Sarah. "What's the technical term for this murder?"

"A tissue-engineered transplant." Drake gestured to have himself wheeled to the window beside Colter, and he stared somberly down at Solomon. "They've got this list for human heart transplants. I'm low on it, but I need a new heart. This damned thing is shot." He patted his chest.

"You're perfectly fine!" exclaimed Sarah. "You've got the LVAD. You can go forever."

"LVAD?" asked Colter.

"Left ventricular assist device." Still looking down at Solomon, Drake tapped his chest again, then a bag attached to his wheelchair, from which wires led to his chest. "Electrically powered pump implanted in my chest. Keeps me going for now." He wheeled around to face Sarah. "But pretty soon, even that won't help. My heart's going. Besides, I've got no heartbeat! I want a fucking heart! And that animal will give me what I want."

"You want to take his heart?" asked Colter "But you can't transplant an animal's heart. It gets rejected, right?"

Ignoring Colter's question, Drake smiled and with an effort meant to impress her, wheeled himself over to the young woman. "Besides, my dear wife, Clair, deserves more than an old guy with an electric pump." He turned back to Colter. "I don't want the animal's heart, exactly. I want the extracellular matrix. I've given a shitload of money for research on tissue engineering, and it's paid off. The surgeons take the animal's heart and give it to the tissue engineers. They biochemically remove the living tissue leaving the matrix—the heart's scaffolding. They seed the matrix with my heart cells. It grows a new heart. *My* heart."

"You couldn't use another animal heart? Pig?"

"That's taking a chance, the scientists tell me. There might be immune factors in the pig heart matrix that trigger rejection or other complications. And why should I take that chance? I've got my own primate donor. Ninety-nine percent human, genetically."

"Tell him the rest," commanded Sarah. "Tell him what you plan to do to *all* chimpanzees!"

Drake took Clair's hand. "You mean what I'm doing *for* every person who needs a new heart, don't you?" He waved his hand. "There are maybe a thousand of these animals in captivity, in so-called sanctuaries. If my tissue-engineered heart is successful, that means they could give a thousand people brand-new hearts."

"You know they're listed as endangered, and—"

"Endangered? The ones in captivity? They're non-breeders. Their life or death won't make one bit of difference to the species' survival." Color was returning to his face as he continued. "But I have a plan that will. I'll give half a billion dollars to preserve chimps in the wild, increasing the population so—"

"So you can murder them, too!"

"—so they can be sustainably harvested and also farmed for organs. Not just hearts, but *any* organ that can be grown on a primate matrix. It'll be a medical triumph!"

"Okay, the government prohibits experimentation on the captive animals."

"This is not some lab experiment," spat Drake, clutching the arms of his wheel chair. "This is directly using them to save human lives."

Colter felt a bit overwhelmed by the new information. He sought to bring the debate back to his arena. "Legally—"

"Legally, it's an animal," interrupted Drake. "And legally it's mine. This is America. See these flags?" He turned the wheelchair from the windows, gesturing expansively at his collection on the walls. "They were taken into battle; they flew over the White House, over Congress. They even went into space. They stand for American rights, including the right to private property."

"Nice speech, Walter, but Solomon is not mere property."

"Bullshit. The animal is mine to do with as I please."

"Not to murder him," said Sarah. "Mr. Colter will see to that."

Drake glared at her for a moment, but the fatigue of his illness began to overcome him, and he slumped in his wheelchair. His face grew even paler, a sheen of perspiration blooming on his forehead. He feebly waved his hand at Lunt. "Show these people out." Then to the young woman. "Clair, I'm tired now." Clair rose gracefully from the sofa, smiled a silent good-bye, and wheeled Drake away into the other room. Lunt said a few words into his earpiece and decisively opened the door to the hallway to escort them back to the car.

Once Colter and Sarah had returned to the limousine and it began descending the mountain roads, Colter decided it was time to get some answers.

"May I ask what's going on here? I don't know much about the history of your relationship with your son, but I'd expect you to be happy that he was trying to save his life."

"My son," said Sarah, saying the phrase like it was an epithet. "His late father, Edward, was a newspaper reporter when I married him. We both had big dreams. We wanted to tell the world about all the injustices, and we built a newspaper chain that did that. With my family's money and his drive, Drake Newspapers did that. We added radio and TV stations, and we really built something. When Ed died twenty years ago, we thought Walter would carry on that tradition, but he turned it all to trash. Sensationalistic trash. He dishonored his father."

"Well, Sarah, that's no reason to try to stop him from doing this. It's an animal, after all."

"No!" she exclaimed. "Solomon is not *just* an animal! And Walter knows I've worked for the welfare of animals all my life. He's dishonoring me in this, and mainly he's dishonoring himself. It's not the first time. He's done things that never made the newspapers, certainly not his own. Sleazy things. I just won't have this act, this murder, added to that list. In fact, I'm going to make this into something good, something historic. I'm going to redeem him."

Colter didn't quite get her meaning but decided the declaration was a bit of raving on the part of an old woman whose eccentricities came close to matching those of her son.

"Sarah, here's what I'll do. I'll look at the contract between your son and the lab. If necessary, I'll bring in the best contract people, and we'll try to tear it apart. But I warn you that his lawyers may well have outsmarted the university lawyers. If that's the case, the animal belongs to him, and he can do what he wants."

Sarah leaned toward him, her stern expression challenging him. "Losing your nerve? That's one reason I got you out here . . . to show you who you'd be up against. To see if you'd blink. I guess you blinked." Emma sat silently beside Sarah, glancing from one to another as they spoke, as if watching a tennis match.

"It's not a matter of nerve," countered Colter. "It's a matter of contractual obligation."

"Contracts don't matter here. That's not the way I want you to go."

"What do you mean?" Again, there was that reference to some tactic he didn't grasp.

"I don't care how ironclad the contract is. I want you to take on this case from a different angle." She placed her wrinkled hand on his and squeezed it. "I want you to prove this animal has a legal right not to be killed."

Colter couldn't resist a disbelieving chuckle, not a good reaction to a client who had put fifty thousand dollars into his bank account. "Legal rights for animals. That's—"

She kept her hand wrapped around his. "Not all animals, just apes. They're intelligent; they should have rights."

"The case would be laughed out of court. You don't need a lawyer; you need a . . . ." He trailed off. Suggesting she see a shrink would be overstepping his bounds. "Look, I've had some animals for clients, that's true. But they walked on two legs and qualified as humans."

"They told me you were a clever son-of-a-bitch. They didn't tell me you lacked guts."

"Look, I'll go all out for you. I'll tear the contract apart if I can. Maybe we can go after them for cruelty to animals. But I won't walk into that quicksand."

She removed her grip and folded her hands carefully in her lap. Colter thought he detected the faintest smile on Sarah Huntington's face. Perhaps she was recalling other men in her life who had refused her something. He wondered how many of them had disappeared into the morass of Sarah Huntington's obsessions.

. . .

With a few satisfied food grunts, Solomon finished a carrot that had been part of his dinner and sat quietly on the high rock in the gathering twilight, enjoying the evening. This was a good place, as Abby had promised. He liked the smells of the flowers and the breezes and the larger space, with all the climbing things. But he still didn't want to be here. He missed the others, even the aggressive Jonathan.

He had awakened here, groggy from the needle-sleep, with Abby sitting outside the cage reassuring him. She had already set up the talking machine in a room attached to his sleeping cage. He touched the symbols on its screen to make words asking if the others would come, too.

She sat on the other side of a big window, and said no not yet, without telling him any more. She immediately started their work, practicing words with him to talk about the new place. She showed him a new feeling-word she had added to the talking machine. "Lonely." She said it meant a kind of sad feeling from not having others near. He still didn't understand the word, so they talked about it, and he touched the symbol for lonely she had added on the screen and made the machine say the word many times. He would understand it eventually, because Abby said she would work with him every day.

Solomon asked if Abby was sad, and she said no. But after knowing her since she was a child, he saw the slow, listless way she moved, the lack of a smile, and decided she wasn't saying what was real. Was she lying or wrong? He knew both words and thought he understood what they meant.

After Abby had given him his dinner and left, two human strangers had come to stare at him through the hard, clear wall across the cage. He had screamed in fear and anger, and smashed against the wall, venting his frustration at them, also showing he was still the alpha male. The small female had come here before, but he didn't know the male. He decided the male must be one of those who'd brought him here, where he didn't want to be. So, he decided he would "hate" the male—another word Abby had taught him.

He had returned to thinking about Abby's sadness, when a movement behind the clear wall caught his attention. The man in the chair with wheels had appeared. He had come once before, when Solomon was just waking from the needle-sleep. The first time, Solomon had screamed and slammed against the wall, but now he accepted that the man would just sit there quietly for a while and leave. So Solomon continued to sit on the rock, and the two of them silently watched each other, as each one's image of the other faded in the gathering darkness to become merely a vague patch of reflected light.

CHAPTER 6

Wednesday morning

"Gorilla warfare!" laughed Darrell Beckman. "Bobby, this would clearly be a case of gorilla warfare!" He took care not to spill his morning coffee on his bespoke pin-striped suit vest. With his blond good looks and his meticulous dress, he seemed a younger, blonder clone of Colter, except for an Ivy League sheen to his manner and a slightly cocksure confidence. Beckman had found much to laugh about in his twenty-two months as Colter's junior associate. After the coolly cerebral years at Duke Law slogging through case studies and moot courts, he'd found an amusing contrast in the bizarre world of southern California criminal justice. But his amusement hadn't dampened his ambition to become a high-profile criminal-defense attorney, as he had confidently announced when he first took the job.

Beckman took another sip of coffee, leaned forward in the leather armchair in Colter's office, and set the personalized Duke mug with his name inscribed in script down on the table to give himself freedom to gesture. "Can't you see the possibilities? You've got this big mansion with this monkey in the back, and this billionaire and his mother fighting over whether he gets this monkey's heart. God, Bobby, that sounds like a scene out of some black comedy! You could sell this to Universal. They'd call it *Gorilla Warfare*. You've got a moneymaker all the way around here!"

Colter smiled and drank his morning coffee from a white mug with script gold initials RWC. He leaned back against his desk, continuing his description of the events of the previous afternoon. "It gets better. She also wants me to overturn centuries of legal precedent and make a case for legal rights for this animal."

"Oh, I can see it now," said Beckman, propping his ankle on his knee, showing his Gucci loafers, and furrowing his brow in mock seriousness. "Apes get the vote. Somebody packs a district with them and bribes them with bananas. Pretty soon, we got a gorilla in congress. . ." He paused for effect, grinning. ". . . and the average I.Q. goes *up!*"

Sheba gave Colter an impatient let's-get-down-to-business look, and he turned to her. "So, did you get in touch with Digger?"

"Yeah, he's back from Palm Springs late tonight, and he'll see you tomorrow. He said that Sarah Huntington is big-time. Connected all over the country. He says she did have a bad falling-out with her son after the husband died. And, he says there's all kinds of stories around about Walter Drake. He said he'll start working the case tomorrow and have a prelim by the time you meet."

"Well, we've got to give Sarah Huntington her fifty thousand's worth," Colter stood and paced the room, his hands in his pants pockets. "Darrell, you research what the statutes and case law say about animal cruelty. Maybe we've got something there. Check the animal-protection people and see who they like as expert witnesses."

He turned and pointed an admonishing finger at Beckman. "But don't under any circumstances give out the details of the case. If this thing gets out now, it'll blow up in our faces. We just want to get this nonsense settled quietly, justify the fee, and get done with it. Our human clients might not take it kindly if they knew we were taking new clients from a lower branch in the family tree."

"Right, right," agreed Beckman, nodding vigorously. "Hey, not even the great Bobby the Barber could shave his way through that case, no matter how much it paid."

Beckman didn't grasp the significance of Colter's long pause after Beckman's joking reference to Colter's courthouse nickname. But Sheba picked up on Colter's raised-eyebrow expression, peering at him dubiously over her half glasses. She knew the offhand remark had activated a few of Colter's easily activated ego switches—including ambition, pride, greed and love of publicity.

"Bobby," she warned in a low voice.

He responded by holding up both hands and ducking his head reassuringly. "Okay, Sheba, okay. I'll just see the researcher and get a look at the contract, and that's it," he said in his best Sheba-pleasing businesslike manner. "What's my time like?"

"You've only got lunch free." Sheba ticked off from memory the long list of client meetings, depositions, and social events that crowded his schedule that day.

"Okay, then lunch at the Jonathan. She's director of the Primate Language Research Center at California Technical University. Abigail *Somebody*, I think Sarah said. Just tell her it's the issue of Drake's donation and Solomon's future. She'll understand."

They continued to plan the day, including an emergency make-up dinner that evening with Rachael. Sheba informed Colter that she had sent roses and a gold bracelet in apology. He had called her for late drinks after returning from Drake's, but she was out. So, he'd repaired to the bar in one of his favorite Beverly Hills restaurants, Mr. Chow, where he spent the evening sipping single malt scotch, and cultivating a pair of attractive women, one whose boyfriend spent considerable time away on business and didn't appreciate her. He ended up treating them to the restaurant's classic fiery beef filet mignon and procuring their phone numbers, which he entered in his BlackBook app.

•   •   •

Lunchtime found Colter sipping a vintage merlot, letting the rich complex flavor of the wine suffuse his palate, and looking over the menu. He was lulled into a luxurious noontime serenity by the wine and the soft light filtering into the grill room of the Jonathan Club through the tall windows. Also pleasing were the ornate paneling, the delicate clink of crystal and silverware, and the deft movement of white-jacketed waiters among white tablecloths.

The morning had been tough; particularly a round of hard bargaining on behalf of Johnny Califano. Colter couldn't get Califano off scot-free, but the prosecutor had laughed only half-heartedly when Colter suggested bargaining down to a charge of discharging a firearm in the city limits. The prosecutor knew his back was against the wall, and, in the end, Colter had gotten Califano a reduction to misdemeanor assault with a deadly weapon, which brought a mere six months in the county jail. Califano had shaken his hand and promised to "go straight" from now on. Back in his car, Colter had laughed louder than the prosecutor. Straight to what? A higher post in the organization of Gregory DiNofrio and a condo next to DiNofrio's in Long Beach, so Califano could sit on his balcony and watch drug shipments coming in?

His attention left the wine, attracted by the approach of the tuxedoed maitre d', followed by an attractive young woman in jeans and a t-shirt imprinted with a gallery of chimpanzee faces. She was slim but with pleasantly rounded hips and a hint of shapeliness beneath the t-shirt. Her oval face, milk-white skin, silky dark-brown flyaway hair and wide-set brown eyes gave her the look of a Gainsborough model. She wore no makeup but had naturally dark eyebrows and lashes, a delicate flush to her cheeks, and lips the rich color of a peach bruise. She nodded a thank-you to the maitre d', stuck out her hand, and launched a breathless introduction/apology.

"Hi, I'm Abby Philips. Sorry about not being dressed for downtown, but we had an emergency at the lab, and I didn't have time to change. Just when you wear your good clothes, that's the day you've got to go into a cage. This morning I had to untangle Caliban from a rope he got wrapped around himself, poor old guy. And they always seem to pick my outside-meeting days to get into a screaming match with each other and get too upset to work."

Colter took her small hand and felt a firm feminine grip. "I take it you're talking about the chimps and not the professors." He had expected a laugh, but she only smiled a tentative smile. "No problem, of course," he continued. "Sit down and relax a bit." The waiter appeared immediately. "Glass of wine?" asked Colter.

"Just water."

"Saratoga? Perrier?" asked the waiter.

"Just LA tap." As the waiter filled her blue goblet, she carefully freed the napkin from its elaborate fold and spread it across her lap.

They looked over the menu and made small talk about life in Los Angeles, and he realized her city was very different from his. Her lunches would be homemade sandwiches taken at her desk; his were client or lawyer lunches at his club or a trendy restaurant. Her days were spent wrangling huge screaming apes and doing research; he spent his in the sophisticated company of more decorous suited lawyers arguing over miscreant clients. The waiter arrived, and he ordered veal marsala, recommending it to her. Then he discovered another difference between them.

"I think I'll just have a garden salad. I'm a vegetarian. Like the saying goes, I never eat anything with a face."

"Well, the veal comes from the other end," he joked, realizing when she smiled politely that it had fallen dead flat. He tried to recover by launching into business. "So, you're the director of the center?"

"Two years. Since my father died. Did you know my father? Brandon Philips?"

She seemed surprisingly composed, given that one of her prized research animals was threatened with becoming an organ donor. Colter decided her detachment arose from a scientist's no-nonsense pragmatism, both financial and intellectual, and began his discovery-style interview. "Well, no, I didn't know him, but tell me about the center."

She looked a bit confused but launched into a description of the Primate Language Research Center. Founded by her father in the 1970s to explore the language capabilities of apes, mainly chimpanzees, the center had enjoyed federal funding for its first decades, she said. But the center, like others of its kind, had lost out when language studies went out of vogue.

"Thank God for private funding," Abby said, as their food arrived and they began to eat. "We think we're breaking entirely new ground. We're going beyond anything ever done. We're not just establishing a dialogue with chimps about the everyday things . . . food, behaviors, so forth. And we're not studying language syntax, but deeper concepts. We're trying to learn what—or really *how*—chimps think about abstractions, since we've shown they do. You might call it philosophy or ethics or even religion." She remembered that she had eaten only a bite, and took up her fork. "You have to let me show you the center and the animals, and what they can do." Between bites of salad, she went on to describe the animals and the language studies, coming at last to Solomon. She called it "saving the best for last."

"Yes, well, we should get down to the matter of Solomon," said Colter, taking a bite of the veal marsala, its delicate flavor helping him overcome any self-consciousness at dining with a vegetarian.

"Oh, Solomon's the star. He's the most advanced. We're coming close to talking about some really subtle abstractions. He's a very special guy."

"I guess I hadn't really appreciated that," said Colter, recalling Solomon's screaming assault the night before.

"And, well, Mr. Colter, I just want you to understand that the agreement with Mr. Drake about Solomon was a very special case. Mr. Drake offered to build Solomon a far more expansive enclosure, with better facilities for my work. And to bring in other of my chimps if it works out. Y'see, Solomon is getting along in years. And he needed to be separated from another male who was challenging him and could've badly injured him. Is Mrs. Huntington thinking about a similar arrangement for another animal?"

"God no! I hope nothing like this ever happens again."

She chewed her salad for a moment, puzzled. "I'm sorry, but I don't follow. I thought you were helping Mrs. Huntington develop her own plan for a gift. Your secretary said you were representing her and wanted to talk about Solomon. You're an estate lawyer, aren't you?"

"No, sorry, I'm a criminal lawyer."

"Why would she need a criminal lawyer?"

Colter realized with a shock that Abigail Philips hadn't learned of Drake's plans for Solomon. "You don't know?"

"Know what?"

He took a deep breath. "Dr. Philips—

"Abby, please."

"I think you'd better brace yourself."

"Has something happened to Solomon?" She put down her fork, leaning toward him expectantly. She seemed too delicate to withstand what he had to say next.

"No, but something may. Walter Drake proposes to . . . use . . . Solomon."

"As what?"

He took a deep breath. "As an organ donor. His heart."

At first Abby's face showed only confusion, as if his words had become garbled in the journey between them. But as the realization hit, her jaw grew slack, opening as she breathed the shallow quick breaths of someone going into shock. The color drained from her face, and her gaze darted around the room, as if the truth had hidden itself somewhere else. Her small hands began to tremble, grasping one another as if seeking mutual comfort. "Wha . . . What?"

"You didn't know? Can I get you something?"

She stammered but only managed to choke out, "Explain this."

"Well, as I understand it, Walter Drake offered a ten-million-dollar endowment gift to the center, in return for ownership rights to Solomon."

"Yes," she breathed, her voice betraying a rising fear.

"Sarah Huntington somehow found out that he didn't intend to offer a refuge for the animal but to use its heart as the scaffold for an engineered heart. . . for himself." Abby slumped forward clutching the table. Colter didn't know whether to rise to help the stricken young woman or shield her shock from the other people by continuing to talk.

Trying to compose herself, she slowly lifted the water goblet, spilling some with her trembling and took a drink. "We . . . had an agreement. I could work with Solomon. I could stay there for periods. He . . . he would be well cared for."

"Until the time came for the operation." The last word pushed her into panic.

"My God! What have I done?" she whispered hoarsely, pushing herself to a standing position, then sitting back down, tears welling in her eyes.

"Can I get you something?" Colter repeated, not knowing what else to say.

"I've killed him. I've *killed* him!"

"Wait a minute. You haven't done anything. *Drake's* the one, not you. You made a decision that seemed right. You couldn't expect this."

Now she was staring at him vacantly. He was now no more than a visual point of reference while she processed the shock of what she had learned. Tears fell from her pale cheeks, leaving faint wet marks on the white tablecloth. A large bald man at the next table peered at him with accusing eyes.

But as abruptly as the color had left Abby's face, it returned, growing to a bright red flush.

"GOD DAMN HIM!" she bellowed, her voice choked with emotion. She launched to her feet, overturning her water glass, causing the other diners to swivel their heads in her direction as if yanked by a single string. She noticed her napkin, still clinging to her lap, threw it onto the table, and turned to rush out, nearly colliding with a waiter carrying a tray. She'd almost reached the dining room door by the time Colter recovered and ran after her, catching up to her in the entry foyer.

Amidst a crowd of discreetly curious power-dressed men and women, he clutched her arm and turned her around. "Where are you going? What are you going to do?"

She wiped her dark hair from her face and glared up at him, her eyes glistening, her expression hardened into utter fury. "I'm going out there! I'm getting Solomon back!"

"Whoa, wait a minute. There are just a few legal issues here. I need to—"

"Screw legal issues." She tore her arm from his grasp.

"You could get yourself into more trouble than you can imagine." Her passion had aroused Colter's sympathy. But he was also pained at the prospect of fifty thousand dollars flying out of his bank account if Sarah doubted that he had vigorously represented her interests.

"Then so be it," she said tersely. "If you're worried about what'll happen, you're welcome to come." She shoved the glass door open and disappeared into the downtown noontime crowd.

"Shit!" Colter pushed through the door and quickly followed.

CHAPTER 7

Wednesday afternoon

Abby careened up the narrow winding road to Drake's estate, swerving the blue Subaru Outback violently to the right to avoid an oncoming Rolls Royce, and nearly sideswiping a tree. Colter had needed all his driving skills to keep his BMW close behind her as she swerved in and out of freeway traffic on the high-speed run from Los Angeles. She skidded around the last turn and slammed on the brakes, coming to rest inches from the steel barrier at the Drake estate entrance.

By the time Colter had scrambled out of his car and to her side, she had already leaped out and confronted the guard.

"Let me in!" she demanded, fists clenched, her chest heaving with rage. "I want to see Solomon! And I demand to see Walter Drake!"

The guard towered over her, pausing, and with insolent slowness communicating her request. They stood face to face, staring tensely at one another until he heard the answer. "He says you can't come in. He says you're barred from further access."

Abby moved toward her car, as if planning to try to crash the gate, but Colter stepped forward and laid a hand on her shoulder, turning to face the guard. "You remember me? I'm Sarah Huntington's lawyer."

"Yeah, so?" The guard hooked a thumb over the butt of his holstered pistol.

"Tell them that they must honor the binding contract with Dr. Philips stipulating that she has full access to Solomon. *Anytime* she deems appropriate. Is that correct, Dr. Philips?"

"Uh . . . yes . . . it's absolutely clear," said Abby, trying to shift mental gears into accepting Colter as her advocate instead of the dubious messenger of horrible news.

Colter looked at his watch and back at the guard, who shifted his weight. It was an almost imperceptible clue to indecisiveness that Colter had turned to his advantage many times across the plea-bargaining table. He tersely instructed the guard.

"Tell them they've got ten minutes. Tell them that if they refuse her access, they're violating that contract. And that makes the contract null and void. And that means the animal must be returned." The assertion was a bluff, but Colter depended on the impact of his best authoritative lawyer's voice and the likelihood that the guard hadn't taken a course in contract law.

It worked. The guard obediently communicated the message. As they waited for an answer, a dark-blue Mercedes SUV rolled up to the other side of the gate, and four large men in blue blazers emerged, one of them Fred Lunt.

Colter checked his watch and called to Lunt, "Five minutes left." He took out his primary cell phone, poising his finger over the screen. "Then I make a call and arrange for a court order to impound the animal pending a court hearing and a Santa Barbara County sheriff's deputy to enforce it. Y'know, courts here are really friendly, since I helped the son of the chief county judge get off on a DUI charge."

After only four minutes, Lunt began to talk to someone over the earpiece in a low voice. Colter stowed his cell phone and opened Abby's door, and she started to climb into the Subaru. He pulled his second cell phone from his coat pocket and handed it to her.

"This is if we get separated and you need to call the cops."

"You carry two of these things?"

"More, actually. They're my lifelines," he said, smiling.

Lunt finished his conversation and announced through the fence. "She has to be under escort at all times. And she can't see Mr. Drake. And you can't go in, Mr. Colter."

"He's . . . part of my research team," said Abby. "The contract says I can bring research assistants. He's a research assistant."

"He's a lawyer," said Lunt.

"Well, I just made him a research assistant." Her defiant gaze at Lunt convinced Colter that this delicate-looking woman could hold her own in any encounter with any intimidating creature, ape or human.

Lunt considered the situation for a few tense moments and then, with an annoyed wave of his hand, signaled for the barrier to be retracted and the gate opened. Abby and Colter pulled their cars through as Lunt and the other security men climbed back into the Mercedes. The SUV executed a rapid U-turn and accelerated down the roadway toward the mansion, with Abby and Colter following. By the time Abby and Colter reached the mansion, Lunt and another security man stood planted before the front door, looking as solid as the steel door itself. A third man appeared from the direction of the cage, a short bull-necked man with close-cropped hair and a barrel-shaped build that didn't fit well in a blazer.

"Mr. Giacomo here will be your escort," said Lunt. "You're not to leave his side or go anywhere he says you can't. The contract may say you can have access to the animal, but that's it. This is, after all, private property." He turned and disappeared into the mansion, and Abby and Colter made their way around the mansion toward the cage, followed by a silent Giacomo. Colter took the time to call Sheba and cancel the rest of the day's appointments. This looked to be a long afternoon, with many billable hours.

As they walked, Abby leaned toward Colter and whispered, "Did you really get the judge's son off?"

"No, but if he'd hired me, I would've," Colter whispered back. "Good idea making me a research assistant."

"You *are* doing research. Legal research."

Colter didn't respond but reminded himself that he was here as Sarah's lawyer. He planned to be involved only until he'd played out all the reasonable strategies, none of which involved advocating for an ape.

They reached the cage, and Colter hung back as Abby moved up close to the steel mesh. An eager, soft hooting arose from inside, and Solomon appeared from the other corner, galloping toward Abby. He reached the chain-link fencing and poked his thick leathery fingers and toes through the mesh, his mouth open in a kind of half-smile.

"Solly, God, it's good to see you!" exclaimed Abby, her voice rising in pitch, as if speaking to a baby. "You okay? Got your play face on? We're going to talk now. Let's go to the work room. C'mon, guy."

She skirted the cage along the brick walk, toward the building attached to the cage on the other side. But Solomon lagged back, having spied Giacomo and Colter. His hair rose from his massive body, and he swaggered stiff-legged toward them, beginning a rising crescendo of pant-hooting, ending in an angry, ear-splitting scream.

"He's not pleased at our presence," said Colter, as Solomon turned and loped away toward the low entrance into the building.

They reached the building, entering a door on the side away from the cage. Abby led them into a room with several chairs and a computer terminal sitting next to a large Lexan window. Solomon appeared on the other side of the window, saw the two men, and slammed his body against it with a loud boom, hair still jutting out, jaw set. This was Colter's first close-up encounter with the animal without intervening cage mesh, and he stood fascinated by the powerful, heavily muscled creature. This was an animal built for the jungle, beautifully adapted for a three-dimensional life stalking the ground and swinging far above it. Solomon paused in his angry display, his dark bulk filling most of the window. He stared at Colter with riveting amber eyes set in a broad face with a fringe of gray whiskers. Abby clicked a switch on a microphone and spoke soothingly into it, trying to calm him, but he continued his tirade, showing formidable canines.

"Fuckin' ape," muttered Giacomo.

"He doesn't like you, either," said Abby coldly. "Look, if I'm to work with him, you'll have to go into the observation room." She gestured to a door across from the window. The two men entered the room to find a one-way mirror and a closed-circuit television showing a close-up of an agitated Solomon beginning to settle down on a low platform in front of a computer touch-screen glowing with an array of colorful symbols.

"Solly, calm down." Abby's soothing voice sounded over a speaker mounted on the observation room wall. "C'mon, my handsome boy, let's talk. Are you okay? Are you hungry?" The video feed showed Solomon tapping the screen with the back of his thick index finger. There was a long silence, during which Giacomo squeezed his bulk into one chair, and Colter sat down at another.

"No, I'm not hungry," intoned a mechanical-sounding voice over the speaker. Some of the words sounded like Abby's voice; others were clearly from other people. So, the words seemed strung together like separate beads on a necklace. She and the other researchers had apparently recorded their own words for the speech system.

"Jesus!" breathed Colter.

"Was that him?" asked Giacomo. "Was that the monkey talking?"

Abby responded over the speaker. "I can hear you through headphones I'm wearing, but Solomon can't. Those were my recorded words, but Solomon chose them to express himself."

She continued talking with Solomon. "Solly, how do you feel?"

Solomon tapped the screen's symbols, lighting them up. At the end of a sequence, he poked a small image of a chimpanzee with its mouth open, and the sentence sounded. "I hate the men."

"Calm down, now. You can see they're not here. I won't let them hurt you, Solly."

"Hurt you, Abby?"

"No, they won't hurt me. Solly, I love you."

"I love you, too, Abby. I want you here more time."

"I'll come here as much as I can."

"I remember when we tickled."

"I do, too, Solly. You were very young then."

"My leg hurts."

"Is it an injury or an ache?"

"It is an ache. Can a friend come here?"

"I'm sorry, Solly. Not now, but maybe later."

"I want to see Bruno, Sandy, Wendy, Wombat, Earle, Jonathan?"

"I hope you can. You remember all your friends, don't you, Solly?"

"I remember Bruno, Sandy, Wendy, Wombat, Earle and Jonathan. I don't know the man here."

"The man who brings you food? His name is John. We'll put his name in the machine for you. Solly, do you remember the new feeling-word I taught you?"

"Lonely."

"Yes. That's the feeling you have now."

"Lonely is like nothing."

"Yes, Solly, it's like having nothing inside you, when your friends are not here."

"Where are you going? Abby, where are you going? Come back and talk."

On the video screen, Solomon leaped off the platform and disappeared.

It took a moment for Giacomo and Colter to realize that Abby had left the computer room. Giacomo leaped up and threw the door open. Seeing the empty chair beside the computer, he drew a chrome nine-millimeter pistol and ran out.

"Hey, there's no need for that!" shouted Colter, sprinting after him.

"She's gonna let the animal loose! That big fucker could do anything!"

"Yeah, and so could Drake, if you shoot it."

Giacomo held up the pistol. "He comes after me, he's a dead animal. Where the hell did she go?"

As they circled the cage, Solomon scrambled up the side next to the mansion, hanging on, screaming and shaking the mesh with his powerful limbs. They reached the observation area to find Abby struggling with one of Lunt's security men at the mansion's back door.

"He's a damned coward if he won't face me!" She tried to pull loose, but the burly, crew-cut man held her arms tight, beginning to drag her away from the door.

"Hit her," Colter instructed the man, over Solomon's enraged screams.

"What?" asked the startled guard, as both he and Abby halted their struggle in surprise.

"*Slug* her," added Colter.

"What the hell you talking about?" Giacomo, himself taken aback, holstered his pistol and moved between the group and the back door.

Colter shrugged, "Doesn't matter. I've already got a winnable assault-and-battery case against you, but it would've made it better if you'd hit her. Left a bruise maybe. On the face, please." Colter smiled his best lawyer's crocodile-smile, toothy and predatory. "Who knows? Maybe I'll even arrange a bruise before we go to the police station. I'm really good at assault cases."

"*Bastard*," spat the guard, abruptly releasing Abby and backing up next to Giacomo.

"We have orders not to let either of you in to see Mr. Drake," said Giacomo.

Abby took a deep breath and calmed herself. "Tell the coward he won't get away with this. Tell him I don't care how much money he has, we'll fight him, and we'll win." She moved to the cage to quiet Solomon, who raptly watched her every move.

"What do you mean *we*?" Colter thought, as he stood facing the two security men, waiting for Abby to finish soothing Solomon.

Giacomo impatiently gestured for them to move back around the mansion to their cars, and Abby reluctantly left Solomon hanging spread-eagled and forlorn on the side of the cage. As they moved out of sight of the cage, the chimpanzee began a series of deafening pant-hoots.

"I'll come back, Solly." Abby whispered, a promise to herself as well as Solomon, "I'm not about to leave you here." Her jaw was set in determination, but her lips displayed the slightest tremor.

Chapter 8

Wednesday evening

The gloomy nighttime drive over winding back roads in the hills above Los Angeles ended with Colter pulling his BMW to a stop behind Abby's Subaru. Her headlights illuminated a chain-link gate attached to a fence on which hung two weathered painted signs, one identifying the anonymous acreage only as "California Technical University Smithfield Research Forest." The other sign warned that trespassers would be prosecuted. Abby's arm extended from the window of her vehicle, slipping a gate card into a reader. The gate slid slowly open with a metallic rattling. They drove down the narrow road for about half a mile and into a small gravel parking lot next to a modest one-story beige-painted concrete building, lit only by a single light fixture over the door.

The lot was empty except for a rattletrap blue Toyota pickup, whose lettering on the tailgate had been painted out, except for "yo." Colter parked his car beside Abby's and followed her toward a steel door in the building, the cool, dry night breeze brushing softly past them in the darkness.

"Pretty isolated out here," he said, as she opened the door. They entered a long fluorescent-lit hallway, empty except for a stainless steel cart halfway down and with walls covered by children's colorful, scrawled drawings of leaping apes and monkeys.

"The idea is not to have traffic," said Abby. "The chimps need their peace and quiet." She seemed to have recovered her composure from the earlier ordeal, perhaps drawing strength from returning to this place.

As they walked down the deserted hallway, Colter felt himself suddenly on edge, alerted to an animal presence by some sense he couldn't place. Of course, he knew intellectually that the chimpanzee colony was here, but this intense feeling of their physical presence was body-knowledge, some primitive, instinctive sense of foreboding. He heard no sound, saw no animals, smelled no odors in the well-scrubbed place. Perhaps some unknown pheromone tickled his awareness, activating some deep emotional center in his brain.

He puzzled over his unease as he followed Abby into an open office whose door sign said "Abigail Philips, Director and Alpha Chimp." In a small reception area, a slim, long-haired young man wearing jeans and a stained blue polo shirt lounged at a worn metal desk, sneaker-shod feet up, computer keyboard on his lap, typing numbers into a database.

Abby introduced the young man as Keeli Mannix, a research technician who worked with the chimps. He flopped his feet onto the floor and amiably shook hands with Colter.

"Everything okay?" she asked.

"Oh, yeah, it's cool," said Keeli. "They're fed and quiet. Jonathan's still kind of freaky. I think he's still looking for Solomon. He's worried that Solly's hiding somewhere, ready to pull something on him."

Abby visibly stiffened at the mention of Solomon, busying herself by shuffling through mail on the reception desk. "Uh, would you tell everybody we'll have to meet tomorrow to discuss Solomon. Maybe about nine."

"What's up?" Keeli cocked his head, alerted by Abby's tension.

"I'm not ready to talk about it yet. Mr. Colter and I have some work to do."

Keeli shrugged and said he'd finish up his data entry and call it a day. Abby led Colter into her cramped office, dominated by a paper-laden wooden desk that looked as if it had been rescued from an old schoolroom. Beside the desk stood a four-drawer filing cabinet piled with manila folders and scientific journals, with still more piles covering the scarred asphalt tile floor. The folders on the floor showed scrawled titles such as "Syntactical modalities," "Primate Symposium," and "JA paper." A large stuffed chimp perched smiling and limp on a wooden chair in the corner, and the book-laden shelves also overflowed with chimp dolls, chimp statues, chimp windup toys, chimp photos, chimp drawings, and even a chimp lamp, which was an upright log with chimps climbing its surface. Above the desk, the modest wall space left uncovered by bookshelves held a chimp calendar and a yellow cascade of sticky notes, which had spread like ivy to cover the side of the file cabinet and the computer sitting on a cheap, pressed-wood computer stand beside the desk.

Abby waved Colter to the chair from which he removed the stuffed chimp before sitting down. She closed the office door and sat at the desk in a gray metal desk chair, furrowed her brow for a moment, then bent to shuffle through the third pile from the left on the floor, coming up with a manila folder marked "Drake gift." She pulled out a sheaf of papers with the characteristic blue cover that marked it as a legal document and handed it to Colter.

"I know this is too much to ask, but . . . well . . . I won't be able to sleep until I know whether the contract can be broken. Whether there's a loophole."

Colter flipped through the pages and gave the noncommittal "hmmm" employed by both doctors and lawyers. "Well, I couldn't give you a definitive answer tonight. I—"

"I know, I know. It's just the uncertainty. If you see a loophole, that's great. If there's not, then I can at least know I've got a harder fight. Gives me a direction. You understand?"

"Yeah, sure. I'll look at it."

She jumped up. "Great! I'll go see to the chimps. You sit here and look it over. Take your time. Find a loophole, okay?"

"Sure. Loophole guaranteed. You have my word as a lawyer."

Abby almost smiled, as she hurried out. Hers would be a pretty smile if she ever used it, thought Colter, sitting back and scrutinizing the contract. He stretched out his legs, crossing them at the ankles and switched into his attorney-attack mode. Every word, every phrase presented a possible opportunity, and he worked his way slowly through the verbiage, undeterred even by the raucous chorus of hooting echoing from down the hall, no doubt chimpanzees greeting Abby.

Fifteen minutes later, she slipped silently back into the office and sat down at her desk, leaving him to read, conspicuously busying herself by flipping on her computer and reading her e-mail.

But the instant he laid the contract down on his lap, she turned from the computer to stare at him expectantly.

He sat up, sighed, and slowly shook his head. "Sorry. Nothing obvious. Some damned smart wording here. I hate to disparage my colleagues at the bar, but the university lawyers let Drake's people slip some things through that should have been caught."

Abby clutched the worn plastic arms of the old desk chair, as if to hold herself in place. "You're sure? Can you give it another read?"

"Well, I'm not the final authority. I know some corporate lawyers who I'll ask to really give the contract a shaking and see if something falls apart. And I'll send it to an animal-welfare lawyer I know, Amy Meyer, who does work with the ASPCA. She can see if what they're proposing to do somehow violates animal-cruelty statutes. But your best shot is probably with the contract itself."

"That's still a good possibility, isn't it? Isn't it?" Her voice cracked slightly at the end of each question, a punctuation of both hope and desperation.

"I can't kid you. I know contracts, too. This one explicitly states your rights to visit Solomon to work with him. But it also says that in return for his donation, Drake receives full, permanent ownership of Solomon. True, he is responsible for Solomon's welfare. There is language stipulating that Solomon must be maintained in good health and not subject to cruel treatment. But the relevant word is 'maintained.' If Solomon is being maintained in good health, the ownership means that Drake has a right to dispose of Solomon as he sees fit. The subtle wording his lawyers slipped in means he could go out to that cage and shoot Solomon and not be held responsible. . . because Solomon had been *maintained* in good health and not subject to cruelty up to that point."

Abby dropped her head onto her hands, rubbing her face. "God, it's my fault. I should have seen that. I should have—"

"It's not your fault. You're not a lawyer. I'd bet the university was so eager to get that money, their lawyers missed the legal traps that Drake's lawyers set. Or. . . maybe. . . decided not to see them."

"No, that's no excuse. It's my fault. I should have looked out for him."

Colter decided she needed to be alone, and he stood to go. "Look, I'll take this with me." He waved the contract. "I'll talk to you tomorrow."

She looked hopefully up at him. "So, you can take another tack, right? There's another way, right?"

"Sorry," he said. But he knew that terse answer wasn't enough. He felt compelled to say something else. Her pleading brown eyes made him add, "Y'know, Sarah Huntington is desperate, too. She even asked me to change thousands of years of legal precedent, to try to get legal rights for Solomon. To try to establish that he has a right not to be used as a donor. But that would be . . ." He trailed off, realizing that he'd made a stupid mistake no lawyer should make: he'd opened an avenue that he didn't want to take.

Abby's brow furrowed as she absorbed the idea, her eyes staring at him but not seeing him for a long, silent moment. "Yes!" she finally exclaimed, her expression brightening with hope, coming straight up out of her chair. "You could do that! There's a group that's been trying to do that. The Nonhuman Rights Project. Apes are intelligent. More like humans than most people realize. They have emotions. You could do it that way!"

"Abby. . . no. . . sorry, that's just such a long shot that it's foolish to try."

"But you could try. Her money would pay for that. You could try."

He patted her shoulder, turning to go. "I'll call you tomorrow. We'll take another look at the contract." He stepped through the outer office and into the hall.

But she followed, determined not to let him dismiss the possibility. "But you'll think about the legal-rights strategy?"

"It just wouldn't work, Abby. No judge would hear it. And the idea that apes would have some legal rights . . . I'm sorry. The closest we might come is to say Drake was being cruel to Solomon. We'll check the statutes." He turned to walk down the hall toward the outer door, and she stood silently in the doorway to the office. He felt her desperation, like some emotional wind at his back, and, strangely, he found himself caring about it.

"You should see the chimps," she announced abruptly.

"What?" He turned back to see her standing flat-footed in the hall, her hands fidgeting at her sides, looking vulnerable.

She pointed back down the hall, a gesture meant to be nonchalant, but which looked oddly forced. She cleared her throat. "If you're thinking about a cruelty strategy, you should see how Solomon lived here. He had other chimps to interact with. He had a different life. You might see something that gives you a point to argue."

Colter considered the idea, as she took a couple of steps away down the hall, turning and looking back. Colter realized she would tell Sarah about their meeting, and he didn't want her reporting that he had neglected some possible avenue to advance the case.

"Sure. . .well. . . I guess it might be useful."

"Have you had a tuberculosis test recently?"

"Uh, yes. I went to Africa on a case."

"Okay, good. It's Department of Agriculture regulations. Protects the chimps. That's a really nice suit."

Startled at the non sequitur, Colter looked down at his two-thousand-dollar bespoke pinstripe. "Yes, it is, why?"

"Well, the guys can get messy. Throw stuff. And they're great pickpockets. Watches, cell phones, so forth. We've got some jumpsuits in the locker room. Why don't you change into one and leave all your stuff there. Anything they might steal. It'll all be safe."

He agreed and emerged shortly from the locker room dressed in a worn jumpsuit that reminded him of the prison garb some of his clients had worn. Feeling naked without his phones, he followed her down the hall, to a heavy, locked steel door. They entered an anteroom with a metal mesh door into a hallway with cages on either side. He felt the unsettling sense of animal presence even more powerfully here.

An excited hooting rose from the cages, a deep guttural grunting resonating from large chests. A loud bang reverberated, like large hands smashing against metal.

"This isn't dangerous?"

"No, they listen to me. I'm the alpha."

She opened the mesh door, and, along the hallway, large black fingers and toes appeared through the steel mesh of the cages—a welcoming party. They walked along the cages to see dark-eyed inquisitive faces pressed against the mesh, lips pursed in pant-hooting. There was no smell in the well-scrubbed hallway, but Colter detected some subtle, indefinable subliminal animal scent. Maybe pheromones shared across eons of evolution?

At the sight of Colter, the pant-hoots crescendoed to raucous screams, accompanied by a random, deafening banging and clattering. Massive bodies flung themselves around the cages, dark blurs of hairy, muscular animals.

"Cut it out!" scolded Abby. "This is a friend of mine. Just cool down, guys."

But they didn't, and she had to shout above the ear-splitting racket as they walked down the row. On either side of the hallway, a mesh tunnel ran along the ceiling and across the far end of the hall. The tunnel was divided by sliding doors so that the animals could be moved about and isolated at will. Four television screens hung from brackets in the ceiling, angled down, with two each facing the cages on either side. Their screens were dark.

"This is Jonathan on the left. Hi, big guy." Jonathan lumbered forward, and then away, in agitation, not sure whether to approach Abby or retreat from Colter. "Bruno on the right. Tough fella." Bruno launched his bulk with a crash against the cage door, climbing up and swinging away. "Old Grandpa Caliban on the left." The old chimp with rheumy eyes and a sagging round belly raised a great gray-bearded head and regarded Colter with dignified aplomb. "On the right is Sandy." The female chimp stared calmly at Abby with expectant eyes, touching her large fingers to her lips. "Here on the left is Earle. He's the clown of the bunch." Earle obliged by swinging wildly back and forth on a thick white rope, blowing lip raspberries and launching himself from either wall, spinning around in mid swing. "On the right is Wendy and her baby Wombat." The female chimp clutched the cage with her feet, her arms enfolding the small body of her baby as its big dark eyes stared timidly out at them. Abby reached the last cage on the right, empty and well-scrubbed, but she remained pointedly mute, a silence so significant that it seemed to hold its own, even against the hooting of the chimps. She turned away to another empty cage on the left.

"And, finally, here was Solomon's cage." She took out a ring of keys and unlocked the door, opening it wide. In the next cage, Earle finished his acrobatics and climbed down the cage wall to sit and watch them, picking assiduously at his crotch.

Colter inspected the space. "It's a lot smaller than his new place," he said, shaking his head. "It would be hard to convince a judge that he's being abused."

"They don't stay in here. The doors on the other side of their cages lead to a big outdoor enclosure where they all stay most of the day. And there's the lab wing they go into to work with the computers."

"Okay, thanks, I've seen enough."

"You haven't really seen his cage. Try it out yourself. You'll see that it's perfectly livable."

"Thanks, no." Colter had to shout above the din that started up when the chimps could no longer see Abby. "Look, what I need to know is . . ." He stopped as Abby cupped an ear toward him.

"They'll quiet down if we get in the cage," she shouted. "They'll think you're just another chimp, come to stay for a while."

Colter shrugged and ducked inside the cage, pushing aside a large plastic tire hanging from a rope. Abby walked across to stand by the sliding stainless steel door to the outside. Their neighbor Earle stood against the mesh, his large hands hooked high above him, watching with interest. The racket did begin to subside.

"I want you to see this," said Abby pointing to the door. "I've got to open the outer door. Let me get the switch." Abby moved toward the cage's front entrance, and Colter turned to face Earle, who leaped away pant-hooting, grabbing his blanket and flinging it into the air. Earle paused, and Colter heard the clink of a metal lock being snapped shut. Abby turned toward him, a set of keys dangling in her hand.

"WHAT THE HELL ARE YOU DOING?" Colter leaped toward her, but she backed against the door, her lips pursed in defiance, and thrust her small hand through the mesh, pitching the keys away down the corridor.

CHAPTER 9

Wednesday night

"Are you crazy? You locked us in here!"

Abby silently crossed the cage and sat down on the concrete floor against the back wall, staring intently at him, pursing her lips, as if trying to figure out where to begin. Colter whirled and threw his weight against the cage door, then backed up and kicked it, the loud clang bringing a startled yelp from Earle next door.

"That door can hold a full-grown chimp, it can certainly hold you. Now just relax. It's okay." Abby's voice was quiet, soothing, as if she were talking to a child. Or a chimp.

"Call somebody, damnit!"

"How?"

"Okay, why did you do this?" Colter moved to stand over Abby, who hugged her knees to her chest and stared straight ahead. But before she could answer, a wet slug of water splattered against the left side of Colter's head. "Christ!" he yelped, backing away from its source, Earle, who retreated immediately to the back of his cage, making a pant-chuckling sound that could only be a chimpanzee laugh.

"Don't worry, it's just a mouthful he got from his drinking trough. It's a little trick he plays on visitors."

"He's not the only one who plays tricks. What's this about!"

Earle scurried forward and spat another chimp-temperature mouthful, wetting Colter's jumpsuit before he could duck.

"Cut it out Earle, or no TV!" bellowed Abby. Then to Colter: "He really likes *The Simpsons*." Earle returned with another mouthful, standing on all fours, rocking back and forth, preparing to launch. "You spit that, I'll get the ice cube tray, then." She held up her hand and shook it, making a rattling sound. Earle let the water dribble from his mouth and retreated, hooting gently, squatting with his blanket clutched to himself, watching them intently. "Earle's afraid of the dividers in ice cube trays. We can't figure out why, but it's a way to get him to behave." Now Abby regarded Colter as accusingly as she had Earle. "You were going to drop the case, weren't you?"

"And this is a *really* good way to persuade me to stay on it, right?"

"I figure if you got to know these chimps better, you'd understand why you could win a case on rights. They're intelligent."

"Like Earle?"

"Humor takes intelligence. Earle's our smartest chimp, in fact. He was playing a joke on you."

"Well, this is no joke. This is kidnapping."

"Oh? Well, I *accidentally* locked the door. Can't prosecute me for that."

Colter laughed a sarcastic "Hah." He sat down on the floor with his back against the side wall, as far from Earle and Abby as he could get. "So what do you hope to accomplish by keeping me here all night?"

She stretched out her legs and regarded him with serious brown eyes. "These animals play jokes on one another. They laugh, they cry, they jump for joy, they admire beautiful sunsets."

"How can you know? Maybe they just look like they're doing those things. It's called anthropomorphizing."

Now Abby tucked her legs beneath her and squatted lithely on her calves, facing him in an almost begging position. "But there's objective proof. . . scientific studies. Look, they have the same basic physiology as us. The same genes create their bodies, the same hormones trigger their emotions. Adrenalin, testosterone, oxytocin, dopamine, serotonin. We humans behave just like chimps. Human males. . . including yourself, counselor. . . are more attracted to ovulating women, just as chimp males are attracted to ovulating female chimps. We use the same body language as them to communicate. Dominance, submission, fear, love. We live in social groups just like they do. So, you see, they *are* enough like us to make your case."

"Physiology. . . behavior. . . social groups. . . none of those denotes intelligence," said Colter. "That's the criterion for legal rights."

Now Abby stood in triumph, pacing the cage. "That's why Solomon is so special, so unique! He is the *only* chimpanzee in history who has been taught language from infancy! My father got him just after he'd been weaned, during the same critical period that human babies learn language. Dad immediately began teaching him to use a computer to produce spoken words. And he taught Solomon the meaning of those words, even abstract words. And how to put them into meaningful sentences. And I continued that work." She gestured at the other chimpanzees. "All these guys have been learning language, too. They're good, but not as good as Solomon. He's the ambassador for legal rights!"

"Tricks," said Colter, shaking his head. "They'll call them tricks. Like a dog does tricks. And, his lawyers have other powerful arguments they'll throw at you. There's the slippery slope argument. You give legal rights to chimps, then the animal people will want rights for dogs, then pigs, then mice. Hell, they'll say *bacteria* deserve protection."

"Bullshit," she said, waving her hand dismissively. "There's no such thing as a really slippery slope. There's always. . . well. . . *ledges*. People can decide where to draw a line, and this is it. Great apes. Other people may have other lines, but there are always lines."

"Okay, then how about this? You're sacrificing chimps, true. But you're saving *human lives*. The scientists have figured out how to make human hearts with tissue-engineered chimp hearts. So, if this ability can save human lives, they should do it."

Abby abruptly stood up and paced the cage, turning angrily toward him. "I'm a scientist! I know how science works, believe me! Scientists can figure a way around limits. If you set this limit. . . that they can't sacrifice chimps. . . they'll find a way to save lives without that sacrifice! We just have to set this moral limit! Take that as a given, okay?"

"And exactly why should we make them develop a new way, when there's a proven one?"

Abby ignored the question, her mind racing to another argument. "Look, we must learn to respect the Earth. We're in deep shit now. . . climate change. . . pollution. . . and we can start by respecting the creatures who are the most like us on it."

"So, you'll save the Earth by saving these apes?"

"Like I said, it's a *start*; it's a change in thinking about ourselves. . . that we're a part of this planet, dependent on it, not lords over it."

"Look, I'm just not going to discuss this anymore. It's not a winnable case. I'm stuck here all night. I'm hungry. I haven't had dinner and looks like I'm not going to. Jesus, you'd better come up with something better than this little ploy with the next lawyer."

Earle moved away across his cage, but Colter still kept a wary eye on him.

"They murder, you know. They make war. Does that persuade you they're like us? They cheat, lie, steal. And they know that it's wrong."

"Fine, well, we keep them in jails where they belong."

Earle knuckle-walked toward them with something in his hand and Colter stood up, ready to dodge.

"Earle!" Abby warned, but the young chimp squatted on the other side of the cage and held up a banana, pushing it through a hole in the mesh. Abby's expression softened, and she looked smugly at Colter. "He's offering you dinner."

"Thanks, but I prefer it on a plate."

"It's all you're going to get. And he's sharing from his dinner. Go on, take it. He's trying to apologize."

"Yeah, well, maybe he thinks I'll sic an ice cube tray on him." Colter finally relented, moved across the cage and gingerly took the banana from the ape, backing away to the other side and sitting down. Earle's mouth widened in what could have been a smile, showing some of his lower teeth.

"That's a play face. Now thank him."

"Right. Thank you, Earle. You're a prince." Colter peeled the banana and took a bite, resigning himself to a night in the cage. When his mouth was clear enough, he said "So, you're an expert on chimp emotions?" To his surprise, his anger at being caged for the night with this woman and surrounded by hulking animals was waning. Besides, his interest in both was piqued. And, of course, he decided, these were billable hours.

"Yes. Their emotions. Their beliefs. It's what I'm trying to get at with my communications."

"Beliefs? Chimps don't believe in anything beyond their next banana."

"That's what the people say who call me a 'woman' scientist. They say I'm just projecting my own female prejudices onto the animals.

They said that about Goodall, too. But that's bullshit. That's their own prejudice talking. Prejudice against what I'm proving." She walked to the front of the cage, calling to Wendy, asking her how her baby was doing. Anticipatory hooting rose from down the corridor.

"You're not a real barrel of laughs, are you?" Colter remained seated, finishing off the banana. The last time he'd had bananas was at Brennan's in New Orleans. Very nicely prepared bananas Foster. He doubted whether Earle had ever experienced bananas Foster.

The timer-activated lights clicked off, leaving them in darkness except for a row of dim nightlight fixtures along the ceiling that cast shadows into the cages. Abby took a deep breath, as if the darkness was a welcome relief, and Earle carefully scrunched his blanket beneath himself, settling down for the night. "It's hard for me to be happy after what I've seen. I guess the best I can manage is not unhappy."

As Colter's eyes grew used to the dimness, he could see the outline of her face. It was a pretty face, but so grim.

"What have you seen?"

"Too much death. You don't need to know."

"Dr. Philips, you're being an unresponsive witness. Do I have to treat you as hostile?" She had turned so he couldn't see her face, but he knew she didn't smile at his joke. He did sense that he might have at least brought her slightly out of her somberness.

"Okay. I'll tell you about my first time." She shifted in the dim light, turning toward him, leaning sideways against the wall and again hugging her knees. Colter was sure the story of her "first time" wouldn't be the same kind he would expect from other women he knew—those golden women whose beauty had enfolded their lives in shimmering protective privilege.

"Sure, I like stories."

"I grew up here, basically, around the chimps, and I had an early appreciation of what they were like . . . their intelligence, their complexity. So after I got my doctorate, I decided to go to Africa to do research on their behavior in the wild. I wanted to see how they were naturally—whether they showed the same complex mental abilities. And I guess partly it was kind of a tribute to my mother. She was an anthropologist, and she was in Africa when she disappeared. I was eight."

Abby paused and shook her head slightly, trying to free herself from a deeply painful memory and back to her story. "Anyway, I did some observations at Gombe Stream National Park, Jane Goodall's site. And I think it was good work. But then I took a trip to Uganda. There's another preserve where they were trying to rehabilitate chimps confiscated from the animal trade. I decided I needed to give something back to the animals."

"The animal trade?"

"Yes. There's an active trade where poachers shoot mothers and take the babies to export. Anyway, the sanctuary had this big island in the middle of a river, where the rescued chimps could live naturally as a colony. So, one day I was in Kampala, in the marketplace, and I heard a scream. It sounded like a baby. So I went down this narrow alley, and behind this little shop in this tiny concrete courtyard, I found a baby chimp. She was chained to a stake and sitting in her own filth, and some kids were hitting her with sticks. She had sores all over her body, and you could see her ribs sticking out. She had cigarette burns on her hands, where the owner would offer her a banana, and when she reached for it, burn her. She had this sort of straight line of burn marks on one palm."

"God, why would they keep her like that?"

"Well, she's *just* an animal, you know." Abby's voice caught slightly with the angry sarcasm. She had to pause before going on. "We were told not to buy chimps in the market, because it just encouraged the poachers. But I couldn't help it. I gave all the money I had to the guy who owned the shop, and I took her with me in a box. It took a month of medicines and food to get her back to some form of health, but, even then, she was still so very frightened. Imagine doing that to a baby. So very terrified of everybody. She would just huddle in the corner of her cage, whimpering. But I worked with her every day. I called her Sadie. I don't know; something about her made me connect with her like no other chimp. Sadie my little lady, I called her." Abby coughed and straightened a bit, embarrassed at allowing emotion to overtake her.

"She got better?"

"Over about six months, I got her to start interacting with me. She decided I was like the mother that had probably been killed before her eyes. But I knew she had to go back to live with other chimps, so I started to take her out in the boat to see the other chimps on the island. She would scream in fear and cling to me at first. But gradually, she got interested in them."

"So you let her out onto the island?"

"Wasn't that simple. The males will kill newcomers unless they're introduced carefully. And Sadie didn't know the first thing about living in the wild. So I went onto the island. I actually had the workmen make me a cage to live in. And Sadie and I lived in the cage until I was sure Sadie would be accepted. Oh, you should have seen it when this old female we called Big Mama finally gave her a hug. Even the alpha male, Shando, didn't mess with Big Mama, so I knew Sadie would be all right. Big Mama and I managed to teach Sadie about what to eat and how to relate to the other chimps."

"So then Sadie went with her own finally."

"Yeah, after about four months, so I moved off the island. I'd go back every week or so to observe, and Sadie would come over to see me and we'd hug like old friends. But she was really accepted into the group, and she knew that's where she belonged."

"And she lived happily ever after?"

"No." Abby choked the word out. "One day I went out with the food boat, and Sadie didn't come down to the shore. Neither did Big Mama. I went onto the island and looked for them. It took an hour. I found Big Mama. She'd been shot. Her head was gone, and they'd chopped off her hands and feet."

"God, who would do that?"

"The poachers sell the adult parts as souvenirs."

"You must have gone nuts."

"Well, I got one of the local game wardens to tell me what he knew about poachers. He told me that a couple of guys in a village about ten miles away had been rumored to be poaching bushmeat—"

"Bushmeat?"

"Anything a poacher shoots is known as bushmeat."

"So, I took one of the local boys as a guide and drove out there. We found a hut out in the forest with an old truck piled with carcasses. Antelope, a water buffalo, some smaller animals. These two guys were out front, cooking a stew. I got the boy to ask them if they'd captured a chimpanzee in the forest. I wanted to give them a chance to admit it without getting into trouble. I figured they were going to sell Sadie to an animal dealer, even though Sadie had grown out of the cute age that pet owners like."

"Did they admit it?"

"Oh, no. They said they never hunted chimpanzees. Said they hadn't been near the sanctuary, even though I didn't mention I was from the sanctuary. So I noticed some pieces of carcass and intestines that looked like a chimpanzee's. I told them I wanted to buy an antelope carcass and sent the boy off with them to pick one from the truck. While they were at the truck, I got a look in the stewpot. I saw a hand."

"A chimp hand?"

"It had cooked for a while, and the meat was coming off the bone, but the skin was still intact. On the palm was. . . a straight line of cigarette burns."

Colter felt himself becoming ill. "What did you do?"

"I screamed. I got sick. Then I went after the poachers with my fists. One of them took up a gun. Luckily for me, I'd chosen one of the older boys to take me out there. He was strong enough to drag me away. He persuaded the one with the gun he couldn't kill us because the game warden knew we were there."

"That was your first time? You meant the first time you lost an animal."

"That was my first time. I stayed another three years. We saved a lot of animals. But Sadie always haunted me. Then my dad had his first heart attack, and I came back to help him with the research here."

"It's easier here? I mean in terms of losing animals."

Abby stood up and went to the front of the cage, putting her fingers through the mesh. In the next cage, Earle stirred and lifted his head sleepily, questioningly.

"No, not easier. Just different. Caroline wasn't easier."

"Who's Caroline?"

"She lived in the cage that's empty now. I grew up with her. Solomon and I both did. She was Solomon's mother. She died a year ago, and I just couldn't bring myself to bring in another chimp for that cage. Couldn't afford to, anyway. Funds were cut." She turned back toward Colter. "I can't lose Solomon. I won't."

Colter felt something start to slide away within himself. A resolve he'd had since his father died. A resolve not to commit himself to anything beyond the safe pursuit of money and celebrity. But he immediately shored up his resolve with a lawyer's cynical opinion that this woman who had cleverly tricked him into this cage had also tried artfully to play on his emotions. He retreated safely back

74

to his pecuniary mode, reminding himself that this case offered the certainty of money and the distinct probability of more contacts. He rose to his feet, joining her at the front of the cage, leaning against it and folding his arms. She stared across the dim corridor at the sleeping form of Wendy, with her infant Wombat visible only as a little, light-faced lump nestling in his mother's arms.

"Okay, let's just say I'll spend a little time looking into this legal-rights strategy."

Only a hint of pleasure played around her mouth. "Good. That's good."

"Well. . . we'll just see if it's good. Or if it's a dead end," said Colter. He immediately regretted using the word "dead."

Chapter 10

Thursday night

igger Murray never sat on bar-stools. He'd fallen off too many in his day, and the resounding thud of his beefy frame onto the barroom floor tended to alarm the other customers. So, when Colter spotted Murray, he was installed stably in the third booth along the wall in the downtown bar. The place was filled with a funky beer-smelling warmth and the raucous noise of cops who'd spent their shift politely saying "Yes, ma'am," and "No, sir" to pissed-off people and needed to let off steam before they went home to families. Murray sat absorbed in the business of drinking, the stubble-faced sixty-seven-year-old man with wild, sparse gray hair, a little pug nose, and squinty, knowing eyes.

Two young cops at the bar paused in their talk to give Colter a decidedly cold stare, as he slid into the booth across from Murray.

"Bobby!" Digger exclaimed with the warmth of a few shots of whisky and of a man greeting his godson. He grinned, showing a perfect set of false teeth. "Gladda see ya, boy. But we probably shoulda met someplace else. You got too many friends from the force in here tonight." He shifted his ample middle-aged padding, which sheathed his jowls, arms, chest and stomach, where once had been thick muscle. He had one pudgy hand wrapped around the handle of a beer mug, the other gently gripping a shot glass. He wore a short-sleeved shirt and wide, red-checked suspenders that Colter had given him not just as a fashion statement but so that his pants would have a fighting chance of staying up over his belly.

"Seems like old times, Digger."

"Yeah. I remember when your mom used to come by and pick up your dad after his shift. Damn, you were a scrawny little fart. We've all grown since then." He rubbed a hand contentedly over his belly.

"I had my first legal drink up there on that barstool."

"Sure, I remember. The first part of the night, anyway. Your dad was so proud that night he lit up the whole damn place."

A middle-aged straw-blond waitress appeared at Murray's side, amply filling out her jeans like denim sausage casings. And just as amply filling a white blouse with the name "Connie" on it. "You look thirsty, ace," she said to Colter. He ordered a scotch on the rocks, asking for Glenfiddich but settling for Dewar's.

"Con, sweetie, you remember Jimmy C.'s boy?"

"Yeah, sure. Haven't seen you for a long time."

"He don't drink here no more. He's a big lawyer 'round Beverly Hills. Look at that suit, Con. By God, that's a big-time lawyer's suit."

"Real fine, son." She grinned at Colter and laid her hand on Murray's shoulder. "Someday this old crook here'll need a good lawyer." Murray slithered his hand around as if to pinch her rump, but she slipped deftly away as she'd probably done countless times before.

Colter leaned forward. "So, have you been doing your job for a change?"

Digger took a sip of the whisky, followed by a healthy swig of beer. "Hell, son, that's why I'm here. To rest up. I did a lot of checking around on Mr. Walter Drake. Bottom line, Bobby, don't fuck with that guy."

"Could you be a little more specific?"

"I got a shit-pile of specifics out in the car. A fat envelope full of rap sheets and other stuff, and files on my laptop I'll e-mail you. As usual, you never saw the rap sheets, right?" He took another fortifying swig of whisky with a beer chaser. "That fucker Drake would sell his own mother. In fact, in a manner of speaking, he did." Murray's voice grew stronger, more sonorous. He was a cop reporting on a case now. "Sarah and Edwin Drake built up a good solid newspaper chain. Got into radio, TV, newswires, and did real good on all of them. So, when old Ed died, his will gave a big chunk of stock to their only son, little Walt. Well, he got greedy after a while and got into a battle with Mom and ousted her from the company. Expanded it into this big damn conglomerate. Added web sites, theater chains, and so forth."

"So, he's greedy. How about the other deadly sins?"

"He's done them all, and broken a few commandments and some statutes of the state of California. And he ain't real fair with wives, either. He's gone through three of them and left every one broke. I heard some bar talk out in Palm Springs. One of his wives was cheating on him one time with a tennis instructor. These days, the guy drives a lawn mower at the Palm Springs Country Club. I talked to him."

"Lost his job?"

"Lost his knees. They ran into a chunk of steel rebar. Twice."

"The jealous type."

"The fuckin' lunatic type. The Malibu cops got a thick file on him, but he never spent jail time. Had a bunch of shyster lawyers. Sorry, Bobby. . . present company excepted." Murray took another one-two sip of his shot and beer. "Drunken driving, fights, abusing women. But that was many years ago. Last ten or so he started changing."

"How?"

"Got religion of some kind. Maybe all kinds. He had lots of holy guys, spiritual advisors, living at his estate. He got reclusive, and that's when the problems with the law stopped. He'd have to tell you about what else is going on in that brain of his."

"That must have been when he started that cult-religion cable channel." Colter's drink arrived, and he sipped it, enjoying the smoky, bracing tang of the cold scotch. "Okay, how about Sarah Huntington?"

"Like it said in the newspapers, she is connected big time. Houses in LA, Newport, and a little Caribbean island. The second time she married after Ed died, the guy was even richer than she was. When he died, she got another big chunk of change. And she got herself even richer. Real estate, artworks. Hell, she even made money on Broadway."

"And Abby Philips and her lab?"

"Well, she doesn't have a rap sheet."

"Jesus, Digger, I could have told you that."

"Never hurts to check. Anyway, I made some friends out at the university. You'll see a couple quarts of Jim Beam on my expense report. Anyway, the administration was going to shut down her monkey place. They were just waiting for a respectable time after her dad died. Drake's money persuaded them to keep it open, but they're still looking for an excuse."

"Why do they want to shut it?"

"Don't know for sure. Probably mainly money. Always is. But it's also because the idea of her trying to find out what the monkeys are thinking doesn't sit right with some donors . . . or the other faculty, for that matter. I got into the online archive at the student paper. I'll e-mail you the articles. Talked to a bunch of grad students. There's a case of beer on the expense account, too. They call her 'Doctor Toolittle' around campus. They said the valid data on the monkeys' thinking is *too little* and that she's putting words in their mouths. You know she's got all kinds of computers and stuff to talk to them and have them talk back?"

"I've been there," said Colter. "In fact, for quite a while. Spent a little close time with the animals." He recalled a touch of wry amusement the uncomfortable, unsettling night on a blanket on the concrete floor listening to the heavy breathing of the slumbering apes, watching the slow rise and fall of Abby's chest as she slept. In the shadowy light, he'd admired the curve of her back turned toward him, aware of the roundness of her bottom. They'd awakened to the sound of a morning TV talk show, with Earle squatting up against the front of his cage, eagerly watching the news. The young woman who'd come to bring breakfast had been startled to find two sleepy humans locked inside one. He'd experienced some sort of initiation that night—but what kind, he was not sure. He knew he felt a strange reluctance to leave the blowsy-haired Abby, with her thank-you-God coffee in hand, launching herself blearily on her morning animal duties.

Connie brought him back by arriving with another scotch and clunking it down on the scarred table.

"I didn't order that," said Colter.

She smiled in embarrassment. "Yeah, well, a couple of guys over at the bar bought it for you. They said the deal is, you can drink that, but it's your last one, and then you leave."

Colter scanned the bar to see four muscular men glancing pointedly in his direction as they talked. He recognized three whom he had cross-examined at one time or another in the course of getting clients off. He had been more than rough on them.

"Tell them thanks, and, when I finish my business, I'll be happy to oblige them."

Digger downed his drinks and ordered another shot and beer. "Lucky I'm here, Bobby, or you mighta gotten that drink somewhere besides on the table. So, what're you going to do about Drake? Like you told me on the phone, does the old lady still want you to go to court with some half-assed case about legal rights for these monkeys?"

"Apes. Monkeys have tails. I'm considering doing it."

Murray's face registered puzzlement, as if he thought the words had been altered as they penetrated his pleasant alcoholic fog. "Considering doing what?"

"Taking the case."

"A monkey's . . . ape's case?"

Colter took a sip of the free scotch and smiled. "Think of it, Digger. Setting a legal precedent like that. She's willing to pay. Having a communicating chimpanzee for a client."

Now Digger sat back, staring in disbelief. He rolled his gaze blearily around the room, as if trying to gather some reality into the conversation. "Christ, Bobby, your client walks on his knuckles and shits on the floor!"

"You know, Digger, I've had worse. I've got to do some research, get up to speed on the precedents, but this could be one hell of a case."

Digger's drinks arrived, and he downed the bourbon shot in a gulp and took a healthy drink of beer. "Yeah, well, you could also get your nuts run up the courthouse flagpole."

CHAPTER 11

Friday morning

"You want to do *what*, Mr. Colter?" Judge George Kermit Wainwright carefully set aside the worn gavel given to him by Ronald Reagan and scowled formidably down at the lawyer standing before him. Wainwright's face was all sharply defined geometry—a pointed chin, ruler-straight thin lips, a small, down-curved nose, and planar cheeks stretched tight by high prominent cheekbones. His facial topology contrasted starkly with the smooth dome of a shaved bald head.

Wainwright had enlisted every stringy muscle of that face to form a fierce expression of displeasure aimed at the lawyer before him. He leaned forward, his black judge's robe hanging on his spare frame neatly as it might on a coat hanger, barely disguising the leather-tough gauntness beneath.

"You're asking for guardianship for this animal?" he asked. Wainwright's voice, the aural equivalent of a truckload of gravel spilling down a metal chute, resounded in the spare, high-ceilinged courtroom. Judge Wainwright liked the acoustic and visual qualities of the plain light-oak-paneled walls, the long, wooden hard-backed gallery benches, the unadorned jury box, the heavy dark oak tables with hard chairs for the lawyers and defendants. He liked a blank space that he could fill with his authority. The only decoration Wainwright allowed was a massive, black wrought-iron chandelier, which hung over the center of the room, its six-foot metal arms spread broadly above the lawyers and their clients. Wainwright liked that chandelier because it reminded him of what a judge should do: shed light on the proceedings yet pose the constant, ominous threat of crashing down with its full weight on the lawyers below.

Wainwright provided comfortable chairs only for himself and the jury. Theirs, empty now, were low, padded fabric armchairs. But he ensconced his bony frame in a high-backed leather chair that displayed him properly to the courtroom. The chair had a spread-winged eagle carved into the dark oak top, so that it peered fiercely over his head, lending its sanction to his pronouncements.

He liked being the centerpiece of this hard-edged bastion of the law, of having his voice echo commandingly out across the courtroom, while the lawyers' voices, directed toward him and his eagle, were muted.

"Yes, Your Honor. I ask that Dr. Abigail Philips be appointed legal guardian of the chimpanzee known as Solomon," said Colter, standing easily beside the plaintiff's table, dressed in a gray pin-striped suit, so as not to breach Wainwright's unwritten rule that only the judge wore black in his courtroom.

Wainwright added a raised eyebrow to his scowl. "Mr. Colter, surely you've got enough law in your head to know that animals can't have legal guardians. I've got a German shepherd I like a lot, but I know I couldn't give him a legal guardian."

"That's the point, Your Honor . . ." Colter tensed, preparing to commit himself, feeling a conflicting swirl of dread and eagerness battling inside his head. Now he would drop the bombshell that might explode in his face, shattering his career into wretched shards. But it might also produce glorious, triumphant fireworks. He could almost feel a palpable pressure of Sarah Huntington's personality, as she sat ramrod-straight at the plaintiff's table, hands folded, watching the proceedings with her usual imposing intensity. He could almost feel Abby's desperate hope wash over him, as she sat in the front row of the gallery with three fellow researchers. Wainwright cocked his head impatiently, resembling the bird carved into the top of his chair. Colter took a breath. "Your Honor, I intend to argue that, as an intelligent creature, Solomon should have the right of legal person-hood. And such personhood would bring a right to life. And this is a life-or-death situation for him. Now, we're not saying a legal person is the equivalent of a human being, but—"

"What?" chorused both Wainwright and a voice from the defense table.

The defense-table voice—that of the Drake family attorney Albert Kane—continued, deep and sonorous and with infinite, tired patience. "Your Honor, this is a simple contract dispute that Mr. Colter is trying to confuse with this frivolous tactic." Kane stepped from behind the defense table, a slightly stooped man of medium build in a comfortably worn charcoal suit with an undistinguished blue patterned tie. He looked weary, with a hangdog face and ample bags under lackluster middle-aged eyes that had seen the world in all its perfidy. Even his hair, sparse salt and pepper and combed over a balding pate, seemed ready to surrender its pretension to being an adequate scalpful. Kane shook his head sadly, using that resonant voice, that doleful face, and those sad basset eyes as evidence that his long, arduous existence on earth had made him privy to the real truth, the whole truth; and that he had brought himself into the courtroom as a kindly avuncular presence to explain that truth. "Your Honor, my *human* client's life is at stake. I ask that Mr. Colter not be allowed to threaten that life."

Kane had served a lob and Colter zinged this one back. "Your Honor, I can show clearly that the court's consideration of this motion will not jeopardize the life of Walter Drake. But it will allow the court to decide the fate of an animal that I can show legally deserves the right to live."

"Ah, yes. Now we come to the point of the matter." Kane clasped his hands before him and smiled benignly. "Animals don't have legal rights. There are animal-cruelty statutes, but this animal is not being subjected to cruelty, nor will it be. Surely Mr. Colter knows they are property, pure and simple. And, apparently, Mr. Colter is not disputing the ownership of this animal. We should let our philosophers handle this legal-personhood business."

Wainwright harrumphed and returned his doubtful gaze to Colter. "Mr. Colter, this claim of legal rights. You're really way out there." He folded his hands and shook his head, clearly wondering to himself why this canny lawyer had chosen such an untenable legal position.

"Actually, we do dispute the ownership," said Colter. Wainwright's face registered a flicker of interest that the argument was returning to familiar legal grounds. "We dispute the concept of so-called ownership of an intelligent creature like a piece of furniture. Rather than ownership, the status should be one of guardianship." Wainwright's expression darkened once more. Colter felt any possible advantage slipping away.

"I'm sorry," said Kane, shaking his head. "But this is just not a matter for the court—"

"Counselor," Wainwright shot the word at Kane like a hard-pitched rock. "*I* will decide what is a matter for the court to consider."

Kane spread his hands in puzzlement.

Colter barely suppressed a smile. As the Drake family retainer, Kane was more used to tinkering with contracts and settling minor fracases with the local police. He hadn't argued a case before Wainwright, and he had inadvertently pushed a button he didn't know existed. Colter decided to make sure the button stayed pushed. "Your Honor, if I may be allowed, I think I can make a case for legal personhood. I think the court can decide whether it's on point." He studied Wainwright's face, seeing it begin to screw itself into the contrary scowl that signaled the judge had just about decided to tear off on one of the legal excursions that had distinguished his quirky tenure on the bench.

Wainwright paused for a long time, looking from one lawyer to the other, his impartial judge's mask returning, giving no hint of his thinking. "Tell you what," he finally said, picking up the gavel, twiddling it between thumb and forefinger. "Both of you give me a legal memorandum, say, by Monday. Let's just take a look at what we have here, legally."

"But Your Honor, my client is a sick man—" began Kane, but Wainwright cut him short with a bang of the gavel, stood up, and swept out.

Kane shot a confused look at Colter and began to gather his materials into his briefcase, shaking his head.

"What does this mean?" asked Sarah, standing up as her assistant Emma appeared at her side.

"It means we're in the game." Colter snapped his slim briefcase shut and indicated he didn't want to say any more in the courtroom.

Within five minutes, they were settled into Sarah's limousine, insulated from the turmoil of LA traffic, gliding down Wilshire toward his office. Sarah sat across from him, Emma beside her. Abby sat beside him, dressed in a conservative blue gabardine suit that looked like one that a scientist would wear to present a paper at a scientific conference.

"We could have been knocked out of the box right away, but we were lucky enough to get this judge," said Colter. "He's known for going his own direction. We can only hope that he takes the direction we want."

"Do you need help?" asked Sarah.

"What exactly do you mean?"

"I could ask some friends of mine to . . . explore his situation. They are big donors to campaigns."

"You should do nothing. Wainwright is a man who doesn't appreciate his situation being explored."

"Is there anything I should do?" asked Abby. "Shouldn't you introduce information on ape intelligence? Don't you have to prove this?"

"Absolutely. I need all the ammunition you can get, and quick. I'll need all the scientific papers showing intelligence. And give my assistant Sheba the names of every expert who'll be willing to submit an affidavit about apes' mental abilities, their behavioral similarities to humans. . . all that stuff."

After more questions about strategy, they dropped him off at his office, with Abby inviting Sarah to see the primate lab. They would prove a headstrong pair, Colter decided, but he'd defended mass murderers, so he could surely handle two willful women.

As Colter entered the office, Sheba drummed the nails of her right hand on the desk, her left curled around a Venti Starbuck's cup. She pointed to her headset and continued to talk. "I said I'd let you know when he came in, and I will . . ." She paused, looking questioningly at him.

"Who?" he mouthed the question silently.

"Carly Moffat," Sheba mouthed back. "She heard."

Colter made an "Oh, shit!" expression. He hadn't wanted the reporters to find out until he knew whether he stood a chance of arguing the case. Moffat—a chunky ball of fire who reminded him of the Pillsbury Doughgirl on speed—covered the courts for City News Service. She must have picked up the story in the coffee room where she hung out, sliding dollar bills into whatever vending machines held a bailiff's or court clerk's favorite junk foods. Or, perhaps she had been assigned to make sure the story got prime attention by Walter Drake, a major stockholder in the service. He nodded assent to Sheba.

"Girl, you are in luck. He just walked in this minute," Sheba said into the phone. "He'll be right on."

He took the call in his office. Carly was her usual pushy self and Colter his usual charming, crafty self. Yes, he told her, he had claimed legal rights for a chimpanzee. Yes, the defendant was Walter Drake. Yes, the memos would be presented Monday. No, he was not crazy. No, he would not comment beyond that, because he wanted to save his arguments for court. He hung up and turned around to see Sheba and Beckman standing there, looking expectant. "It's started," he said. "Darrell, you've never seen a media feeding frenzy up close, I take it?"

"On TV. I've seen the big trials."

"Let me tell you, in person, it's a sight to behold. This time, City News Service is the lead piranha. It's the service for the local media that alerts them to stories. Carly will probably file her story in half an hour, and she knows damned well how her boss wants it slanted, so it won't be friendly to us. It'll be on the wire immediately, and we'll start getting calls. Today's Friday. We'll let it build until Monday. Sheba, tell reporters that, before we'll talk to them, we'll present our arguments to the court."

"So what are our arguments?" asked Darrell.

"How the hell should I know? I really didn't think we'd get this far, but, lucky for us, Wainwright went off on one of his tears and decided to review our arguments. Bless the little old fart!" Colter took two breaths, accelerating the lawyer's part of his brain to strategizing speed. He told Sheba and Darrell to sit down while he paced the floor, reeling off a set of assignments, telling them about legal precedents to research, history to gather, affidavits to prepare, favors to call in, people to investigate. After fifteen minutes, during which Sheba and Darrell both typed furiously on their iPads, he stopped.

"Damn! You gave us about a month's worth of stuff to do," said Sheba.

"The legal research alone would take a week," said Darrell.

"Well, when you finish it in three days, you'll just end up with bigger legal muscles," said Colter.

"And what are *you* going to do?" Beckman asked, standing up and straightening his vest.

"Well, I'll bug Meyer at the ASPCA again about the contract. She said that, on first read, it looked ironclad, especially because the chimp is apparently living in the lap of luxury on Drake's estate. But maybe she's had some new ideas. And I'll get some corporate lawyers to look at the contract from a business angle. They cost enough, so they ought to have something intelligent to say. And then I've got a dinner date."

     •   •   •

Solomon paced back and forth on the high rock in the afternoon sun, grunting peevishly. His dinner was late. The big man who brought him fruits and vegetables had not come, and Solomon was very hungry. And when he was hungry, he became angry. He wanted Abby to come, so he could tell her with the word machine that he was hungry. And angry. His grunts grew deeper. When the big man came with his food, he would show that anger.

He heard sounds coming from the side of his cage near the house—not the side where his food would come. Many people appeared, some carrying large black things that were not food.

"Solomon, c'mon over here and meet the press," he heard from behind the hard, clear wall where the people stood. It was a stranger's voice, and he feared strangers. It was a man, and he feared men the most.

His hair rose, and his heart began to thump with the complex emotions of fear and anger. His muscles tensed with the need to proclaim them, to affirm his power to himself and to them. From deep in his chest, he launched a powerful pant-hoot, letting the rage and fear come to a boil, letting it erupt in a screaming, loping rush toward the hard wall, in a flying leap and a vicious slam against it. The thunderous crash made the people shout and shrink back, some even running away. Solomon rebounded, landed on all fours and scrambled off, bashing a barrel across the cage, swinging up into the climbing tree, kicking the ropes and suspended tire. From the high tree, he pant-hooted again, the sound reverberating off the high wall of the house. He would have no more of these frightening people.

· · ·

"Are you coming to bed?" Carrie Wainwright stood in the door to the large book-strewn study, a comfortably ample, aging woman tightening the sash of her robe around her waist. The judge issued a noncommittal grunt that, to a wife of forty-five years, constituted a clear signal that he was grappling with a serious problem. He had retreated into his study after a too-quiet dinner, during which his only spoken words were to ask for more meat loaf from the cook. And afterward, he'd taken a longer-than-usual walk with Patton, which delighted the big German shepherd but increased Carrie's concern. She didn't like him worrying over cases. They escalated his touch of grouchiness into anger, made his blood pressure go up. Now he sat in one of the big leather arm chairs, his slippered feet splayed on the ottoman, his reading glasses on, peering down at a book. When she saw the book was the big family *Bible*, she decided she'd better draw him out. She knew it was time. Their decades together told her he wanted to talk. She knew that whenever he wanted to talk about something bothering him, he would sit just so, assuming a subtly expectant posture. And he'd glance at her over his glasses in just that certain way. She stepped past Patton, who didn't open his eyes or move from his place on the rug, and sat down in the other leather chair. "The *Bible*?"

"Yes. Wanted to refresh myself on a few passages."

"For court?"

He smiled. "Y'know, even though witnesses swear on the *Bible*, nobody ever reads it there. The court's still a godless place, not open to the Scriptures. No, I'm seeking guidance."

"About what?"

"Listen." He adjusted his glasses and wrinkled his brow in concentration, finding his place on the page. "Then God said, 'Let us make man in our image, in our likeness, and let them rule over the fish of the sea and the birds of the air, over the livestock, over all the earth, and over all the creatures that move along the ground.'"

He glanced at her and held a bony finger up while he fumbled for a passage marked with a bookmark, a small strip of paper torn from a yellow pad. "And listen to this one. I remembered this one." He read. "Now I will hand all your countries over to my servant Nebuchadnezzar, king of Babylon; I will make even the wild animals subject to him." He sat back and peered solemnly over his glasses at his wife.

"And how do they apply?"

"Carrie, I feel like Nebuchadnezzar. The Lord's given me a task." The judge's wrinkled hands seemed to float above the open *Bible*, as if trying to gather in the right words to express such an emotional concept. "He's given me a mission—I know it. To keep the walls strong." Carrie Wainwright made a puzzled face. "Don't you see?

Too many walls coming down these days. Walls that should remain solid. Cloning, genetic engineering, and all that. Walls crumbling. And today, another one threatened that I'm to protect. This arrogant, ungodly lawyer came into my courtroom and said he was going to argue that a lower animal . . . an ape . . . should be elevated to be man's equal."

"My God, no!"

"Carrie, I think I'm meant to be an agent of the Lord. I'll let this lawyer argue his case. I'll let him lay out all his diabolical reasoning." George Kermit Wainwright made a fist. "And, by God, then I'll squash him." The judge slammed his fist beside the open *Bible* with a thump loud enough to startle the dog.

CHAPTER 12

Saturday morning

"You're going to wish this was stronger stuff than coffee." Sheba pulled three Venti Starbuck's coffee containers from their cardboard tray and set them on the table. Her ample frame was draped with a blouse with big bright sunflowers that challenged the California morning and billowy black silk pants that reflected her funereal message. "I tell you, ain't no amount of coffee going to give us the ideas to work out of the deep shit you got us in with this case. Kane let the press in to see the ape. His PR people got Carly Moffat to push the hell out of the story—not that it needed it. You see the videos?"

"I was busy last night."

"You're going to be busier now." Sheba pushed her iPad toward Colter. He watched videos of a hairy, screaming beast slamming into a Lexan wall. Following the footage, reporters did stand-ups editorializing about how a lawyer was actually asking for legal rights for this animal that could save a human life.

"Expected this," said Colter resignedly, handing back the iPad.

"And there's the damned phone messages. We got newspapers, news web sites, wire services, TV, news magazines. This thing is spreading worldwide." She took a sip directly from her Starbuck's cup, while the two lawyers carefully poured their coffee into their personal mugs.

"We'll worry about the press later," said Colter, sitting on the edge of his desk across from them, taking a sip of coffee. His casual sky-blue polo shirt, light-gray cotton pants, and topsider shoes were rendered more businesslike by an expensive dark blue blazer. He raised his brow expectantly and thrust his face forward. "So?"

Beckman had just taken a healthy drink of his latte as he sat tiredly on the couch, the all-nighter of research casting a faint shadow of haggard fatigue on his taut young face. He dressed this day in studied preppie casual, with a J. Peterman plaid shirt, baggy Dockers khaki slacks, and tasseled loafers. Colter's terse query roused him to alert-lawyer mode, for he plunged his hand into a fat leather briefcase and hauled out three thick folders, one by one, plopping them on the coffee table. He flipped open the first one.

"Okay, we've got the scientific papers that Philips published, showing her work yielded proof of Solomon's language abilities and intelligence. And we're working on affidavits from all the scientists she gave us. . . on chimp intelligence, self-awareness, emotions, sense of past and future. And the genetics stuff."

"That's all well and good, but what about the history of law?"

"Okay, we went back—"

"How far back?"

Beckman chuckled. "How's four thousand years?"

"So you think you've gotten to the roots of the law?"

Sheba chimed in "Hell, we go back any farther and we're citing the laws of cave men rootin' around on all fours!"

Beckman laid out neatly typed summaries. "If the good news is the science, here's the bad. Roman law, biblical tenets, Hobbes, Locke, American common law . . . they all say the same thing. Animals aren't legally equivalent to humans. Simple as that. They're property."

Colter rolled his eyes to the ceiling. "Damn! I wasn't looking for a history lesson. I already figured there was a pretty good legal reason Solomon isn't living in Sherman Oaks. What I wanted was holes in the law. What about animal-rights law? What does it say? Find out the rulings that went our way."

Beckman shrugged and pulled out yet another folder, a thin one. "Aren't any. . . yet. Steven Wise and the Nonhuman Rights Project are filing suits to free chimps held in bad conditions. But Solomon is living the good life. So, they've gotten no rulings that are on point— where there's a human life at stake. So, it'll be incredibly tough to convince a judge to overturn centuries of precedent *and* risk having the defendant die because of it."

"Well, Wainwright wouldn't have allowed the case if he hadn't been interested in the legal arguments."

"Still, Bobby, it's just too big a risk. Remember, you told me yourself 'If you can't pulverize them with precedent or flatten 'em with facts, bury 'em in bullshit.' We don't have any precedent or facts on our side, and we don't even have bullshit, Bobby."

"Damnit, the animal-cruelty statutes have to apply here!" exclaimed Colter, pacing the office wall to wall, as if he was trapped in a cage himself. "Isn't killing the chimp treating him inhumanely?" The phone began to buzz again, a reporter, no doubt, but the answering service was intercepting calls this morning.

Beckman shook his head. "First, you said yourself—the contract gives him the right. And it's humane if you do it right; by starting with anesthesia. I talked to the docs at UCLA who do animal research. . . pigs, dogs, monkeys. When they do animal-transplant studies, they basically anesthetize the animal with drugs, and it doesn't wake up. Quiet and peaceful."

"Well, it sure isn't going to be peaceful for me unless you give me something. Sarah Huntington's not going to be very willing to pay my fee for trying to go before Wainwright and get a judgment with my smile."

"How about sympathy?" asked Sheba. "Poor monkey and everything."

"I know that won't work, especially since Wainwright no doubt saw the damned videos of the ape going. . . well. . . apeshit." Colter stopped his pacing and regarded the two bleary associates. "Look, you've done fine. Leave all the stuff, and I'll go over it and try to figure out some strategy."

"So, I'm outta here," Sheba announced, her tone brooking no argument. "My baby's got a game." She stood to leave, her coffee cup in one hand, her satchel in the other.

"Sure, of course. Sorry. I've got reading to do. And thinking."

"Well, hope you get a brainstorm by Monday morning." Sheba and Beckman stacked their files on Colter's desk, and he sat down in the voluminous leather desk chair Sheba had dubbed his throne, leaned back, and plopped the first folder onto his lap.

His facial expressions over the next two hours showed a steady rise in muscle tension in the forehead and mouth, and a more frequent clenching of the jaw muscles. As he worked his way into the thick stack of legal memoranda, his frustrated frown rose to its zenith along with the sun. Then, about three-quarters of the way through the stack, the tiniest glimmer of an idea began to relax the muscles.

As Colter allowed the faint notion to crystallize into a courtroom strategy, a sly, self-satisfied half-smile rose. He flipped the last folder shut and pitched it on the desk, picking up a yellow legal pad in one hand, twiddling his Mont Blanc pen in the other and turning the chair around to gaze for a long while out over the street. Retreating into deep thought, he barely noticed the Sunday traffic and the strollers languidly making their way to late Sunday brunches at the bistros along the street. Periodically, he roused himself to jot a point on the pad.

An hour later, he exclaimed to himself, "Hah! You clever devil!" as the strategy finalized itself in his mind and on paper. He scanned his notes, scribbled a few additions and swiveled the chair around to pick up the phone. "Showtime!" he declared with a carnival barker's lilting inflection, as he stabbed at the phone buttons.

CHAPTER 13

Monday morning

"Are you *serious*, Mr. Colter?" The shouted question from a reporter punctuated the demanding babble of a dozen others. They crowded tightly around Colter, brandishing notebooks and tablet computers, waving microphones, pointing cameras and scrambling up the steps with him, as he hurried to the Monday morning session.

"I'm always serious," Colter grinned, trotting up the steps, followed by Beckman, fueled by his morning coffee and a rush of adrenalin. His answer unleashed a rapid-fire tattoo of other questions:

"You really think monkeys have rights?"

"What's your strategy?"

"You think you'll win?"

Colter stopped and turned, an onslaught of microphones thrusting toward him from all directions. "Look, this is a case of an outrageous attempt to kill an intelligent, feeling animal that deserves to have his day in court. I intend to make sure he gets a hearing. As for my strategy, you'll just have to watch the session." *Nice sound bite,* he thought. He'd rehearsed it enough.

"So, you getting a lot of bananas for this case?" asked Carly Moffat, peering up at him with an insolent smile.

"Say hello to your boss," answered Colter, smiling back and jogging away up the steps.

Inside the great stone courthouse, he pushed through the heavy oak door and into Wainwright's courtroom, pleased at the packed house and at the remote-control video camera bolted to the bracket above the jury box. It panned toward him, its glowing red light signaling a new level of notoriety. The television stations had petitioned to have the proceedings televised, and he would no doubt show up on the evening news as the foolhardy-yet-sympathetic lawyer who had taken an unwinnable-yet-humanitarian case. Except for the minor problem that the news video had shown Solomon as a violent beast.

At the plaintiff table, Colter busied himself pulling his notes from his satchel, while Beckman brought up the background material on his laptop, should Colter need it.

"You got all the information I sent?" Abby stepped up to the table wearing her dark-blue gabardine suit and a darker expression. "All the papers? The names?"

"Yes, and it's all in the brief my assistant just filed with the court," he smiled reassuringly. "But this case won't be won on scientific grounds. I need to convince the judge on legal grounds. Even on emotional grounds. I've worked out a strategy to do that. I've decided it's one that has the best chance of persuading the judge."

"Mr. Colter," said Sarah Huntington, appearing beside Abby. "You may need all the little tricks in your bag. Have you seen who's representing my son?"

Colter turned to watch Albert Kane shamble tiredly into the courtroom. Nothing new there. But then behind Kane strode Michael Showalter Jenkins!

Colter's brow muscles, which had relaxed since the previous day, bunched reflexively into a gnarled knot that felt as if a thumb had gouged into his forehead. He willed himself to a semblance of confidence.

"Ah, Jenkins." He truncated the comment, concerned that his voice would rebel and quaver, revealing his surprise. He felt the smallest crack in his confidence, like the abrupt subterranean fracture of an earthquake fault.

Michael Showalter Jenkins resembled Albert Kane only in that they were both middle-aged males of the same species. But Jenkins showed what Kane might look like with an injection of international fame, utter confidence, a laser-sharp mind, and the depth of legal knowledge that struck abject, palpitating fear into his opponents' hearts.

Jenkins stood augustly erect and imposingly built, with a barrel-chested physique suggesting that if he couldn't out-argue an opponent, he could out-wrestle him. In fact, an editorial cartoon in the *Los Angeles Times* had once shown him body-slamming an LA County prosecutor whom he had trounced embarrassingly in court. Jenkins' thick, brushed-back silver hair constituted a mane that translated every nod, shake, and cock of his head into a singular event. His jaw seemed always set, held infinitesimally higher than it needed to be, as if he were constantly alert for prey, usually opposing lawyers attempting to sneak through a verdict against one of his clients. His steel-gray eyes held the potential for explosive anger, but an intelligence to channel that power into exquisitely lethal legal arguments.

"Who's Jenkins?" asked Abby.

"You haven't watched much TV, have you, dear?" asked Sarah. "He's defended some big ones. A Secretary of State, a couple of

Senators. He's argued before the Supreme Court. Won every time. You ready for him, Mr. Colter?"

"Of course," answered Colter, perhaps a little too emphatically.

Jenkins finished shaking hands with several people in the courtroom and nodded his maned head at Colter, a slight smile crossing his lips. Colter managed to sustain a mask of calm, and nodded back. They both remembered the Roberson murder case. There were two defendants, one represented by Jenkins, one by Colter. Jenkins' stunningly clever legal maneuvers sent his not-guilty client to luxuriate in a beachfront home in Palm Beach. Colter's client, however, was working a vegetable farm for the next several decades in Tehachapi State Prison.

The bailiff, a thick-set, middle-aged man, solemnly announced George Wainwright's arrival, and the court stood as the old judge appeared and assumed his place overlooking the court. He rapped the gavel smartly and began.

"Good morning. We have before us today a serious case with serious questions of law. And despite the intense public interest and the potential for sensationalism . . ." he glanced at the television camera aimed at him. "I want this case argued with professionalism and decorum."

Colter took a deep breath and looked down at his witness list. Should he change his strategy? Too late now, even if he wanted to. He'd already briefed Sarah on it over the phone and had to persuade even her that the unorthodox approach was what this case needed. No, it was still a good strategy. It would sure rattle some cages—an appropriate metaphor, he thought. He smiled to himself as the crack in his confidence began to heal itself.

Kane introduced Jenkins as the new lead counsel, bringing the wry comment from Wainwright, "The court is, indeed, impressed that so prominent a legal mind has entered the case. We look forward to your arguments."

"Ah, well Your Honor, I only wish I had the privilege of an extended period before this court." Jenkins sat behind the defense table, his hands forming two precise finger-tents on the polished dark oak surface. "However, for the sake of my client, we must dispose of this matter quickly." His voice rose to resonate portentously through the courtroom. "Your Honor, I beseech the court not to allow a nattering legal debate over a matter of property ownership when a man lies literally on his death bed, waiting for a life-saving heart. Not even the plaintiff disputes the contract by which Mr. Drake owns Solomon."

"Your Honor," said Colter emphatically, rising from his seat. He made sure his opening words stepped on Jenkins' just enough to establish his primacy. The two lawyers had begun to take each other's measure for the battle. "Indeed, we do dispute that contract, to the extent that nobody can own this intelligent animal. This is a major point of law, not to be taken lightly."

Wainwright leaned forward, clasping his bony hands in front of him. "Tell you what. Before we start these arguments, I want to hear from the defendant's physician. I need to understand the state of the defendant's health."

Smiling slightly at the judge's apparent disposition toward his side, Jenkins obediently called Drake's cardiologist to the stand. Dr. Kevin Rehnquist, a clean-cut, dark-haired man with a physician's air of quiet authority, took the oath and sat down. His legs crossed, his hands folded neatly in his lap, he testified in careful clinical detail about Drake's grave condition, his weakening heart, his patient's doubtful prognosis on the mechanical-assist device, and his desperate need for a transplant.

But Colter was ready. Sheba had done her intelligence-gathering at Drake's hospital well, schmoozing with the nurses over coffee and gathering hints that she could piece together into a picture of Drake's condition.

"So, doctor, how long before the death sentence on Solomon needs to be carried out?"

"*Mr. Colter,*" scolded Wainwright.

"Sorry, Your honor. . . before Solomon's heart must be removed."

"Well, it takes weeks after harvesting the animal's heart to prepare the extracellular matrix, seed it with Mr. Drake's cardiomyocytes, and generate—"

"In fact, doctor, would Mr. Drake be well enough for the transplant if the generation process were to begin now?"

"Well. . . he has just suffered a setback. We need for him to regain some strength. But, in a matter of a week or so, he will begin—"

"*A week or so.* So, we have some time to argue this case properly."

"Doctor. . ." cut in Jenkins. ". . . can you be precise about how much time Mr. Drake has?"

"No. It's only an estimate. While we expect him to improve enough for a transplant, his condition could change. The generation process should begin as soon as possible."

But Colter had already scored a telling blow. He stood to emphasize this point. "I am not minimizing the importance of Mr. Drake's need for this operation, but it is clear we do have some time. Given that he is not medically ready for the treatment anyway, there is an issue of equity, and of law, that should be explored."

Jenkins rose to speak, but Colter waved his hands in a request to continue. Now, he would land another legal blow.

"And Your Honor, we are talking about an experimental procedure here. This has only been done on pigs. And the National Institutes of Health has already ruled that experimentation on chimpanzees—particularly of this lethal type—should not continue." His voice rose to its calculated dramatic height. "As the head of the NIH has declared, chimpanzees are our closest relatives in the animal kingdom and deserve special consideration and respect."

But Jenkins was ready with a rebuttal. "Your Honor, this is no mere experiment. The organ-generation technology has worked brilliantly in the preclinical studies. The transplant procedure is standard and, in fact, will be more successful than the usual transplant because the heart will be constructed from Mr. Drake's own cells. And this is no mere experiment to prove a scientific theory. This is a procedure to save a man's life. Certainly, chimpanzees deserve respect, but certainly saving a man's life must take precedence."

"Your honor, the NIH would certainly not approve this experiment, since it leads to Solomon's death," declared Colter, but he realized he had made a blunder the instant he said the words. Jenkins was ready.

"Your honor, the NIH has no standing in this case. The animal is privately owned, and no federal money will be used in the procedure. And again, this is no laboratory experiment. This is a clinical procedure to save a human life."

A tense silence settled over the courtroom. The lawyers and the entire gallery stared expectantly at Wainwright, who raised his head to stare at the ceiling in thought.

"I want to see this process," he declared. "I want to see for myself whether this is lifesaving or just some scientific folderol."

CHAPTER 14

Tuesday morning

Abby backed away from the window into the operating room and averted her eyes. Colter followed and gently grasped her arm to support her.

"That's what they want to do to Solomon!" she breathed. "I can't. . ."

The others, however, continued to watch the masked-and-gowned surgeons using a chest spreader to ratchet open the rib cage of the anesthetized pig, revealing the healthy pink, glistening, pumping heart and other organs. The group alternated between the view through the window and a video monitor in the small observation room that showed a brightly lit overhead view of the operation.

Unlike Abby, Wainwright retained a judicial impassiveness, asking the white-coated scientist standing beside him, "So this is done under complete anesthesia?"

"Yes, Your Honor. The animal is first given a sedative when taken from the pen, so it is comfortable when being positioned on the operating table. Then, it is given the standard anesthetic used in this procedure—ketamine. There is no pain whatsoever."

Wainwright nodded, a gesture acutely observed by both Colter and Jenkins. Each gesture, each expression was a clue to how he might rule on the validity of tissue-engineering a heart—and thus whether Solomon would live or die.

Behind them in the observation room of the large laboratory/clinical complex that Walter Drake had funded stood Wainwright's bailiff, whose steady gaze never left Wainwright. And beside the bailiff, a court reporter sat on a portable stool, busily typing the dialogue into her stenotype machine.

Sarah Huntington stood ramrod-straight at the window, her scowl portraying her utter disgust at the process. She reacted only with a subtle gasp when the surgeons sliced the beating heart from its arterial connections in the pig's open chest, suctioned away the flowing blood, and placed the now-still organ into a large jar filled with a slightly milky liquid.

"We've seen enough here," announced Wainwright. "What's next, Dr. James?"

The scientist, a small, narrow-faced man with a mop of dark hair, gestured to the door. "The laboratory," he said. "That's where we take the heart to carry out the tissue-engineering."

James escorted Wainwright down a long hall into a spacious fluorescent-lit laboratory to a bench lined with jars like the one they had seen in the operating room.

"These show the next steps in the process," explained James, his enthusiastic tone contrasting sharply with the intense mood of the rest of the group. "This first chamber contains a newly harvested organ," he said, pointing to a jar holding a pinkish heart resembling the one they had just seen removed from the pig.

"And these others?" asked Wainwright tersely.

"We add a detergent and other chemicals that remove the cells," said James, walking down the row of jars, which contained hearts that were successively paler. "Finally, we end up with just the extracellular matrix," he said, pointing to the last jar, which held a glistening, light-yellow translucent mass the shape of the heart. "It's a framework consisting of the proteins, collagen and other structural molecules. *This* is the foundation on which we build a brand-new heart."

Wainwright merely gestured to move on, and it was enough to send James into the next room, leading the group to another bench—this one containing a fully formed, vigorously beating heart, pumping blood into and out of a connected glass reservoir.

"For this heart, we've harvested endogenous cardiac stem cells—immature heart cells—from one breed of pig." He held up a small bottle of clear red liquid. "And we infused them into the matrix. And once they proliferated sufficiently, we started exercising the heart. We pumped blood through it along with growth substances, and after maybe a week, it formed the electrical conduction system of a normal heart and started beating on its own. Now it will be implanted into a different breed. To test compatibility."

"Let's see the proof of this pudding," said Wainwright. James at first looked puzzled, unused to such homilies. Then he brightened.

"Ah, yes, the transplant recipient." He led the group out of the large glass-walled building across a farmyard to a barn containing long rows of pens. They entered the barn to a chorus of grunts and enveloped by the musky odor of animals. "Here's our latest," said James, leaning over a metal railing and pointing to a large black-and-white pig lying on its side. A stitched scar ran the length of its belly. "This guy is an

Angeln Saddleback breed. But his heart is grown from the matrix of an American Yorkshire. There was no bad immune reaction, even though a normal transplant would have been rejected without anti-rejection drugs. So, this shows us the matrix isn't specific to a related breed."

"He's healthy?" asked Wainwright, peering down at the animal.

"Oh, yes," answered James brightly. "He's only one week post-transplant, so he's still recovering. But pretty soon, he'll be running around just like normal."

Colter felt slipping away any hope he had of questioning the validity of the procedure. He took a chance lawyers usually don't— asking questions for which he didn't know the answer. But he had to stop this litany of success.

"But you haven't done this on humans at all, have you, Dr. James?"

"No. Mr. Drake will be the first. But the procedures are exactly the same as a heart transplant. And, of course, we expect a great success rate, given that it's essentially Mr. Drake's heart. . . because it's made of his heart cells." Colter tried another tack.

"You said the matrix isn't specific. So, why not use the pig heart matrix for a human transplant?" he asked, moving up beside Wainwright, conscious that Jenkins had positioned himself on the other side. The court reporter sat on her stool behind them, busily typing away.

"Oh, very different species, very different matrix," said James crisply. "See, the matrix isn't just an inert scaffold, like the frame of a house. It's got all kinds of proteins and other biologicals we might not even know about that signal the cells to grow and form tissues and organs. True, pig matrix has been used in small-scale wound-healing. But to build a *whole organ*? Not optimal. Not wise. Then there's the different shape of the heart. . ." James wrinkled his brow and shook his head decisively.

"Okay, then, how about using a human heart? One that's too damaged to donate?"

"Damaged heart, damaged matrix," shot back James. The scientist's quick retorts were confirming Colter's growing suspicion: James had been well-coached to give assertive answers that would resonate with a judge. He talked like a scientist, which he was. He had the credible air of a scientist. But he was no dispassionate guide; he was an expert witness for Jenkins.

The pig stirred and shifted, grunting slightly. James continued his recitation. "We tried matrix from abnormal hearts taken immediately post-mortem; we tried healthy cadaver hearts. None produced viable organs. We just don't want to take a chance on a man's life using anything but a healthy matrix taken from an animal that is humans' closest biological relative."

Suddenly, Colter remembered what Abby had said about scientists that night in the cage. How they overcame limits, explored what they could get funding to explore. He took a breath, planning his attack.

"You say you tried nonviable human hearts, cadaver hearts," he said. "How hard did you try?"

"Well, we did some experiments—" James began, but Colter cut him off.

"You did some experiments? That's it?"

"We just found problems with the tissue viability."

"And why didn't you try to solve those problems?"

"Well, the animal became available, and Mr. Drake said he would support pursuing that avenue. And the pig studies gave us reason to believe—" again Colter interrupted.

"But if Solomon wasn't available, what would have happened to the research?"

James paused, his eyes darting around as if looking for an answer. "Well. . . we would probably have continued to explore the use of non-viable human hearts."

"If Drake supported that work. Also, the fact is you've never tried a chimpanzee heart, because you didn't have any chimps to experiment on. So, this is a first time, right?"

"Uh, yes, but we firmly believe it's the right clinical decision," said James emphatically, recovering his composure.

Now Jenkins chimed in. "And it is true, Doctor, that the aim is to save a human life. And the best chance is to use the animal that Mr. Drake clearly owns."

James nodded vigorously.

Wainwright nodded, too, and Jenkins' faint smile told Colter the duel was over, even though all Wainwright said to the lawyers was "You'll have my ruling tomorrow."

"This collection of documents details the entire R and D effort," said James, producing a thick file of reports and scientific papers. Wainwright gestured that they be given to his bailiff, who stepped forward quickly to receive them. The spare judge abruptly turned and led the group out of the barn and toward the line of cars that would take them away from the laboratory.

CHAPTER 15

Wednesday morning

"I have examined the documents. . ." pronounced Wainwright in the court the next day. ". . . and I have considered the field trip yesterday. I find that the proposed medical procedure, although experimental, is a legitimate clinical trial. Thus, there is no reason to suppose that it violates any NIH guidelines against chimpanzee research, although it is true they are only guidelines. Nor does the procedure I witnessed present any prima facie evidence of animal cruelty. Let us now proceed."

In the gallery, Abby lowered her head and, sitting beside Colter, Sarah shook hers sadly. But Colter maintained a head-high, confident stance. He had expected the ruling, and he would go ahead with his unorthodox strategy.

"Yes, Your Honor. For my first witness, I call Carl Schaller," he announced. The name set off a shocked buzz in the courtroom. Those who recognized Schaller's name whispered to those who didn't that he was the notorious convicted serial killer and rapist. Jenkins' maned head jerked toward Colter, his brows furrowing.

"Objection, Your Honor! What possible use could this man's testimony serve? This is no expert witness!" Jenkins knew Schaller all too well. His shrewd defense of Schaller was the principal reason the gaunt, glowering man who hobbled to the witness stand in chains and an orange prison jumpsuit was available to testify and not dead of lethal injection.

"I call this man to testify about his crimes," said Colter. "He is certainly an expert in that area."

Wainwright stared suspiciously at Colter, then at Schaller, then back at Colter. "Since this is such a peculiar case, I'll allow some latitude. But you had better show relevance quickly."

Schaller settled into the witness chair and wiped his long stringy hair out of his eyes with manacled hands, one of which had a crude prison tattoo of a blood-dripping cross etched onto the back.

"Mr. Schaller, you were convicted of killing and raping twelve women and girls, is that correct?"

"That's what they got me on."

"Did you have a trial?"

"Nice trial." He grinned, showing tobacco-stained teeth. "All kinds of evidence. Everybody got to know about my . . . amusement."

"And your lawyer was Michael Jenkins?"

"Worth every dollar."

"Who else is in prison with you?"

"You mean what crimes they did? Oh, we got mother-killers, child molesters, bank robbers, a guy who blew up 'nother guy's house with his family in it."

"And they all had trials?"

"Wouldn't be there if they didn't."

"Are there any chimpanzees in there with you?"

"Jeez, it's a prison, not a zoo."

Jenkins stood, shaking his head. "Your Honor, I just have to object. This is leading nowhere."

"I *will* show relevance," said Colter.

Wainwright leaned forward in his chair and picked up his gavel, as if about to use it. "Overruled for the time being. But make your point, Mr. Colter. My patience is limited."

"Mr. Schaller, I ask whether you think it's fair that you and your fellow inmates, the perpetrators of heinous crimes, had the benefit of full trials and the protection of your rights before the law before your incarceration, even though innocent chimpanzees, who have done no crimes, are incarcerated for life without trial, without any legal recourse."

"Now I must object yet again," said Jenkins, holding his hands wide apart, palms up, in puzzlement. "This witness has shown no relevance."

"I am trying to establish the boundaries of the legal system, Your Honor," Colter shot back. "I'm advocating breaking new legal ground here. I have to establish the parameters of what exists now."

"Mr. Colter, do you see a jury here?" Wainwright swept his right hand to take in the courtroom. "I'm fully aware of criminals' rights and chimpanzees' lack of them."

"Please, Your Honor, allow me to illustrate the limits of the legal system, so that I may show how negating this contract and granting Dr. Philips guardianship does not really compromise them but only extends them logically."

Wainwright toyed with his gavel and scowled at Colter for a long moment but overruled Jenkins, allowing Colter to call his next witness. A swarthy man in a blue suit took the stand. Upon Colter's request, he removed his shirt to reveal a thick mat of black body hair. The courtroom gallery snickered, Jenkins objected, and Wainwright used one lick of the gavel to overrule him and quiet the court.

"Do you vote, sir?"

"Yes," answered the man squirming in his chair and clearing his throat nervously as a few residual giggles peppered the courtroom.

"Do you own property?"

"Yes."

"Do you enjoy all the other legal rights of a citizen?"

"Yes."

"And this, even though you are just about as hairy as my client."

Jenkins rolled his eyes and objected, but Wainwright overruled him once more and sat with an unfathomably stoical expression on his face.

For three more hours, Colter called a parade of witnesses to the stand, each sharing some element of an ape's qualities, each testifying to his or her rights.

A young deaf-mute woman signed through an interpreter that she voted, held property, and enjoyed legal rights, although she had no more vocal abilities than a chimpanzee.

A middle-aged woman sat demurely in the witness chair and explained how she cared for her severely retarded son, who sat in the gallery fidgeting, his gaze wandering around the room, absent-mindedly fiddling with his unaccustomed tie. Her boy, she explained, had the intelligence of a six-year-old, yet enjoyed full legal rights as a citizen.

A young man in a wheelchair rolled himself up beside the stand, explaining that his motorcycle accident had robbed him of his ability to walk but not his ability to vote and even to become president if he wanted to. He was attending college, in fact, and wanted to be a famous lawyer "like Mr. Jenkins . . . and Mr. Colter," he added as a charitable afterthought.

"Are you quite done, Mr. Colter?" asked Wainwright with exaggerated cordiality.

"Just a final point, Your Honor. I have presented witnesses that are hairy, mute, mentally limited, and incapable of walking upright. I have even presented a witness that committed unspeakably horrific crimes. And all of them enjoyed legal rights before the law. However, this innocent animal, who has capabilities that these humans lack, cannot even be given the right to have a guardian that can protect his life. I think I have shown that this inequity should be rectified."

"You have shown us a circus," Wainwright shot back, a flush of anger abruptly coloring his face. "I decided to bend the rules in taking this seriously as a case in law. I allowed you latitude in calling these . . . witnesses." Wainwright hissed the last word with contempt. "But you clearly saw it only as a chance to grandstand. I expected this case to benefit from a more substantive legal argument, but perhaps I shouldn't have." He paused, leaving the last words hanging as a rebuke to Colter.

Colter suddenly became acutely aware of the courtroom camera's unblinking glass eye aimed at him and tried to maintain a mask of determined confidence. "Your Honor—"

"Mr. Jenkins, are you ready to argue your case?" Wainwright interrupted him

"Your Honor, I had not prepared to call witnesses, since this is a property matter, plain and simple," Jenkins said, launching his opening argument. "The plaintiff, in fact, does not dispute the validity of the contract which states that the chimpanzee Solomon is owned free and clear by my client." Jenkins stepped from behind the table, holding a thick sheaf of papers bound in a royal blue folder. "And the memorandum I submitted has addressed this eccentric argument that the animal has some sort of rights that would warrant a legal guardian. I cite the ancient principle of "*hominum causa omne jus constititum*" . . . all laws are established for man's sake. That has been the rule of law as far back as Roman and Greek laws and even into the Old Testament, William Blackstone's seminal work on the Laws of England, and finally American common law." Jenkins held the papers aloft. "And finally, the U.S. Supreme Court in 1896, in *Geer versus Connecticut,* assumed that animals are legally *things.* Not persons. Our legal system clearly holds that a person's life is more important than an animal's. We sacrifice farm animals for our food and experimental animals for our medical health every day."

Wainwright nodded, as if in relief at encountering some common sense. "Gentlemen, it's getting late. I've got other cases this week. So, I'm setting the next session on this case for Monday. I'll hear any final arguments . . ." He stared pointedly at Colter ". . . that is, valid *legal* arguments if you have any. . . at that time." He smacked his gavel sharply to adjourn the session, rose and left. Colter felt a chill from Sarah and Abby as they exited the courtroom, wading through reporters to Sarah's limousine. The two women held their silence until then. But only until then.

"What the hell was that?" demanded Abby as the limousine pulled out toward Colter's office, followed by Beckman in Colter's car.

"That was a case presented the way I thought it needed to be presented," answered Colter, his voice measured.

"It was a weak case by a weak lawyer, I now realize," said Sarah coldly, motioning to her assistant, who handed her a notebook. "I've called another lawyer. He's done animal-rights law. He doesn't go in for circuses, and he actually believes in what he's doing. He'll step in and—"

"Sarah, I can carry this case. Today was a warm-up. I was feeling Jenkins out. I know how to—"

"You know how to put on a good show. I want somebody who can meet Michael Jenkins on an equal footing. I want somebody who takes this case seriously. You didn't do either one today."

"Look, I've got more arguments than I used today. Let me at least outline my future strategy. Tomorrow. Okay?"

Sarah peered out the window, thinking. "Tomorrow afternoon," she said finally. Then to Abby, "Agreeable to you?" Abby nodded somberly.

• • •

"I let a man hang himself today. It felt good. I shouldn't have, though." Wainwright took another bite of the very nice roast chicken that the cook had prepared that night.

"Oh, dear!" His wife set her fork down in surprise. "George, what on earth do you mean?" She sat across from her husband at the antique carved oak table in the spacious, high-ceilinged dining room with the damask wallpaper and the richly embroidered blue silk curtains.

"I'm sorry, sweetheart." Wainwright made an annoyed face at himself for being so enigmatic. "I didn't mean to blurt it out like that without explaining. I've just been thinking about it. It's that case with the animal. The lawyer decided to do some showboating."

"Oh, yes. I watched it on the news. You mean calling all those strange witnesses?"

"I shouldn't have let him."

"But it was his choice, wasn't it?"

Wainwright had forgotten his meal, a troubled look rising like a shadow on his face. "You've heard the old saying 'The devil is in the details?' Well, if I'm going to really defeat the devil in this, I need to have him lay out all the details. I want him to be strong so that, when he falls, it means something."

"Didn't you tell him . . . the lawyer . . . you wanted more?"

"Jesus felt the same way I do, Carrie. Did you know that? I went back and read the Book of Mark before dinner. Where Jesus was in the desert for forty days and forty nights, being tempted by Satan and threatened by the wild beasts."

"I'm sure Jesus would understand, dear."

"And it tells about when he went to Gerasenes and met the man with unclean spirits. Carrie, he allowed the demons to go into pigs. And he let the pigs drown. Jesus, too, believed that animals were below us. They should be kept below us." His hands gripping the table, Wainwright let his eyes wander to the ceiling, recalling the verse. "Now a great herd of swine was there on the mountain-side feeding. And the spirits kept entreating him, saying, 'Send us into the swine, that we may enter into them.' And Jesus immediately gave them leave. And the unclean spirits came out and entered into the swine; and the herd, in number about two thousand, rushed down with great violence into the sea and were drowned in the sea.'"

"Yes, very dramatic, dear." Carrie regarded her husband uneasily. She picked up a small crystal bell and rang it. "Cook has some very nice cake tonight. Would you like some?"

CHAPTER 16

Wednesday evening

Colter stopped in the darkness outside the computer room, listening to the two voices for a while. The soothing voice of Abby alternated with the mechanical-sounding intonations Solomon coaxed from the computer, his sentences stitched together from words spoken by several voices. In particular, he recognized Abby's voice among most of Solomon's computer-generated words, as if she'd contributed bits of herself to the chimp, to give him the gift of speech. Back and forth they went, talking about everyday things, about Solomon's feelings, like two friends catching up on each other's lives.

He felt as if he were intruding, and when he stepped through the door into the room, Solomon clearly concurred, for, at the sight of Colter, the huge ape began pant-hooting with a rapid crescendo, rising to a scream. He leaped off the stool, slammed his body against the other wall of his indoor cage and rebounded to smash against the Lexan window that separated them.

"Solly! Cut that out! It's Mr. Colter. He's trying to help you." Abby moved closer to the window, peering through it to catch Solomon's attention. But he had already fully committed to a display, which consisted of rushing away into the darkness of his cage then returning to slam against the window with a resounding thud, and racing away again.

"He still doesn't like me very much." Colter stepped into the room, staying well away from the window, even though he knew it could withstand Solomon's blows.

"Well, more than anything else, he feels that you threaten him."

"*I* threaten *him*? He's not exactly the most comforting guy I know."

"You're a big, dangerous human. You're an alpha male to him, and he doesn't trust you." She clicked on the microphone. "Solly, this is Colter. You don't have to be afraid. He's helping you. I'll put his name in your computer." She used the computer mouse to click on an icon marked Record and spoke the word "Colter" into the microphone.

"So now he can say my name?"

"He needs an icon for you." She looked him up and down critically and turned to the console, bringing up screenfuls of symbols, using the computer mouse to scan through them. "I'd say a dollar sign on a shark fin."

"Very funny." Colter smiled. Abby was attempting a truce but still keeping the slightly jagged edge on their relationship.

"Okay, how about this? A man and a book." She fiddled with the mouse and the keyboard and came up with an icon of a man holding a book. She touched the screen, and her recorded voice intoned "Colter."

"Man with a book. That's me, exactly. At least he'll know the name of the guy he doesn't like." Colter remembered the bag he was holding and held it up. "Sandwiches. I got you a vegetarian medley, whatever that is."

They walked into the quiet, cool night, skirting the large cage, where Solomon remained in a high state of agitation, climbing a rope, swinging to the pipe framework, and batting angrily at the hanging tire.

"Solly, settle down. You'll ruin my meal," scolded Abby. Thankfully, the chimp retreated back into the computer room.

They sat on the bench in the observation area, unwrapped the sandwiches, and opened bottles of water Colter had brought. Abby pointedly peered at Colter's sandwich but didn't comment on the fact that he'd chosen a vegetarian medley as well.

"Are there still reporters at the gate?" asked Abby, leaning back and taking a bite of sandwich.

"Maybe a dozen and some TV vans. They'd give anything to get in here and tape an interview with you and Solomon. All they've got on the news now is him going nuts and stock footage from old features on you."

"I'm not giving interviews now. But I see you are."

"I've been doing quite a few. I'm still trying to decide about the morning talk shows. We need to counter the bad video. And it's good for the case."

"You mean good for you. I think they call it 'spin control.' I saw . . . and read . . . a lot of criticism of your tactics. I think the word 'ringmaster' was used once or twice."

Colter took a big bite of sandwich and chewed to keep himself from snapping back at her in annoyance. Half a dozen chews, and he admitted to himself that his pique would be partly because he'd begun to care what she thought. He also calmed himself with the notion that her argumentative criticism might be because she cared about him, not just Solomon.

"I did what I thought was best."

"You should have checked your strategy with me."

"You should have told me that your work was controversial . . . Dr. Toolittle."

Now it was Abby's turn to chew in peevish silence. "All this kind of work is controversial." Her voice grew husky with anger. "The same people criticized Jane Goodall when she insisted on studying chimps as creatures with minds, with personalities. I'm building on that work. At least I believe in what I'm doing."

"And I don't?"

"Not really much evidence of that so far."

"So what would I do different if I believed in this case?"

Abruptly, "Colter Colter Colter Colter" in Abby's voice began to sound over and over from the speaker mounted outside the work-room. She laughed in surprise, a warm, feminine, confident laugh that Colter hadn't heard before.

"He's discovered the new icon, and he's trying out your name," she said. "He's figuring out what to think about you. That's how he absorbs new concepts."

"It's nice to be a new concept." Colter continued to work his way through his sandwich.

Abby took a sip of water and leaned back, looking up at a sky with stars fighting to be seen through the glow of Santa Barbara's lights. "If you'd thought about the case, if you'd committed to the idea, you would have presented a very different set of facts."

"Like what? What would convince this judge who's been schooled in a legal tradition a couple of thousand years old?"

"*Facts*. Like that humans and chimps differ by only a percent or so in their DNA. Like putting biologists on the stand who believe our family tree's all screwed up. They say that the branches are wrong. They say chimps should be classified as *Homo troglodytes*, not *Pan*

122

troglodytes. You want to talk about history? How about that, in the 17th century, when chimps were first discovered, they were called *Homo sylvestris* . . . man of the woods. You can use facts like that to change his mind."

"I need law, not facts."

"Jesus, what a cynical statement!"

"I'm sorry, but sometimes that's what it's about. Precedent, emotion, prejudice. Sometime that's the law."

From the speaker came the words, "Colter is a man. Colter is a man. Colter is bad. Colter is a bad man."

. . .

When Colter let himself into his condominium, the small lamp by the couch was on, casting a warm glow across the beige leather furniture and competing with the decorative garden lights outside the room's wall of glass. The lights softly lit the lush garden of large tree ferns, bird-of-paradise, jade plants and neatly trimmed ivy. Colter was puzzled at first. He hadn't left the light on.

But then he sensed that Cindy was in the condo, smelling the faint aroma of her perfume. She must have come back from her magazine shoot and let herself in to surprise him. He felt a subtle clash between the pleasure of her presence and the memory of the time spent in the darkness with Abby. The latter seemed to take on more importance as he thought about it.

"You here?" he called. He'd learned not to use a name. Once he'd called out the wrong one.

Without answering, Cindy stepped out from the bedroom, a tall, willowy, honey-blond woman wearing a powder-blue silk pants suit, her wide blue eyes revealing utter terror.

"Bobby," was all she could manage to utter before her voice failed her.

"What's the matter?"

From behind her stepped a small, pale, haggard man, his head a ragged stubble of hair that matched his unshaven face, a haunted, drained look in his eyes. He wore a tattered long-sleeved shirt that shrouded a skeletal frame, as did the gray worn pants.

He brought up a long stiletto gripped in a pale hand, pointing its needle-sharp tip toward Cindy, who stood dead still, hands at her side, fright draining any hint of a model's poise.

"He followed me in," she said, panic choking off the last word.

"I knew you lived here. You're killing us," declared the man in a trembling voice. "I seen you on TV and what you're doing, and I know you're killing us."

"Sir, I don't know what you mean," said Colter evenly. "If you'll put the knife down, we can talk about it."

"You always talk. You talk all the time, and you don't see that the researchers could make lots of hearts from the animals. They could make them for all of us. I'm at the bottom of the list because I was a drunk, my liver's shot. And there's not enough hearts. But I could get a heart now. You have to stop."

"Stop what? I'm sorry, but I don't understand. If you'd put the knife down—"

"The court case. You don't stop, I'm going to stop you." The man whipped the knife around toward Colter, shuffling forward, now with the deadly point aimed at Colter's chest. "I'll hurt you so bad you'll have to stop." Cindy took the opportunity to slip away into the bedroom. The man swallowed hard, as if something were obstructing his throat, coughed a dry raspy cough, and looked dully down at the knife. He brought up his other hand, and with a swift slash laid open a deep cut across his palm that welled with blood that began to dribble a line of red onto the pale-gray Berber carpet.

"Christ! What did you do that for?"

"That's what you'll see. Your blood on the floor. I'll wait until your girlfriend has the cops comin', the ambulance. Then I'll open you up. Then *you'll* need a new heart." The man clasped his hand against the shirt, wiping a thick stain of blood that stuck the shirt to his prominent ribs. He waved the knife back and forth, stumbling toward Colter.

Colter backed away, his mind desperately casting about for ideas. He began to figure a strategy. He mentally pictured the kitchen, pictured the counter and what it held, calculated his chances.

He bolted away through the kitchen door to his right, careening off the refrigerator to divert his momentum, lunging for the wooden knife rack, grabbing a handle and scrambling out the other door into the dining room. Behind him, he heard the man react with a surprised grunt and the sound of crashing furniture as he lurched clumsily after Colter. But by that time, Colter had dashed across the living room to the bedroom door. He glimpsed Cindy standing beside the bed, her cell phone in her hand, and he whirled to face the man, who advanced toward him, knife held straight out, his other hand red with blood.

Colter brought up the kitchen knife and saw with relief that he had managed to grab a large, impressive carving knife and not the paring knife. "Come on," he growled. "Mine's bigger, and I'll make sure your heart beats its last beat!"

"Just say you'll stop," gasped the man, the point of the stiletto making wary arcs in the air, searching for an opening. "You need to let them use the monkey, or the science people will stop working on the new hearts."

"Right in *your* damned heart," repeated Colter, realizing that his hand was beginning to shake. He steeled himself against the man's attack. The faint warble of a siren penetrated the room. "Hear that, pal? Really soon, there'll be a lot of guns pointed at you."

The man took a step back, doubt clouding his expression, tears welling in his eyes. "Damn. Can't do it, even to you. Just think who you're killing. That's all I ask." He bumped against a chair, and jumped to the side, as if it were an attacker. He turned and fled, holding the knife pointed back over his shoulder, as if it would act as a rear guard. He was gone out the garden door and over the fence.

Sobbing, Cindy ran to Colter, and he embraced her. "Jesus," he breathed. They stood in each other's arms for a long while as the sirens grew louder and then stopped, followed by the squawk of a radio, the slamming of car doors. A kaleidoscope of flashing lights from patrol cars outside danced across the walls and ceiling.

"It's the police," came a voice from his front entrance. "Are you folks in there? Are you okay?" A beefy uniformed cop entered the room, his heft reassuring, as was his belt festooned with all the paraphernalia of police and a nine-millimeter pistol in his hand pointed at the ceiling.

"He just ran out," said Colter. "Did you get him?"

"Sir, are you and the lady okay?" Once Colter nodded yes, the cop continued. "We've called for backup."

"Blood on the carpet in here and down the hall," said a voice behind him, and another cop walked into the room, shorter and slimmer, but hefting the same comfortingly deadly pistol.

"He's gone?" asked Colter.

"Apparently," said the large cop. "But the units we've got coming will do a thorough sweep of the neighborhood."

Finally, the large cop reported that nobody had been found and promised to have a patrol car regularly check up on him. The uniformed cops were followed by a pair of suited detectives to whom Colter and Cindy spent the next hour telling their story as the crackle of police radios continued to punctuate the quiet night.

The burly senior detective, who reminded him of a younger, soberer Digger, warned Colter to keep his doors locked. As the detectives were about to leave, Cindy asked them to wait. She turned to Colter.

"This case about the chimp. You've been all over TV. I hope you understand, Bobby, but I can't take this kind of thing. I just can't. He may come back. There will be more stuff. And there'll be all these reporters. I just can't."

Colter hugged her. "I understand. I don't expect you to take it. It's not your problem. It's mine."

She asked the detectives to walk her to her car, and she followed them out.

Colter closed the door and locked it. He laid towels over the blood on the carpet and turned out the lights, sitting for a long time on the couch in the dark, slowly drinking an entire bottle of merlot, from a crystal glass. The warm glow of the wine and the sight of the softly lit garden helped calm him enough to consider sleep. But that sleep came only with difficulty, as the shards of the day's memories intruded, reminding him of the mess he'd gotten himself into.

CHAPTER 17

Thursday morning

"I count about six hundred 'fuck you' Tweets, three hundred 'damn-you-to-hells,' and eight hundred 'bless-yous,'" said Sheba, sitting at her desk scanning the Twitter feed. "The damn-you-to-hells are mostly from religious folk and the bless-yous are from animal lovers. Actually, some of the fuck-yous are from animal lovers who think you screwed up the case. Okay, now for the phone messages. Lots of threats. Then, you got thirty-one requests for interviews, and all the talk shows say they've got limos waiting to take you to their studios anytime you want. I put them roughly in order of audience size. And the answering service says they're going to charge you double this month for taking so much shit."

Colter sighed and set down his briefcase, peering at the message list over her shoulder. "Give the threats to the cops." He handed her the business card that the lead detective had given him the previous night before leaving. "I had a visitor," he said, briefly telling her the story of the man with the knife.

"Then you'll be glad Digger's in your office. He's got a list of the few retired cops who don't hate your guts and are willing to work as bodyguards."

Colter picked up the briefcase, looking forward to seeing Digger, but Sheba waved her multi-ringed hand commandingly for him to stay.

"I got really bad news. There were three kiss-offs from big clients. California Indemnity and Alpha Megastores. They said they didn't want to catch hell from any customers who found out you were on their retainer. And Johnny Miller has dropped you, too."

"Well, damn!" grumped Colter. He had been making ten thousand a month off the two firms, from retainers to handle court work on claims for the insurance company and customer lawsuits for the store chain. And Johnny Miller? To be dropped by a notorious gang boss? That was especially galling.

He entered the office to find Digger sitting at Colter's desk, coffee in hand, staring out the window.

He swiveled the chair around at the sound of Colter's briefcase on the desk. "Boy, you sure brought a shit load on yourself, didn't you? Them cameras been out there all morning."

"Yeah, well, it's not easy being a celebrity." With Digger occupying his desk chair, Colter let himself collapse into one of the armchairs. On the rare occasions he sat there, he liked to ponder what an imposing sight he must present to clients. Not this morning.

"Well, you say the word, I'll put a guy up here with Sheba. Another at your place. A buddy of mine on the nine-one-one desk called me about your intruder last night. They still haven't found the perp. But it sounds like he was some drugged-out mook who watched the news and got all riled up. You're going to keep getting them. I saw Sheba's list."

"Yeah, pick who you like and put them on. I appreciate it, Digger."
Sheba appeared with his coffee and went over to pat Digger's shoulder, asking him if he needed more. When Digger declined, saying he preferred room in his cup "for additives," she tweaked his ear, gave him a scowl of knowing reproof, and settled onto the couch.

"I got other stuff to tell you, though," said Digger, hauling himself up to open the cabinet that held the liquor, augmenting his coffee with Colter's best cognac.

"More good news?"

"Drake has put his people out after you."

"People? What do you mean?"

"Lawyers, investigators, flacks. They're pressuring clients, looking into your past. He's got his PR firm assigned to see that your image gets real lousy real fast."

"I just lost three clients."

"Shouldn't wonder. You'll likely lose more."

Darrell Beckman came in, set his cup down on the table, and flipped open his leather notebook. "So, Bobby, what do you want us to do now?" Digger sat back down behind Colter's desk and eyed Beckman with a vague expression of distaste. Their personalities and tactics had clashed on several occasions; and after half a bottle of Wild Turkey, Digger had once called Beckman a "rich little southern-fried turd" to his face.

Colter's coffee began to kick in, and so did his sense of outrage. "Sheba, hire some of the best paralegals you can find. Tell them to go back over the law, the legal philosophy, the history . . . everything. Lay it all out, and I'll review it. Talk to the people with the Nonhuman Rights Project. And get me the number of the head lawyer for the People for Moral Animal Treatment. I'll call and talk to him. They've been fighting these battles for years. I've got to present a new strategy to Sarah Huntington and Abby this afternoon that will keep us on this case. There's too much at stake here—the clients, the fees, the reputation. Digger, you keep checking your sources about what Drake's people are up to." He pushed himself resolutely out of the chair and grabbed his briefcase. "I'll review it all when Darrell and I get back."

"Back from where?" asked Beckman, as Digger drained his coffee, picked up the phone, and began punching in numbers.

"We're going to see Drake."

CHAPTER 18

Thursday afternoon

The cavernous bedroom smelled of disinfectant and the bodily aroma of illness. Walter Drake lay in a huge antique four-poster re-engineered into an adjustable hospital bed, his pale flesh sagging from his frame. The persistent California sunlight was masked by heavy blue velvet curtains, save for one opened just wide enough to cast a muted light across the room. The young woman Clair held the bed's control box, pushing the button to raise the head until Drake nodded wanly to her. She kissed him on the forehead, folded a red call button into his hand and stole quietly away. But the stolid Lunt stayed by the door where he had installed himself after escorting Colter into the room. And beside Lunt stood a young, expensively suited man that could have been a clone of Beckman, who stood at the back of the room. The lawyer was one of Jenkins' senior associates, and his annoyed expression portrayed displeasure that Drake had disregarded legal advice not to talk to Colter.

"You get through the mob out front all right?" asked Drake, motioning Colter to an armchair beside the bed.

"Yes. They certainly would like to interview you."

Drake managed a weak chuckle. "It's ironic, isn't it? I'd love to put a couple of the boys at the gate with M-sixteens and see how well reporters dodge bullets. But the hell of it is, I'd hit mostly my own people. Ruin some perfectly good camera equipment. Maybe someday, I'll be willing to stand the cost." He laid a hand across his stomach, exposing its blue-scarred back inserted with an IV tube connected to a bag of clear liquid.

"How's the assist device working?" The question was more than sympathy on Colter's part, and Drake knew it. Colter was looking for an angle to challenge Drake's need for Solomon's heart.

Drake smiled and patted the device's battery pack lying beside him on the bed. "It's pumping my blood. I've got no heartbeat. Some people say that's always been the case. For people like me, the doctors call this 'destination therapy.' It's a euphemism. It means there's no chance for a transplant, and this is it for me." Having made his point, Drake's eyes narrowed. "I understand you were here last night. With the woman."

"Look, I came here to make sure you understood my position. I know what you're trying to do. That you're trying to ruin me. Well, you'd damned well better stop it." Colter felt a mild shudder run through his body at the thought that he was giving an ultimatum to a billionaire, and a ruthless one at that.

A rush of anger contorted Drake's face, and he strained to inch himself up on the bed, his voice taking on an authoritarian growl. "No, *you'd* better damned well stop it! You're interfering with my God-given right to life. I have a destiny to live out my life before moving to the next, and this animal was presented to me as a pathway to that destiny." Lunt appeared beside Colter, ready to do whatever was necessary to make his employer more comfortable. No doubt that would include roughing up Colter, if necessary. Jenkins' associate moved up nearer the bed, as well.

"It's one thing to fight a court battle. It's another to ruin people."

Again Drake chuckled, but the laugh was stronger, energized by hatred. "This is no game. This is my life, and I'll do what's necessary to save it. Even ruin a rather insignificant lawyer. That's why I *let* you come here. To tell you about. . ." He managed a feeble wave at the young associate. ". . . what was that case, William? What was the name?"

"MacIntire," answered the associate, with a predatory smile.

"Yes, MacIntire. To tell you what we know about that. Mr. Colter, you remember the MacIntire case? Murder case five, six years ago? One of Jenkins' legal researchers dug out the records. He got Jenkins really interested in how you handled it. He's thinking about passing what he knows to my newspapers, TV stations. . . and the cops. Purely in the interest of responsible journalism, you understand."

Colter gripped the arms of the chair hard, his palms growing damp. "There's nothing there. Not a thing."

"Enough for disbarment. Hell, even jail time if it's. . . uh. . . augmented. You know, with some additional evidence."

Colter stood up, towering over Drake, but at the same time feeling as if Drake were looming over him. "You're not going to scare me off this case, Drake."

"Oh, sit down, sit down, Mr. Colter. I believe in sticks and carrots. Sticks force people to react, but carrots inspire them to want to act. That's always been my saying. We can forget the MacIntire matter. Who needs responsible journalism anyway? We'll also forget the Vasquez bust."

"The what? I don't know anything about—"

"No, you wouldn't. It was a police case about fifteen years ago. A couple of cops busted a drug dealer. Lots of cash. But the pile had shrunk by the time it was logged into the evidence room. One of the cops is still around. He works for you as a matter of fact. And as for the other one . . . well . . . your father paid your first-year tuition in law school with a fat check, didn't he?"

"Son-of-a-bitch!" Colter leaped up and immediately felt Lunt's large hand clamp down on his shoulder. He glanced back to catch the cold glint of a pistol beneath Lunt's jacket.

"Carrots, Mr. Colter. I haven't talked about the carrots. My companies have major legal needs. As you saw by the presence of Mr. Jenkins in court, I do not hesitate to employ the best. My best lawyers receive a million a year for a retainer. It's a good investment. I'd like to make such an investment in you."

"Go to hell!" exclaimed Colter, twisting away from Lunt's grip and striding away, past the young associate, Beckman falling in behind him.

"Mr. Colter, I'm a student of go-to-hells," Drake called after him, his breath beginning to fail him. "Been analyzing them all my life. I know, for example, that yours was a *thinking-it-over* go-to-hell, and not a *no-deal* go-to-hell. My people will be in touch with details."

Beckman walked with Colter down the huge staircase and out the front door to the Mercedes. "You should really think about it," he whispered. "This case is a loser, anyway, and he's got stuff that could hurt you badly." Colter was so preoccupied that he didn't notice that Beckman still had his smartphone out, snapping images of the house and grounds, as he had been doing since they first approached the front gate. "Reference purposes," he had told Colter, also persuading him, before they had seen Drake, to take him around to Solomon's cage and the research building.

"You never can tell when an image might show something relevant to the case," he'd told Colter. He was right, although Beckman seemed more than his usual assertive self about taking the photos.

      •   •   •

Beckman continued shooting photos out the window as Colter drove the car down the road from the mansion, through the gate, past the crowd of reporters, and back toward the city. As Beckman continued to talk about Drake's offer, Colter felt as if two tumors had been implanted in his brain, one threatening his life, the other threatening Digger and his father's memory. He remembered his old man, tough as a chunk of concrete when he was on the streets but tender eyed when he looked at his son. He remembered his father's tight embrace that lasted so very long when his mother had died. He remembered when the toughness seemed to grow brittle as his father aged. Then, for the first time he realized that his father's life, and his father's power, had limits.

He also remembered that he'd vowed when his father died of a heart attack not ever to accept being poor. He wouldn't live the kind of frayed, precarious existence that his mother's long illness had brought the family. He wouldn't accept the shabby apartment they'd moved to when his father had to go on disability from the patrol-car accident. The old man would call him a smart-mouth when they argued. Now that smart mouth had made him nearly as rich as he wanted to be. But it had also gotten him into a case that now wrapped around him like a coil of barbed wire.

Drake had been right, God damn him. Colter's go-to-hell wasn't completely a no-deal. He was still wavering back and forth, a moth circling a bright light, first near, then far. How very easy it would be to give up the case, to save his security and Digger's. It *was* a hell of an offer, considering that he'd lost the first round so badly, and all Drake really had to do was wait for Jenkins to finish him off. He even figured a graceful way out if he wanted to use it. He could tell Sarah and Abby that his conscience wouldn't let him sacrifice a man's life—in fact ultimately a thousand human lives—to some doubtful legal principle, which was essentially what he was doing. It was reasonable, he told himself.

So, if he was so ambivalent, why did he sit in his office the rest of the day, poring over the stack of new research Sheba's research team had gathered? Why did he spend an hour on the phone with Harper Childs, the chief lawyer for the People for Moral Animal Treatment, going over legal precedents and tactics? Childs was a genial veteran of the very battles Colter was now fighting.

"You okay?" Childs had finally asked solicitously. "Can we help besides giving advice? You know we're here for you. Whatever you need."

"That's reassuring," said Colter. "I think I've got it."

"Yeah, you handle yourself well. I saw the news shows. Are you sure you don't want us to file an amicus brief, to bolster your side?"

"I thought about it. But I want this to be seen as a David-and-Goliath scenario. It does sometimes influence judges. And you guys are the eight-hundred-pound gorillas in the field."

Childs laughed heartily. "That's the nicest thing anybody could say to somebody from PMAT! Tell you what. We'll stay below the radar. But we'll quietly use our contacts to see that you've got a level playing field with the politicians. You won't hear a peep out of them, I assure you. And our supporters know how to assert their opinions in the media."

Heartened, he went back to work for several more hours, painstakingly outlining a strategy that forcefully argued all the morally right points. And, that afternoon, he used his best persuasive powers to pitch those points to Sarah and Abby, leaving them backing him with only minor qualms. Maybe he was driven by that cursed demon, misguided professionalism. Maybe a touch of arrogance, maybe an attraction to Abby. Or, maybe he was just keeping his options open.

Beckman had left after they arrived back at the office, saying he wanted to check some legal points. Colter had sent Sheba home and was reading through the research again, when he heard voices and the thump of scuffling in the outer office. He stuck his head out the door to see Digger—who had appointed himself to the majority of guard duty—rousting a gangly ferret-faced man in a ratty white baseball cap and a blue windbreaker with an eagle on the back.

"Get the fuck out of here," growled Digger, heaving the man against the wall, backing up and pulling his coal-black Glock pistol.

"Hey, this is business he'll be interested in. He'll want to see this."

"You fuckin' won't want to see what comes out of this gun, if you don't haul your skinny ass out of here."

"Really, this is a good thing he'll want to see. Good business proposition."

Colter stepped out into the office and beside Digger. "Who is this, and how the hell did he get in here?"

"Ah, Mr. Colter, sir," said the man. "I just waited until the janitor brought the garbage out the back, then I slipped on in. I got your problem solved." The man's tongue darted nervously in and out of his mouth in excitement, wetting his lips in anticipation of the pitch that was to come.

"I've got lots of problems. Which one?"

"The chimp, man. I got a replacement. Downstairs. Just come see." He flipped his head toward the elevator. His hands flapped excitedly at the open elevator door, as if they were preparing to enter it by themselves, without him.

"Don't do it," said Digger. "Looks like a trap to me."

"You've got a chimp downstairs?" asked Colter.

"In the truck. Up and up business proposition. You'll see, man." Again the darting tongue made its fleeting appearance.

For a long moment, Colter watched the eager little man display his medley of tics and twitches. Then finally, "Let's take a look."

"I don't like this shit," said Digger. "Bobby, if you go down there, you do it my way. I go first and check it out."

"Well, Digger, then you're out there all alone yourself, aren't you? How smart is that?"

"Damned smart. I know how to use this." He brandished his pistol.

"Okay, you can go first, but I'm at your back."

"Wow! What a relief!" hmphed Digger. "I got a lawyer backing me up in case I got to threaten some killers with a restraining order."

Colter clapped Digger on the back as the three entered the elevator to take it to the first floor. The little man chattered all the way down.

"Name's Willie Baker." He stuck out a hand and pumped Colter's eagerly when it was offered. "They call me Willie the Wild Animal Man. Willie-Boy. Wonder-Willie. Sometimes Free Willie. I'm a promoter. Exotic animals for your amusement and education. Actually, just this one chimp right now, but once I pass him to you, I'm going to get more."

They reached the lobby, and Digger drew his pistol, following Willie into the utility area. They walked out the back service entrance to see parked beside the small loading dock, a faded-blue pickup truck with a tarpaulin covering a high structure in the back. He scampered off the dock and to the truck.

"This is something you'll want!" exclaimed Willie, whipping back the tarp. "This is what you're looking for, right here."

The sickening stench of feces and urine rolled out of a steel cage set into the truck bed, causing Colter and Digger both to exclaim "Jesus!" and avert their heads.

"Don't pay no mind to the smell," said Willie. "I haven't hosed it out today, 'cause I been traveling. I just hose it out, and he smells fine."

Colter peered into the depths of the cage, still partially covered by the tarp. He could see only a dark form huddled against the other end. Willie peered in and then back at them.

"Oh. You can't see him; that's the problem. Let me fix that." Willie yanked the tarp completely off, revealing the form to be some sort of hairy black animal, curled up in the corner. Colter thought he saw the white flash of a face. Willie rummaged in the truck and brought out a long black stick with a button at one end. He thrust the stick through the cage bars and pressed the button with his thumb.

A wail of soul-deep anguish erupted from the animal, and it leaped up and slammed against the rear bars of the cage, crying pitiably. The impact of the large body drove a startled Digger and Colter several steps back, as two large, feces-encrusted hands thrust themselves through the cage bars. An index finger on the right hand was but a stub. A face turned toward them, the fear-contorted face of a large chimpanzee.

"You see him good now?" asked Willie. "I can give him another shot. Take a look at him."

The chimpanzee's eyes, wide with fear, glistened with the gray viscous film of sickness. His brow knitted and un-knitted like an instrument recording waves of pain. A line of drool dribbled from his mouth, and the animal's head lolled from fatigue. His shallow panting was interrupted by a long moan emerging from deep in the throat. Underlying the reek of feces was a sour smell of infection. Scabbed-over sores matted with tangled hair covered his body.

"I call him Lucky," said Willie. "We been going around for a few years, place to place. I show him at bars. And the barkeep gives me a few bucks. But the damn government says they're endangered, or something, and maybe make me give him up. And, as you can see, Lucky's not doing so well. So, I figured, you got the experts. You buy him off me, fix him up, you got a substitute for the other chimp. You want me to pop him a couple of times, turn him around, so you can see the other side?" Willie brought up the cattle prod, and the animal winced and raised his hand, desperately waving it back and forth, whimpering and grinning, showing broken, stained teeth. "See that wave. That's a trick I taught him. He can do all kinds of tricks. Shows he's smart. Like the one you got. I'll pop him."

Colter knocked the cattle prod away. "No, no. Don't do that." He swallowed hard and shook his head. "Lucky," he breathed to himself, shaking his head at the irony of the name given the wretched chimpanzee. After a moment, he took out his cell phone and punched in a number. The other party answered. "It's Colter. Come to my office. Fast as you can. It's an emergency. You'll see." He stepped away from the truck so Willie couldn't hear the rest of the conversation. After a moment, he was back, the phone stowed away. "Let's get him some water, some food."

Digger bought fruits and vegetables from a small market on the next block, and, by the time he had returned, Colter had found a bowl, filled it with clean water and slid it through a slot for feeding. They pushed bananas, oranges, carrots and other vegetables through the slot, and the animal eagerly snatched them up, gathering them into a pile, as if afraid they would be taken back. He ate with an urgent relish that spoke of starvation, yet his body moved with a lethargy that betrayed profound illness.

After a half hour, the darkened alley was lit by the headlights of a white van with the university's seal and the Primate Language Research Center's sign on the side. Abby leaped out of the driver's side, and Keeli Mannix, the long-haired technician, unfolded from the passenger's side.

"Oh, dear God," was all Abby could say when she saw the animal. "Whose chimp is this?"

"Mine, ma'am. He's not in so good a shape, but—"

"You son of a bitch. I ought to have you jailed. I'd like to—"

Willie's face began to harden, but Colter stepped between them. "So, how much do you want for this animal?"

Willie's face softened immediately. "Well, sir, it's a fine animal. Except for the sickness and all. I'd say about ten thousand. I came to you first, but I could go to the rich guy, y'know. I bet he'd pay."

Colter squeezed Abby's arm, and she gave him a disgusted look that said she would stay quiet while the critical business of saving the chimp was carried out.

"Let us take a look at him," she finally said, in a low, strained voice. Willie agreed, and Abby and Keeli moved to the animal, who had returned to the distant end of the cage, curling up and panting and whimpering quietly. They began to talk in low tones.

"Say, Willie, ten thousand's pretty steep for an animal that might not see tomorrow. A thousand."

Willie whipped off his cap and rolled his eyes. "Jeez, you're killing me, here. This guy's worth a mint!"

Digger stepped up and grinned menacingly, using his bulk to its full advantage. "Ain't worth much if you're in jail on animal-cruelty charges and resisting arrest."

"Hey, I wouldn't resist arrest! I'm a legal guy!"

"My buddies who arrested you would say you did. And that you littered and jaywalked and loitered, and drove a car with broken headlights. You'd stay in jail a long time. Especially, if you had any outstanding warrants in another state."

Willie jerked his head about, looking for a way out. "Make me an offer," he finally pleaded. "Make me an offer."

"Four thousand," said Colter. "And an agreement to stay the hell out of the animal business."

"Jeez . . . well . . . yeah, you got it, Mr. Colter. Y'know, I've got other enterprises. I'll do something else. I will. My word's as good as gold."

Abby returned from ministering to the animal. "I'm paying," she declared. "I've learned my lesson about letting somebody else pay for an animal." She took out her smartphone and accessed her bank account, peering intently at the numbers on the screen, as if she could will them to change. "I can do $2,465. That cleans out my account." She looked pleadingly at Willie, who scrunched his face into a frown, darted his tongue in and out a few times, shrugged and shook his head decisively.

"Can't do that. I just can't do that. Y'know, I got expenses."

"I'll pay the rest," said Colter, taking out his checkbook and scribbling a check for the entire amount.

"I'll pay you back," said Abby, intently regarding Colter for a long moment, as if reconsidering an opinion she had until now firmly held about him. She returned to the van to fetch the long, thin tranquilizer gun, filled a large dart with tranquilizer and pumped it full of pressure. She loaded the dart into the rifle's breech, pumping pressure into its propellant chamber. She stepped back, took careful aim through the bars and fired the dart into the animal, who squealed in surprise, but settled down quickly, and within a few minutes fell unconscious. His thick pink tongue lolled out of its mouth, and his breath rattled wetly in his throat. His large simian face relaxed

"Probably the first time in years he's not suffering," muttered Abby.

With a nervous Willie standing back holding the cattle prod in front of him for protection, Abby, Keeli, Colter and Digger opened the cage and struggled to lift the inert animal by his thick limbs. They heaved his bulk onto a litter that they hoisted into the van. Abby stroked the matted hair and talked quietly to the chimpanzee, seemingly unaware of the foul smell. Once the chimp had been securely strapped down and she had checked his breathing, she turned to Colter, her eyes showing a sheen of tears.

"Thank you," she said in a voice husky with emotion.

Colter cleared his throat to rid it of an annoying lump. "Well, I did it for me, too."

She smiled. "I know." She climbed into the van, leaning her head out the window. "Come by tomorrow and visit him. There are some other things I have to talk to you about." She gunned the van, and it accelerated away into the night.

Digger began to colorfully describe to Willie the deep misfortune that would befall him if he ever kept in captivity even so much as a cat.

Meanwhile, Colter stood staring at the end of the alley, where the van had last been visible. He took out his primary cell phone and punched in a number.

"This is R. William Colter, the lawyer. I'd like to leave a message for Mr. Drake. Please tell him I said 'No deal. Go to hell.' Use those words exactly. Thank you. Goodbye."

CHAPTER 19

Friday morning

The radio news jockey announced in his rich baritone that "The World Evangelical Confederation released a statement today condemning the effort by a California lawyer to obtain legal rights for a chimpanzee. The statement emphasized that the Christian religion holds that man was made in God's image and given dominion over the animals. The group said that the lawyer's effort to lower man to the level of animals constitutes a sacrilege. In other news—"

Colter punched the radio button to switch to an easy-listening station, sighed, and downed another gulp of coffee, steering the BMW along a freeway swarming with speeding, weaving early-morning traffic. He'd been up since 3:30 a.m., having decided that he and Abby should go on the morning TV talk shows to defend the case.

To counteract the news reports that showed a violent Solomon, they had shown video of a peaceful chimp, conversing with Abby using a tablet computer. And Abby had advocated passionately for Solomon's right to life.

But they faced adversaries. On one show, they had argued with the head of a militant animal-rights group, who insisted that they hadn't gone far enough. The woman asserted they should be going for rights for animals all the way down to mice, too. On another, the head of the National Institutes of Health warned that legal rights for chimpanzees might well spark rights cases for monkeys and other experimental animals, precluding possible lifesaving studies. On a third show, a Baptist minister accused them of blasphemously attacking a fundamental tenet of the church—that man had dominion over the animals.

But Colter and Abby had given good TV on all the shows, coming across as calm, reasonable people and not the slick, glib lawyer and the firebrand scientist that the media had painted them as. As he negotiated the traffic, he called Harper Childs at the People for Moral Animal Treatment.

"The David-and-Goliath strategy isn't working out," he'd told Childs. "I don't have a rock. Hell, I don't even have a slingshot."

"Son, I've been reading your court transcripts," said Childs. "You're a smart young fellow, somebody who thinks on his feet. I have no doubt whatsoever that suddenly you'll find yourself with just the right slingshot, just the right rock."

If Colter ever needed a shot of confidence, he had one now. As he ended the call, he found himself driving boxed in by looming trucks in the lanes on either side. But he didn't feel nearly as boxed in on this case. Even so, like the traffic, this court case was growing, moving faster, and growing road-rage nasty.

On the crowded freeway, he did manage to bluff his way into the right lane to exit onto the road leading to the primate lab, and after the winding drive, pulled up to the gate, announcing himself over the intercom. Abby hadn't slept at all, staying up with Lucky all night then going directly to the TV interviews, and then leaving Colter to hurry back to the lab, saying Lucky needed treatment.

After he changed into protective coveralls and left his watch and cell phones in the locker room, he found her curled up, napping on a cot beside Solomon's empty cage. Across the way, Caroline's cage now held a sleeping Lucky, oblivious to the periodic hooting and screaming of the other chimpanzees, who hurled their massive bodies around with loud crashes each time yet another human stranger ventured into their cage room. Abby looked so vulnerable curled in a fetal position, her fine dark hair spread out over the pillow, her stockinged feet crossed, like those of a sleeping child.

He sat down on the cot, and she stirred sleepily. With her eyes half-open, she asked, "Is he okay?" Then she opened her eyes and smiled. "Oh, it's you." She sat up, stretching and peering into the cage. "I owe you some money for Lucky."

"I'll just pad my hours. Sarah can pay."

"Normally I'd believe you did it for money, being a lawyer and all. But I'm not so sure now. I think maybe you're getting soft-hearted."

"Nah. No chance. How's my investment? I see you put him in Caroline's cage."

"Yeah." She tilted her head and pursed her lips in sad memory. "I think the old lady would have approved of me doing that. He's lots better. We did a full physical with a blood workup. He had an infection and some untreated wounds. That son-of-a-bitch used more than a cattle prod on him. He was also dehydrated and malnourished. I figure the guy decided that, as long as he was going to sell him, he'd quit investing in food."

"What did you do for him?" Colter stood and peered into the cage to see Lucky rolled up in a blanket in the corner, his chest rising and falling rhythmically.

"Gave him a broad-spectrum antibiotic and a vitamin injection, plenty of water, and began to slowly bring his nourishment up."

"Is he going to be all right?"

She joined him by the cage, clutching the mesh. Next door, Earle clambered up the side of the partition between the cages, to hang there and watch her eagerly. "Physically, yeah. But mentally? He probably wouldn't be if he was human. He'd know what a scum his former owner was and think we were going to be the same. Such chimps may seem like lost causes when they're abused, but they can really rebound with loving care. They're a lot like street kids, runaways."

"Kids that can throw refrigerators," Colter said, bringing another weary smile from her. It was a good sign. Maybe she was going to be okay, too. "You wanted to talk to me about something?"

Just then one of the technicians, a young, slim brunette girl wearing rubber boots, came into the hallway with the morning fruit, and the chimps launched an excited racket, prompting Abby and Colter to retreat to her office to talk. Colter put his suit back on and retrieved his phones.

She sat in the chair in her office, seeming to sag with the weight of what she had to say.

"The university lawyers called yesterday. They've sent me a letter saying they're closing the lab."

"*What? Why?*"

"The case has got some pretty important people mad. Donors, trustees, faculty, some students. They get complaints from even a few of those people, and that constitutes a tidal wave of opinion."

"What can you do? Don't they have contractual obligations to you?"

"Nothing they can't get out of. And I still don't have tenure, so I can get kicked out in a New York minute." Abby stared blankly at the floor and raised her hands from her lap in a gesture of helplessness before they dropped back.

The young girl in the boots appeared at the door, ducking her head in apology and wincing to indicate she didn't want to interrupt.

"Ivy, you need to tell us something?" asked Abby.

"Uh, well, uh, I was cleaning the cages, and I turned CNN on the TV in there," said Ivy. "Mr. Colter, they said there was a breaking story coming up about you."

Abby and Colter went into the lab's coffee room and watched the morning CNN report until Colter's image flashed on behind the news anchor.

"CNN has learned that the Los Angeles District Attorney's office has launched an investigation of R. William Colter, the lawyer attempting to gain legal rights for a chimpanzee, on charges that he bribed a witness. Mr. Colter was not reachable for comment. An unnamed source, however, said that the case could bring disbarment and possible criminal action." The scene cut to a reporter in front of the courthouse reciting the history of Solomon's case and speculating on the case against Colter.

"Bobby, what's this about?" asked Abby. "Did you do anything?"

"No and yes. It's complicated." Colter's face remained impassive, his jaw set, as he took out his cell phone and punched in a number. "I can't explain it now," he said as he waited for an answer. "It would involve you in something you don't need to be involved in." He turned to the phone conversation. "You're in already. I figured you would be. Listen, have Digger and Darrell in my office in half an hour. We've got some figuring to do, and—" He paused, listening to the other end. He uttered a string of frustrated curses at the news he heard and then said goodbye.

Abby took Colter by the arm. "What's going on, Bobby?"

"That was Sheba on the phone. When she got into the office, there was the usual bunch of phone messages from reporters about the investigation. But there was also one from her source at the hospital where Drake is being treated. The bad news is that Drake seems to have gotten worse. They can't wait for him to get stronger, because he's not. Jenkins has filed a brief with Wainwright that the tissue-engineering process has to begin immediately . . . that he wants a fast decision, so when they get it, they can immediately take Solomon's heart."

"Oh, dear God." Abby turned and went through the steel door to the cages, as if to seek strength from the chimpanzees. Colter followed. She reached Earle's cage, and the chimp's stubby fingers extended through the mesh, as he made quiet, breathy pants. "No game today, Earle," she said. "We'll play chase some other time. I'm sorry." She turned to face the eager, bright-eyed chimp. "So sorry."

CHAPTER 20

Friday evening

Solomon leaped against the Lexan cage wall, slamming against it with feet propelled by powerful thigh muscles, creating a thunderous crash that still made Colter flinch, even though he had been the object of the explosive display so many times before. He sat down on the bench in the twilight, as Solomon stormed about the compound, hooting and slapping about barrels, ropes and any other loose objects in his path.

"Yeah, I really need this," said Colter, leaning forward and rubbing his face. He raised his voice, so that Solomon could hear every word. Abby said he understood quite a bit of spoken English, and that she still hadn't completely plumbed the depths of that understanding. "Solly, old pal, I've spent all day working on your case. Tomorrow, I've got to go into court and argue for your life. So, I came out here just to see you and maybe figure out whether I may have missed something, and you still go apeshit."

Solomon responded by swinging down, standing stiff-legged on all fours, hair erect, pant-hooting his way toward another nerve-jangling scream.

"And that son-of-a-bitch in the house up there somehow managed to find out about a case I'm not too proud of and has the district attorney after my ass." When Colter had arrived, Giacomo had stationed himself prominently on the back patio, looking like a fireplug somebody had dressed in a suit as a prank. He had stared pointedly at Colter, establishing officially that he had noted the lawyer's presence. Then he disappeared, probably to return his attention to a six-pack and a football game.

Colter was thankful for the time alone. He'd also shed his bodyguard, one of Digger's ex-cop friends, convincing the bull-necked old man that he'd be eminently safe on Drake's guarded estate, and that the bodyguard's presence would interfere with Colter's rapport with Solomon.

Some rapport. Solomon continued to vent his displeasure, stalking back and forth like a wrestler looking for an opening, preparing for another charge. The looming prospect of one more attack suddenly flipped a rarely activated anger-switch deep within Colter. He felt the rise of a boiling, pressurized rage that he usually kept bottled up within his lawyer's cool demeanor. The rage burst forth in a white-hot fury at this ungrateful beast. He leaped to his feet to give his anger full, glorious eruption.

"YOU ASSHOLE! YOU GODDAMNED HAIRY SON-OF-A-BITCH FLAMING ASSHOLE!" He felt somehow lighter. It felt great to bellow back at the ape, to let it all out, so he stepped right up to the wall and loosed another satisfying fusillade. "FUCK YOU, YOU KNUCKLE-WALKING BASTARD! YOU STUPID FUCKING BANANA-EATING BASTARD! YES, YOU! FUCK YOU!" Ah . . . that *had* been satisfying, Colter thought to himself, breathing easier.

Abruptly, Solomon halted his pacing, sat down, and stared at Colter, amber eyes intent, hair flattening. He absent-mindedly scratched his ample belly.

"Didn't like getting a little of your own medicine, did you?" Colter walked to the left edge of the plastic wall, so he could talk directly through the cage mesh. "Well, okay, now that I've let off a little steam there . . . let myself get a little out of control . . . I would like to add calmly and rationally . . ." Colter raised his eyebrows in an expression of deep sincerity. "Solomon, fuck you and all your ape friends, and fuck the rope you swung in on. Fuck King Kong and fuck Tarzan's Cheeta, too. Let me tell you, ape, if I hadn't committed myself to this case . . . and in fact, if I hadn't come to believe in this whole business . . . I'd be happy to hand them the knife to cut you open and slice your nasty ape heart right out of your fucking chest."

Without uttering a sound, Solomon roused himself from his musing, stood up and took two steps toward the computer room, and then turned and looked back at Colter. Then two more steps and a look-back. He continued the action several times; then he stopped outside the door, beginning to quietly pant-hoot.

"What the hell do you want now?" asked Colter.

Solomon disappeared into the building and came out again, watching Colter steadily.

"You want me to go in there so you can scream at me some more? Well, *fuck you* one more time." But that clearly wasn't what the chimpanzee wanted. He entered the building again, and after a moment, from the speaker came Abby's voice, intoning "Colter. Colter. Come, Colter. Come, Colter."

"So, the big ape finally wants to consult with his lawyer," Colter said to himself. He shrugged and made his way around the cage and into the computer room. Solomon loomed in the window, leaning his bulk against it to flatten his hairy flesh against the smudged surface.

When he saw Colter, his mouth broadened in what Colter took to be an expression of amity, and he hooted softly several times.

"So, what do you want?"

Solomon rocked his head back and forth somewhat comically, rapped the back of his touch screen with his knuckles, and then turned to stare at Colter with expectant eyes. He turned back to the screen and touched a series of symbols with his fat, leathery finger.

"What words?" came over the speaker.

"What do you—?" Colter realized the chimp couldn't hear him, so he sat down at the computer and clicked on the microphone. He'd never been so close to the animal, and Solomon's raw animal presence penetrated even the two inches of bulletproof plastic. "What do you mean 'what words'?"

Solomon stared at Colter for a moment and then back at the screen; then he quickly tapped at a series of symbols. "You say bad words."

"What? You mean the curse words?"

"Teach me the bad words."

Colter laughed. "So, Solly, you're just like every other guy. Can't get by without a few choice curses, eh?"

"Colter, teach me the bad words. Teach."

"How about 'fuck you'? That's probably the most popular one."

"Colter, what does the word mean?"

"It means I hope a bad thing should happen to you."

"Put the word in the computer, Colter, so I can say the word."

Colter smiled and found the "Record" icon on the screen. He clicked on it and said "Fuck you" into the microphone. After a few tries, he figured out how to assign an icon to the phrase. He chose a scowling face, and, after a bit more manipulation of the computer mouse to explore the screen menus, he saw with satisfaction that the "Fuck you" icon popped up on Solomon's touch screen.

Solomon rapped the icon, and "Fuck you," promptly emanated from the speaker in Colter's voice. "Fuck you. Fuck you. Colter, fuck you."

Colter cackled a sarcastic laugh. "Fuck you, too, Solomon. Boy, the proper Doctor Abigail Philips is going to have a fit when she hears that." He and the chimp stared at each other for a moment. Solomon tapped his screen impatiently. A silent question passed from ape to human, two males of a different species, but with the same communication needs.

Colter answered. "Sure, hell, Solomon, let's give you the full repertoire." He set to work, trying out several curses, explaining them to Solomon as simply as he could—sometimes pointing to parts of his own anatomy to illustrate—and assigning an icon to each. He discovered how to create entirely new icons—a necessary capability, given the unique nature of some of the epithets he was teaching. He even discovered how to organize them into a special new category, readily available to the chimp but not obvious to Abby or any other researcher who might use the system. Colter grinned, anticipating the surprise Abby would get the next time Solomon felt the need to express himself more fully.

Finally, he peered through the window with satisfaction to see displayed across Solomon's screen a line of new icons depicting a scowling face, a squatting dog, a period inside a zero, and a human kicking a chimp. Solomon immediately began to test them out.

"Fuck you, son-of-a-bitch asshole bastard," said Solomon in Colter's voice. "Colter is an asshole bastard fuck you. Son-of-a-bitch, Colter. Asshole."

Colter indulged himself in a long, satisfying laugh. "Solly, I've got to teach you a little syntax, but I think you're getting the idea."

"Solomon is not an asshole," came over the speaker.

A loud thump against the glass and a startled scream from the chimp made Colter leap from his chair, bringing him up against the window to peer through it. Solomon had suddenly slammed against the thick plastic and leaped off his stool in reaction to something. Now, on the floor of his sleeping room, he whirled clumsily around, trying to reach his back. As the chimp turned, Colter could see extending from his hairy back the red feathery tail of a tranquilizer dart.

"What the hell!" exclaimed Colter, pressing against the window to try to see out to Solomon's outdoor cage. A rustle behind him made Colter turn to see standing at the computer room door a figure dressed in black, a black ski mask pulled down over his face. Colter tensed to leap as the figure raised a long-barreled pistol and fired.

CHAPTER 21

Saturday morning

The absolute blackness took on the slightest tinge of gray. Colter still felt as if he were only a small, vague patch of consciousness floating paralyzed and anonymous in a sea of darkness. The faint, unintelligible murmur of voices insinuated itself into the darkness. The amorphous sound crystallized into words.

"He's moving. Thank God. You put too much in."

"I figured his weight. Maybe I overestimated a little."

"Guesstimated is more like it. You should have—" The voice stopped when Colter experimented with his muscles, finding them puny devices for lifting the massive deadweight of his limbs. Cool wetness spattered on his face and then the feel of a damp rag.

"You're okay. Just lie still for a while."

Colter tried a few words, but his mouth wouldn't cooperate, and only a randomly modulated groan came out. He opened his eyes, and the grayness lightened into blurry space and vague, moving forms.

Solomon's pant-hooting echoed from nearby, revealing that he was in a cavernous space. Even with the uncertain acoustics, Colter vaguely recognized that the chimp's sound was not the raucous ape-tirade he had grown to know and love.

Limbs still leaden, he gathered his strength and managed to push himself up on one elbow, his head still feeling as if it were only a visitor to his body. He realized he was lying on a cot, swung his legs over, and sat for a moment, still struggling to focus. His coat jacket was pitched on the floor nearby. A sprawling corrugated metal warehouse began to materialize, with the sun streaming in through several small windows. They illuminated a large overhead door at the far end, two cars, a pickup truck, and a large white van with a Ready-Plumbers sign on the side. Near Colter's cot stood a large folding table holding pizza boxes, various food containers, a small television, and a coffee maker. He could also vaguely make out what looked to be the contents of his pockets.

Nearby sat three men and a woman, on a circle of folding chairs. The men included a pony-tailed, multi-earringed young man in his twenties and a lean, muscled, military-looking, middle-aged man with a fringe of gray hair on an otherwise bald head. The middle-aged man still wore a black outfit that marked him as the one who had likely shot Colter. He also wore a belt holster cradling an automatic pistol. The woman was a worn-looking type in her forties with a leathery sunburned face, long blond hair, and wearing a baggy print blouse and loose-fitting pants. The fourth, a slim, preppie-looking man in his thirties, looked out of place among the others. He had what Colter recognized as an expensive haircut and wore khaki slacks, loafers and a dark-blue polo shirt. Something about him seemed familiar, but Colter couldn't quite place it. The preppie got up to come over to him, carrying a chair.

Colter realized that his corner of the warehouse also held a steel transport cage on wheels. Solomon sat inside, eating a sweet potato, eyeing the people with a simian version of Colter's own bleary suspicion.

"You awake enough to talk?" asked the preppie, pulling the chair up near the cot and sitting down, leaning forward, placing his forearms on his knees.

"Jesus," croaked Colter, looking at the other three, who regarded him with annoyance. "What did you give me?" He brought his right hand up to his forehead and a metallic clink told him he was handcuffed to a chain that was, in turn padlocked around a water pipe.

"A light dose of ketamine. You weren't supposed to be there. We had to take you along with the chimp."

"Well, I was. Now you've got a kidnapping charge. What the hell do you think you're doing?" Colter swallowed and managed to bring himself awake enough to notice that strands of black hair had stuck to his shirt. He and Solomon had no doubt been piled into the van together for their trip to . . . where? He took a deep breath, feeling the haze that clouded his thought finally beginning to clear. "What do you want?"

"We just want you to listen."

Colter rattled the chain. "Not much choice for me, is there? You are? . . ."

"Nobody you want to know about."

Colter felt clear enough so that his lawyer's argumentativeness began to kick in. "I ask again, why the hell did you kidnap Solomon and me, and how ready are you to do jail time on this?"

"I doubt that will happen, we'll be long gone. With the money." The young man clasped his hands together expectantly.

"Money?"

"As long as you're here, you'll be useful. We want fifty million dollars for the chimp. That's nothing for Drake. We'll blindfold you, drop you near Drake's house. You take him the offer and the Cayman bank account number. When the money is transferred, we'll text him the location."

"How the hell did you get past security?"

"Do it, or we'll just let you go, and you'll have to explain why you disappeared along with the chimp."

"Let me have a cup of that coffee." Colter needed time to think. And some caffeine to help.

The preppie gestured to the blonde woman, who brought him a Styrofoam cup of coffee.

"So, I do this for you, it puts me under suspicion as an accessory, disbarred, disgraced, and generally screwed."

The preppie shrugged. "You're a good lawyer, I hear. You'll talk your way out of it."

Colter sipped his coffee and considered his situation. There was a way out, but it would take a risk. He let the coffee do its work, and the plan crystallized.

Solomon was not particularly happy, either. The chimp had finished his sweet potato and decided to editorialize on his accommodations by grabbing the cage mesh, jerking his body back and forth to rattle the cage furiously and launching a pant-hooting that echoed off the steel walls to fill the warehouse with his anger. The resounding racket drowned out his captors' talk, rousing the blonde woman to walk over and pitch a banana into the cage. Solomon took the fruit grudgingly, but continued to scream his complaints. Solomon had obviously emerged from the tranquilizer with his full ornery attitude. Meanwhile, the middle-aged muscled man left with the van.

For several hours, Colter watched the group fidget impatiently, periodically drawn to the television to watch reports of his and

Solomon's disappearance. He could not see the screen, but he gathered that the police and the media had launched a major hunt for them, flooding the roads near the estate with cars and the air space with helicopters. Throughout the time, Solomon periodically and loudly expressed his opinion of his situation.

As the light filtering in the windows began to fade, a horn sounded outside the warehouse, and the long-haired young man pressed a button that sent an overhead door rattling up. A Ryder truck backed slowly in, and the middle-aged man got out, opened the back, and dragged out a ramp. He and the others wheeled the cage holding the agitated Solomon across the warehouse and strained to shove it up the ramp into the truck's back. The middle-aged man drew his pistol and came over to aim it at Colter. The long-haired, earringed man released Colter's hand from the cuffs, also freeing him from the chain and handing both to the gunman.

"My friend will ride with you in the back, and he is quite capable of using that pistol," said the preppie.

Colter rubbed his unmanacled hand and stood up, noticing that the table held his keys, his wallet, but only two cell phones! They'd assumed that, like any normal person, he carried only one. They were probably not surprised that, as a hotshot criminal lawyer, he carried a second disposable. But they hadn't dreamed he'd have a third nestled deep in the specially tailored pants pocket. He casually brushed off his pants, feeling the little bump of the cell phone in the personal area of the garment. Its presence advanced his plan considerably.

"Pretty impressive," he said to the preppie, who stood beside the back of the truck as Colter climbed in. The middle-aged man stood at a safe distance, his expression grimly determined, his pistol still trained on Colter.

"What's impressive?" asked the preppie.

"This operation. You managed to penetrate the security of Drake's estate, take the animal and get here, and now you've apparently got a plan to get the money free and clear."

The young man nodded, accepting the compliment. "My colleague here is well versed in military strategy. He's studied the techniques of the Navy SEALS especially closely." He cocked his head to signal Colter to climb into the back of the truck, which he did, followed by the middle-aged man. The young man followed them in and moved to snap the handcuffs on to Colter's wrists.

"May I offer a suggestion that will make it easier for all of us?"

"We're always open to suggestion," said the preppie.

"If you cuff my hands behind me, I won't be able to catch myself if I fall. This is going to be a pretty bumpy ride, I suspect. If I show up with an injury, it won't look very good if you try to peg me as an accomplice. You've got your partner, with an impressive-looking pistol there. I'm not likely to challenge him. Just attach a hand to the chain."

The young man looked questioningly at the middle-aged man, who answered brusquely, "Got it covered. He won't be any problem."

The preppie nodded in agreement and threaded the chain through the truck's tie-down railing, handcuffing Colter's hand. He let himself down from the truck, sliding up the ramp and swinging the doors shut so that the only light came from the inside overhead lamp. As the truck lurched forward, Colter made his way to the front of the cargo area, between the front wall and Solomon's cage. He crouched down to look directly into Solomon's eyes. Solomon swayed back and forth nervously, making soft grunts. His amber eyes seemed to be searching Colter's for an answer.

"Solly, it's okay, pal. We'll get you out of all this." The chimp stuck his fingers through the cage mesh, and Colter stroked them gently, the first time he had touched Solomon. The hands were like calloused leather, with onyx-black fingernails. Solomon allowed the calming touch, but still rocked his head and body back and forth nervously.

Colter noticed that the wheels of the steel cage were held in place by brakes operated by a single lever at the bottom. He also saw that the cage door faced the back of the truck and was secured only by a latch. Those facts enhanced his plan still further. He stood up to see that the middle-aged man had stationed himself in what he believed to be the most strategic spot, his back against the doors. He had braced himself in the corner, one hand grasping a railing, the other gripping the pistol, which he pointed at the floor, ready to bring it up in an instant. Colter leaned against the side wall, positioning himself so that he could flip the cage brake off at just the right time. He waited through several bumps and jounces, hoping that the topography of the trip would enable his plan to work.

Then came the perfect chance! The truck began to lumber its way up a hill, giving him just the gravity assist that he needed. For the middle-aged man's benefit, he frowned down at Solomon, as if he had noticed something amiss about the animal. He crouched down, flipped off the brake, braced his feet against the front wall of the truck, and heaved with all his strength. The heavy cage careened backwards smashing against the truck's door, pinning the man against it. Solomon loosed an ear-splitting scream in alarm, as Colter shoved the brake lever back into place and leaped over the cage, slamming his fist squarely into the man's face. Again and again Colter pounded the man, oblivious to the searing pain in his hand from knuckle striking facial bones. The man managed to remain conscious enough to fire off two rounds from the pistol, deafening blasts that panicked Solomon into loud screams. But the man couldn't free the pistol to aim it, so the bullets only tore holes in the side of the truck. Under Colter's repeated blows, the man's eyes finally rolled back, and his body sagged, held in place by the cage. A solid metallic clunk told Colter that the pistol had slipped from his grip and hit the floor of the truck. Colter quickly rifled the man's pockets, coming up with the cuff key and freed himself.

The truck stopped. Colter heard the sound of the front doors opening. He flipped off the cage brake and hauled the cage backward with all his might, just as the rattle of the back latch told him that the door was being opened. He dropped down and scrambled around the cage, crawling over the man's inert form.

"WHAT THE HELL?" shouted the preppie as he swung the doors wide. He froze when the middle-aged man tumbled out, and he found himself facing Colter, crouched beside the cage, bringing the pistol up to level it at his face.

"Your friend should have studied physics," said Colter. "Gravity's a bitch. Get the driver around here."

The young man's expression hardened into a mask of grim determination. "John!" he shouted to the driver over Solomon's screams. "Colter's got the gun. Get the rifle."

Oddly enough, that was just what Colter was counting on. The long-haired man appeared at the back of the truck, leveling the rifle at him. Both men were positioned directly behind the truck, just where he wanted them.

"Okay, okay," said Colter, turning the pistol around to hold it by the barrel, and extending it toward the preppie. With a smug smile, the young man reached for the pistol. Just before the handoff, as both the men's attention was fully on the pistol, Colter reached over, unlatched Solomon's cage door, and swung it open.

"DON'T DO THAT!" bellowed the preppie. "HE'LL—" Solomon burst from the cage slamming both men against asphalt. The chimp bounded across the road and disappeared into the thick forest darkening with the growing shadows of dusk. Colter leaped from the truck and plunged after him.

Behind him, he heard shouts, two shots from the rifle, and a shout from the preppie, "IDIOT! YOU'LL HIT THE CHIMP!"

As Colter tore his way through the thick, dry underbrush of the southern California forest, he heard more shouting behind him. "Get the dart gun! Bring the rifle! Kill him if you can, but get a clear shot. Don't hit the chimp!"

Colter ran as hard as he could, clawing through underbrush that tore at his clothes, slashed at his face. He directed his course by catching occasional glimpses of a hulking, hairy body bounding ahead of him in the growing gloom, or hearing the ape's occasional hoots of fear.

But the glimpses grew fewer, and the sounds faded. Colter ran on, peering into the deepening gloom, trying to make out any movement. But Solomon was nowhere to be seen. He stopped to listen. No sound behind him of pursuers, none in front of the chimp. Their wild flight through the forest had been so haphazard that they'd managed to lose the kidnappers. But he'd also managed to lose Solomon.

CHAPTER 22

Saturday evening

Solomon plunged through the forest, terror clutching at his chest, remembering the explosions from the black thing, the men fighting, the cage door opening, bursting free of it, screaming in fear, tearing through the thick brush past big trees, down into rocky canyons and back out again.

He had to escape the explosions, escape the cage, escape the strangers who put him in needle-sleep, gave him food, but frightened him.

He also had to escape Colter, the man who made the explosions, started the fighting, was with him when he was taken. The puzzling Colter. They had talked. Colter had showed him words. But he *was* the one who made the explosions. He'd seen people use the things on television, but then they had been only a picture in that window. He knew the object was like the dart gun, except that it hurt, killed. But he had never experienced the horrible noise it made.

Still he fled as the darkness deepened, scraping knuckles on shadowy rocks, stumbling on aging legs and slamming his head against a branch, knowing that the people were still after him ready to make more explosions.

A tree loomed ahead, its massive, spreading branches and thick foliage offering refuge. He stared up at it, muscles drained of strength, chest pounding, lungs burning. It stood so very high. He hauled himself up . . . and up . . . and up, grasping large, solid branches, retreating deep into its thicket of leaves, gathering their darkness around him. Finally, he nestled himself into a broad, comfortable fork in a bower of leaves. Safe.

He peered out through the leaves, trying to see in the deepening twilight the broad expanse filled with bushes and rocks and other large nesting trees. From this hiding place, he would see any of the people coming. The reassuring thought soothed him somewhat, and allowed him to rest and think. He had seen all of these things before—rocks, bushes, trees. He had been outside before, in the enclosure with the others.

But this was a different outside, with no walls and with so very many things in it. He huddled down on the branch. He did feel a nagging anxiety at being here, but also a kind of happiness. He felt a confusion about this vast, overwhelming place but also a sense that it felt so right to be here. Abby had taught him a word about being in a place like this with no walls. She had said it meant not being in a cage; going wherever you wanted to. He remembered the symbol: a chimp holding his arms up, with a play-face on. But it was an effort to remember the word she used. Now he remembered. *Freedom.* He let the word rest in his mind, considering it, until a bone-deep fatigue overcame his body, beginning to melt away his consciousness. He tiredly arranged himself securely among the branches and descended into sleep.

•   •   •

"Oh, Christ," whispered Colter to himself. He stood on the highest rock he could find, scanning slowly around the dark landscape, straining to see any movement, listening for any whisper of sound carried on the dry breeze. Nothing. He sat down and tried to figure what to do next. Gee, maybe a nice cappuccino at a nearby restaurant would help him think. He chuckled wryly at himself. He'd never been a nature person, deciding that the Boy Scouts weren't for him when he found out tents didn't have bathrooms and, God forbid, no wifi. Besides, he'd heard of mountain lions in these forests. And rabid raccoons. And, oh, yes, the rattlesnakes. He scrunched himself up more on the rock and gripped the pistol hard.

But all this fear-mongering, as pleasant a diversion as it was, only delayed the inevitable action he had to take. He laid down the gun and dug into his jacket pocket and took out the cell phone, switching it on. The signal was strong enough, but he hesitated calling Abby, going over in his mind what appeared to be a case against her. This bunch somehow had made it into a secure compound and past a bunch of professional security guards to kidnap him and Solomon. How could they have done that without help from somebody who knew the security setup? Was it Abby? And if it wasn't, they'd likely be watching Abby and Sarah, to see if he contacted them.

He decided his best bet was Digger, so he punched in the old man's cell phone number.

"Yeah," came the gruff answer, over the expected bar noise.

"Digger, it's Bobby."

"What? Shit! You dumbass, what do you think you're doing? Let me get outside where there ain't so many ears." After a moment, he returned, the background quieter. "What the fuck you think you're doing taking that animal and disappearing?"

"Listen, I didn't take him. They took me, too. They wanted ransom, and they stuck me right in the middle of it."

"See what happens when you ditch your protection? Where the hell are you?"

"I'm on a rock. In some woods."

"Big fuckin' help, Bobby."

"I don't know where I am, okay? Solomon escaped, too."

"Jesus, you're not with him? Probably for the best, though. He could tear your fuckin' head off!"

"I'm well aware of that. I'll get myself out of here somehow. Listen, Digger, I need you to poke around and try to figure out who's behind all this." He went on to describe the four kidnappers, while holding the pistol at the ready for both men and beasts. "They were pros, but they must have had help to get past Drake's security."

"Look, don't forget who's out there in the woods with you. I hope the next call ain't from the monkey."

Colter put the phone on vibrate, pocketed it, and considered what to do next. The good news was that the stars were brilliant, a sparkling swath stretching across the ebony sky. The bad news was that they were so bright because the night was moonless, a blackness enshrouding him like a blanket. Sunset had faded, and the trees and rocks around him now vanished into that utter blackness. The night also hid its denizens, and he shivered at what could invisibly slither, crawl, or skulk right up to him. Reasoning that snakes and spiders and such probably didn't like to hang out on big rocks, he took off his jacket and rolled it into a wad, and curled up in a fetal position on the unforgiving surface, with the jacket stuffed beneath his head. His wide-open eyes vainly peered into the night, searching for movement, his hand tightly clutching the pistol.

· · ·

The early light of morning and a growing thirst woke Solomon and made him stretch luxuriously, yawn, and climb down from the tree, working the kinks from his muscles. He ambled slowly through the forest still cool from the night, seeking water. A canyon thick with brush drew him instinctively, and he clutched trees sprouting from its walls and swung down to the broad bottom where a small stream flowed haphazardly among an expanse of rocks. He bent down and began to drink of the cool water, sucking it up in delicious mouthfuls. A clattering of rocks and the muttering of a human voice brought him bolt upright. The man called Colter slid clumsily down the other side and stopped when he saw Solomon. He still held the frightening black thing in his hand.

· · ·

"Uhhhh . . . good morning, Solomon," said Colter in cordial, measured tones meant to soothe. The ape began to hoot in ominous warning, pulling himself up on all fours, his hair rising on his shoulders. Colter looked around for escape. He was trapped in the arroyo, behind him the tall unscalable cliff, on either side the brush-choked canyon, and ahead of him a massive, increasingly agitated ape.

Solomon swayed side to side, his pant-hooting growing louder. He reared up on two legs, baring his teeth, advancing toward Colter, emitting a deafening scream.

"Are you going to tear me apart, fellow? That's really not a nice thing to do," he said, still trying for soothing but feeling his throat constrict. He decided to hell with his worries about Abby being a culprit or being watched. Backing against the cliff wall, he pulled out his phone and punched in her lab number. Solomon continued to advance, his screaming echoing off the canyon walls.

"Shit!" breathed Colter, as the signal faded in and out. The phone rang and rang. Solomon's hair was as extended as he'd ever seen it.

Abby answered, her "hello" faint.

"Thank God! Abby? It's me! It's Colter."

"Bobby, where are you, where is Solomon—" She began to pepper him with questions, but he interrupted her.

"Listen, I'm with him now. We escaped and we're lost in the woods. He's really pissed. What do I do? Quick!"

"What's he doing?" Her voice faded briefly.

"You can't hear that? He's screaming bloody murder at me. He's walking upright. I think he's going to test whether my arms and legs come off. I've got a gun, and if he comes after me, I'm going to have to—"

"Throw the gun away?"

"*Get serious!*"

"I am. It's a threat. Throw the gun away and lie down on your stomach."

Solomon charged, bellowing, and Colter brought up the pistol, which enraged the animal even more. Solomon paused only a few feet away, still screaming, his canines looking like daggers.

Faintly from the phone. "Bobby, I know him. Trust me. Throw the gun away and get down. He has a language of gestures much like us. You've got to learn it . . . fast."

For an instant, Colter wondered whether she was actually trying to get him killed. But finally, he pitched the gun to the side and dropped down on all fours; then he committed fully and flattened onto his belly.

"Okay, I'm down," he shouted into the phone. "Now what?"

"Now smile."

"Oh, *come on!*"

"And show your teeth. It's a submissive expression. Stay there. Let him calm down. Duck your head and don't look at him."

Colter did, and Solomon's screaming reverted to merely a deep, peevish pant-hooting. When Colter stole a glance, he could see the huge ape squat down a few feet away and regard him inquisitively with those intense, amber eyes.

"What's he doing?" Abby's voice faded at the end, and Colter moved the phone around, trying for a better signal.

"He's stopped. He's just sitting there."

"Give him time. Chimps don't hold grudges. Stay there. He'll approach you. Don't move. He may want to step over you."

"The hell you say? Not likely. I'm getting out of here." Colter remembered those canines, those massive arms.

"You stay there, or you'll never be able to bring him back."

After a while, Solomon rose and walked the few feet to Colter. Colter willed himself with all his might to remain still. The ape loomed over him, and Colter's face lay flat against the rock only inches from those massive hands. He turned his head slightly to see the huge gray-whiskered simian face looking down at him and the hairy arms as thick as his thighs. He could smell the slight musk of the animal's body.

Then Solomon was right on top of him. Grunting steadily, the ape lifted his thick limbs one by one to pass over Colter's prostrate body, turn, and wander a few feet down the canyon, back to the stream, where he bent to take a drink of water.

"He stepped over me," Colter whispered into the phone. "What the hell was that?"

"You just submitted to him. You let him know he's the alpha ape, above you. Now crawl toward him and hold out the back of your hand, your wrist."

"We're going to shake hands?"

"No, he's going to put it into his mouth."

"Yeah, right."

"It's a sign of appeasement. You're showing trust of one another. He won't bite."

"I can't just tell him I'm sorry?"

"Do it, Bobby." Her voice faded again. He might be losing battery power on the phone. His mouth was cotton-dry, and he swallowed and tried to generate both saliva and courage.

"Solly," he said quietly. "Solly, old boy, I just want to say I'm sorry I scared you with the gun and all." Solomon turned back toward him and squatted, reflectively scratching his chest and then letting his fingers dabble in the flowing stream. His stone-faced expression gave no indication that he'd understood the apology. Colter raised himself on all fours and crawled toward the ape, keeping his head down. Solomon's hair rose slightly, and he grunted a loud hooting. Colter held out one hand toward Solomon, awkwardly pulling himself along supported by the other. A sharp rock jabbed into his shin and he winced and continued on. Hand out, six feet from Solomon. Five feet . . . four feet . . . he stopped with the hand poised in mid-air not a foot from the ape. Solomon moved toward him, and Colter put his head down, the crunch of gravel telling him the animal had moved up next to him. Would the next sensation be the searing pain as the huge canines crunched through the bones of his hand, tearing most of it away from his wrist?

He gasped as he felt the wetness on his hand, the gentle pressure of sharp teeth, the graze of prehensile lips. He stole a glance up to see the back of his hand almost completely enveloped in Solomon's large mouth, the chimp's brow furrowed slightly, the eyes staring calmly down at him. Then Solomon let go and moved off down the canyon, turning his back on Colter as if dismissing an underling.

Colter sat up on the rocky canyon floor, an uncontrollable shivering gripping his body, as he watched Solomon move slowly away, his thick limbs bearing his mass with a poised muscular grace. It was like watching the departure of a thunderstorm, receding dark and portentous into the distance.

CHAPTER 23

Sunday afternoon

"We're okay, I guess," said Colter into the phone to Abby. "He hasn't torn anything off me, so I guess we're friends. We're still lost. Well, I am, anyway. He seems to know where he's going." Solomon grabbed an overhanging branch and began to haul himself up the side of the arroyo. "Gotta go," said Colter, scrambling after the retreating ape as best he could. "He's on the move." He switched off the phone to save its battery and pocketed it. "Solly, I hope you're willing to wait for me. I'm not as good at this Tarzan stuff as you." But Solomon had already vanished over the lip of the arroyo, so Colter began to pull himself up the side, panting with the exertion. He reached the top to see Solomon's rump disappear around a rock, so he hurried after him. He stayed a respectful distance from the chimp as they made their way across dry, tangled shrubland, dotted with an occasional towering, scraggly tree.

Colter figured this might be the San Gabriel Mountains, but that was a total guess, given that he'd navigated mountains around LA only by road in a sports car, with a distractingly beautiful woman beside him.

Solomon wandered across the landscape, occasionally stopping to taste a bit of grass or bush, sitting and chewing reflectively.

"Yeah, I'm hungry, too," said Colter at one of the stops, leaning against a tree at a prudent distance. "You know, if we were in town, I could take you to some great places. I'm sure you'd get good service, being a big celebrity and all."

After an hour, they crossed a trail, and although Solomon ignored it, Colter recognized its importance.

"Solly, let's go this way. C'mon boy," said Colter, but Solomon seemed immersed in a realm of his own thought. But Colter knew a couple of words that would get his attention if nothing else would.

"Eat, Solly? You want some food? It's down this way."

Solomon stopped and grunted; then he opened his mouth to emit a rapid staccato of breathy, guttural grunts.

"Right, Solly," said Colter, imitating the sound, remembering that Abby said they were food barks. Solomon made his way back onto the trail and paused, cocking his head and looking at Colter in a way that seemed to be questioning.

"I suppose this way's as good as any," said Colter, starting along the trail, which wandered its way up a rocky hillside rapidly warming in the late-morning sun. They hiked along for twenty minutes or so, with Colter periodically looking back to utter an encouraging food grunt. Solomon shook his large head once or twice, perhaps in annoyance. Colter knew he'd better come through soon, or he'd have a very cranky, very strong ape on his hands. As they crested a steep hill, Colter glimpsed a light-blue vehicle among the trees below and the brown path of a dirt road leading away down the wide, flat valley between hills. The murmur of voices and the clink of metal floated up to them.

Solomon abruptly loped past him and down the hill, and a startled Colter sprinted after him, still panting from the climb. Solomon disappeared into the bushes, and a sharp female scream pierced the still air. A young woman fled from the bushes, pulling up her pants, and Solomon came shambling behind her, food barking. She screamed again, and Colter altered his course to aim for the vehicle, a blue Jeep SUV.

"*OhGod! OhGod! OhGod! OhGod!*" exclaimed the slight, brown-haired woman, who stopped suddenly and whirled around, bracing herself and waving wildly at the chimp. "Go 'way! You go 'way! No, wait! Come this way! Come this way! Don't go there!"

"What is it?" asked a worried male voice, as Colter rounded a large stand of bushes to come upon a campsite with a large tent pitched near a picnic table, on which sat an ice chest, assorted foodstuffs, and a cooking stove. To the woman's utter terror, Solomon had ignored her attempted diversion and circled to climb up on the table's seat right beside a young girl of perhaps three and begun rummaging through the food. The round-faced child, with long, brown hair held by a yellow bow, sat transfixed at the large chimp, a sandwich in her small hand. Solomon did a brief reconnoiter of the table and dug two fingers into a bowl of potato salad, examining the white lumpy material and then nibbling carefully. Pleased with the taste, he took several more double fingerfuls.

"Mommy, monkey!" said the little girl in bright surprise, her sandwich temporarily forgotten.

The father, a burly young man in jeans and a t-shirt, appeared from around the side of the tent, saw Solomon and bolted for the Jeep, while the mother stood frozen in terror, repeating "Oh, my God!" She inched forward and then retreated in agonized indecision. "Please don't hurt my baby. Please go away!"

Squatting on the picnic table's seat beside the little girl, Solomon carefully picked through the food, finding a jar of green olives, which he twisted open and sampled, approved of the taste, and poured out a handful, nibbling them up with his dexterous lips.

"Monkey! Hey, monkey!" The little girl reached out and patted Solomon's side to get his attention, but the chimp was busy extracting another olive from the jar. "Big monkey?" She patted again harder.

The father returned with a pistol held high in a double-handed grip, his jaw clenched, circling to get a shot.

"Hold it!" shouted Colter. "Don't do that!" For the first time, the parents noticed him.

"This your . . . your monkey?" demanded the father. "He's about to get shot." The man lowered the pistol aiming at Solomon's head. Solomon, intent on the food, did not look up.

"Just wait a second," pleaded Colter, lowering his voice. "Let me get her. He's gentle, but if you shoot him, he might hurt somebody. And you might hit her. He's not angry. He's just hungry. Now hide the gun. Put it so he can't see it. Guns freak him out."

"He freaks us out!" said the father. "This gun's staying right where it is. What the hell do you think you're doing letting an animal like that wander loose!"

"John, put the gun down!" whispered the mother urgently. "And watch your language! Little ears!"

Solomon finished the olives and realized the girl was patting him on the side. He saw her sandwich and leaned down close to sniff it.

"My God, he's going to attack her!" cried the mother. The father took aim again.

The little girl took a bite and chewed. "You like this? You like peanut butter 'n jelly?" Solomon placed his large whiskered face down close to the little girl's mouth, watching her chewing with intense interest.

"You got ticklies!" The little girl giggled and rubbed her face where Solomon's whiskers had brushed her cheek. "You want a bite?" She held out the sandwich.

The father moved closer to get a shot. "He's going to hurt her!"

Solomon opened his lips and gingerly took a bite of the sandwich and then straightened back up, chewing. He looked up to see the father with the gun, leaped away from the table, and barked in alarm, curling back his lips to show his massive teeth. Colter saw the father tense to fire and immediately jumped between them.

"Damnit, put it away!"

"He's a dead animal!"

Colter glanced back to see Solomon, teeth bared, hair erect, beginning to retreat back into the forest.

"Okay, okay," he said to the father, holding out his hands placatingly. "It's okay, sir. If you put the gun away, I'll get your daughter." Colter backed around the table toward Solomon, turning toward the fearful chimp, who stood immobile, torn between fear and hunger. "Solly, just cool down. Let me get this little girl out of your way so you can eat your lunch. Solly, it's okay."

"John, put the gun away," pleaded the mother. "Let him get Chrissie, for God's sake!"

John uttered a low curse, reluctantly tucked the pistol in the back of his jeans, and backed away. Colter sighed in relief and approached the little girl. "Sweetheart, let's just get you to Mommy and Daddy."

"Can I play with the monkey?"

"Some other time, honey." He lifted the little girl gently and moved quickly toward the mother. "I got her. Now, just move slowly toward the car. She's fine. We're all fine. Solly, you can have the rest of her sandwich."

At the word "sandwich," Solomon's hair slowly flattened, and he moved tentatively back toward the table.

Colter handed the little girl over to her tearful mother, who hugged her desperately as the family rushed to the Jeep, jumped in, and slammed and locked the doors. The man started up the Jeep with a roar, and Colter realized that his only chance for figuring out his location was about to vanish. He ran in front of the Jeep and held out his hands.

"Get out of the way!" shouted the man. "By God, I'll run you over!" He jammed the Jeep into gear and lurched forward stopping inches from Colter's chest; then he began to ease forward again, pushing him back.

"Look, sir, the chimp escaped, and I'm trying to get him back where he belongs. He didn't hurt her. Really, he's harmless," Colter glanced back at Solomon, who had discovered a plastic box of hard-boiled eggs, placed one in his mouth and bit down on it, chewing contentedly and watching the humans with detached interest. Colter placed his hands on the Jeep's hood. "I'll give you five hundred dollars to help us." The Jeep stopped.

"What do you want? Is he from a zoo?"

"John, let's just go," insisted the woman, clutching the little girl, who struggled to push herself up to get a better look out the window at Solomon. "He could get in!"

"You heard of Solomon, the chimpanzee?" asked Colter.

John cracked the window a bit. "Who? The one in the court case? That's him? What's he doing out here? Who are you?"

"I'm the lawyer. We were abducted."

"Really? You're that guy? We hadn't heard about any abduction. We've been out here for a couple of days."

"Where am I?"

"Angeles National Forest. Near Valyermo. You serious about the money?"

Colter breathed a sigh of relief. "Sure, it's yours. All you've got to do is help me get somebody out here to get us." John shut off the

Jeep, glancing warily over at Solomon and slowly nodded his assent. Colter immediately called Abby on the dying cell phone, relaying instructions from John on how to get to the campsite. That done, he turned his attention to Solomon, who was still eating.

"Abby, how do I keep him here? He's going to finish eating and wander off, and I'm not very persuasive."

"I am. Approach him very slowly and hold the phone up to his ear."

"You're kidding."

"No—he's heard me on the phone before."

"Why didn't you just do that before?" Her voice cut off for a moment, and Colter felt a lump of panic rise that he had managed to control until now. But her voice returned, and he asked her to repeat.

"He probably would have hurt you. He was afraid of you. Now, he trusts you. At least it seems that way from this end."

"My life's on the line, and it just *seems* that he won't kill me?" Colter grumped. Finally, he said "Okay" and slowly moved toward Solomon, holding out the phone and praying for the continuing strength of his battery. "Solly, it's Abby. Phone's for you, Solly."

Solomon had just begun rummaging in the cooler to pull out a can of Sprite. He adroitly popped the top and began to drink it down. Colter approached closer, and Solomon reached into the cooler, pulling out a Coke, which he held out to Colter. Colter stopped, dumfounded.

"Well . . . uh . . . thanks." He took the Coke and held out the phone. "But you've got a call." Wincing slightly at the possibility of having his arm torn from its socket, Colter held the phone toward Solomon's ear. The chimp allowed it to be placed next to his head. Abby's voice emanated faintly from the earpiece, and Solomon's expression brightened at the welcome sound. He began to make soft, delighted hooting sounds, setting down the can and grabbing the phone, holding it hard against his large brown-speckled ear. He happily continued to hoot, raising his eyebrows and broadening his mouth in a play-face. After a moment, he held out the phone to Colter, who took it gingerly, allowing Solomon to go back to his drink.

"What did you say?" he asked Abby.

"I told him I was coming there and to stay. I'm sure he understood me, but you have to reinforce it occasionally, or he'll decide I'm not coming and wander off looking for me. Just tell him 'stay' and 'Abby's coming.' And make sure there's lots of food. Chimps are always hungry."

So for the next hour, Colter encouraged Solomon to continue his meal, offering him lunchmeat, cookies, and anything else he could find in the family's food box, continually reminding the ape that "Abby's coming here. We have to stay."

The family remained locked in the Jeep, although the woman relented enough to crack the window far enough so the little girl could push a Hershey bar through for Solomon.

Solomon spent another half hour roaming the camp, nosing through the tent and climbing around on the Jeep.

Finally, the distant sound of approaching vehicles arose from down the road, and the white primate lab van came into sight, speeding toward them, followed by the ivory-colored limousine of Sarah Huntington. Solomon hooted with pleasure at the sight of Abby in the passenger seat and, as the van rolled into the camp site leaped onto its top even before it had stopped.

Abby hurried out and stroked Solomon's hair as he sprawled in delight, putting his face closer to hers, making soft hoots of utter joy. She coaxed him down, and they sat for a long time on the ground hugging and rocking, the chimp's thick arms enfolding her. Finally, she took his large leathery black hand in her small white one and led him over to the picnic table, where they sat among the remains of the campers' food. The technician Keeli Mannix climbed on top of the van with a tranquilizer-dart gun, sitting down and holding it at the ready.

"Solly, you old thing. Are you okay, big guy?" asked Abby. "I don't want to dart you because you just got darted. But old fella, you see Keeli over there? You know he's a good shot and you're a big target, and he'll dart you if you get ornery. So, you just stay a gentleman, okay?"

Solomon eyed Keeli warily but then resumed his happy celebration of Abby's arrival, hooting gently and making his play face, reaching out to clumsily stroke Abby's hair. The limousine's window came down, and Sarah Huntington glared out at Colter.

"Just what the hell is all this? Why did you take the animal?"

"I didn't," said Colter. "People who wanted ransom."

"Who?

"My investigator has started looking into it."

"Where are you going to take Solomon?" asked Sarah.

Abby stroked the chimp's head as he sat happily beside her. "I . . . well, I guess back to the lab. That's where he belongs."

"Can't do that," said Colter. "That would really prejudice the case. It's bad enough everybody thinks I took him, but if he shows up back at your lab, they'll really have a good case that he was stolen. You've got to bring him back to Drake's."

Abby's expression darkened. She sat down and looked solemnly at the ape as he made contented hooting noises. "Let's ask him."

"Ask him what?"

"Where he wants to go. We're arguing that he deserves rights— what more important right than the one to decide his own fate?" She went to the back of the van and pulled out an iPad. "The screen is like the bigger one he uses in the lab. We've used it in the open enclosure to see whether the animals behave differently than in the lab. We continually synch it with his updated vocabulary." She pushed the tablet computer up near to Solomon.

"Abby, we absolutely have to take him back, or we're all in the worst possible shit. I'm saying this as his lawyer."

"Bobby, I've got to do this. Look, we can videotape it. We'll have a record." She motioned to Keeli, who climbed down to rummage in the back of the van, coming out with the video camera. He resumed his post on top of the van, one hand training the camera on Solomon and Abby, the other still grasping the dart gun.

"Solly, do you see this?" asked Abby. "Do you see your small talking machine? Will you talk with me? Say hello, Solomon."

Excited by the adventures of the day, Solomon had difficulty being calmed, wandering around the camp, visiting with the family still locked in the Jeep, and peering into the limousine. Finally, Abby managed to coax him to take the iPad by also offering M&Ms she brought from the van. Persuaded with several of the candies, Solomon finally began to fiddle with the touch screen, and a "Hello," came out of the small speaker, in a male voice.

"Okay, I'll go along with this," said Colter. "But it's against whatever judgment I have left. Just don't use the candy to influence his decision."

Abby motioned him away so he wouldn't distract Solomon.

"Solly, we have to go now. Where do you want to go? Do you want to go back to the big cage at Drake's?" She turned toward the camera. "He knows what that means because we talked about the place when he was there." She turned back to Solomon. "Do you understand, Solly? Do you want to go back to Drake's?"

Solomon began to make a worried whimper in his throat and rapped at the screen, choosing symbols. "No. It's a bad place. Lonely. The men came. Took me." He paused. "And took Colter."

"Where do you want to go?"

"Home. Home. With you. Sandy, Wendy, Earle, Jonathan."

"You want to go back to the lab with me?"

"Yes. Not to the place."

For the benefit of the camera, Abby conversed with Solomon for another ten minutes, showing that he understood the question, understood that he was making a decision to go back to the laboratory. Solomon remained unwavering. Finally, she stood and faced Colter.

"Satisfied?"

"No. I'd be satisfied if you didn't put us in this situation. Okay, let me think." Colter walked away from the van, pacing, as Abby coaxed Solomon into a cage in the back of the van and slammed the van doors. He came back, his expression slightly more satisfied.

"Look, I'll contact the media on the way back. Here's the main talking point. Solomon was kidnapped along with me from Drake's, which proves that he's not safe there. They have poor security. The judge may just buy that. So, if anybody asks, that's the story."

Abby nodded, and the white primate lab van rolled slowly away down the dirt road so as not to jostle its precious cargo.

Colter had Sarah pay the family in the blue van, and he got in with her for the ride back to the city. He borrowed her cell phone and began the calls, starting with City News Service.

CHAPTER 24

Monday morning

"Mr. Colter, you are going to walk out of this courtroom in handcuffs!" Judge George Kermit Wainwright, face flushed with anger, enunciated each syllable with a force that seemed capable of engraving his words on the back wall of his courtroom. He clasped his bony hands tightly in front of him and glared at Colter with an intensity that, if eyesight carried energy, would have drilled through the back of Colter's skull. "And I can promise you, sir, that my contempt citation will be but a mote on your back compared to the other troubles you will have to bear!"

"Your Honor, may I explain?" Colter was all too aware that Jenkins sat easily at the defense table, taking enormous care not to appear cocksure but watching Colter's demise with immense satisfaction. And so did the world. A gallery full of reporters busily scribbled notes, and the courtroom camera's light glowed red, signaling that the proceedings were being broadcast live on CNN, truTV, C-span and the networks. The "monkey lawyer" was very publicly being thrown to the legal lions.

"*Do* you have an explanation, Mr. Colter? *Do* you have an explanation for walking out of my courtroom after that ludicrous performance on Wednesday and then perhaps participating in the theft of the animal whose disposition is under question in this case? Ah, well, then, never let it be said that this court was not willing to hear an explanation." Wainwright leaned back and cocked his head, raising his eyebrows in elaborate mocking courtesy.

"Your Honor, I was kidnapped along with Solomon. I was as much a victim—"

"Mr. Colter, surely you are aware that the police apprehended the perpetrators and that, as a result of their statements, a charge of grand larceny has also been brought against you."

"Yes, well, uh, as Your Honor well knows, I am innocent until proven guilty, and I *will* be shown innocent. Your honor should be aware that the police were successful in large part because of the help of my own investigator, Mr. Murray."

"Perhaps. But given the circumstances, this court frankly cannot understand how the plaintiffs wish to continue with you as their lawyer." Wainwright shifted his gaze to the table where Abby and Sarah sat. "Is this true?"

Sarah stood, her imposing posture portraying all the aplomb of wealth and influence. "Your Honor, we do, indeed, wish to continue with Mr. Colter as our counsel. We believe that his actions in recovering the animal and returning it show that he is blameless in this matter."

"Mrs. Huntington, that may be true, but his actions may also have been that of a clever man who knew he was trapped. But the court will accede to your wishes, as mistaken as it thinks they may be."

"Your Honor, may I also respectfully suggest that Mr. Colter will not be able to adequately conduct this case if he is in jail."

Wainwright paused, his face assuming an inscrutable expression as he glanced back and forth between Sarah and Colter. That poker-face, Colter knew, masked Wainwright's shrewd weighing of the political costs and benefits of letting him continue as counsel. No doubt, on Colter's side of the scale lay the generous campaign contributions that Sarah Huntington had made to Wainwright's political allies over the years. If those contributions evaporated, Wainwright would certainly receive a clubroom skewering from those allies. On the other side of the scale, however, rested the inevitable editorial blasts that Wainwright would suffer, especially from Drake's newspapers and web sites, for allowing such a scoundrel to remain in his courtroom. Colter suspected from the length of the silence that Wainwright was likely tossing a lot more considerations on one side of the scale or the other—considerations Colter could only guess at.

"Mr. Colter," Wainwright finally intoned. "Considering that a life is at stake in this case, Mr. Drake's, and in the interest of seeing the case proceed quickly, I will agree to staying the execution of my contempt citation. You may continue . . . for the time being."

Jenkins cleared his throat and rose with great import. "Your Honor, there is one grave situation that must be settled, however. May I address it?"

"Of course, Mr. Jenkins." Wainwright's voice seemed to mellow at the participation of the respected barrister.

"It is completely unacceptable that the animal is no longer in the possession of Mr. Drake. It was taken to Dr. Philips' primate laboratory instead. I would suggest that it is only reasonable that the animal be returned to the Drake estate, where it can be quickly available for the organ harvesting, should the court's decision allow that."

"Your Honor, I think that until Mr. Jenkins presents evidence that the animal is secure in that facility, he should remain under the care of Dr. Philips," said Colter. "Also, moving Solomon would go against his expressed wishes." The welcome adrenalin rush of arguing a case allowed Colter to forget for the moment the morass of his own problems.

Jenkins chuckled. "The animal's *wishes*? How could the animal possibly express his wishes?"

Colter had hoped for that question. With his trademark persuasion, he convinced a skeptical Wainwright to view the video taken at the campground of Solomon's insistence on being taken back to the primate center. Of course, Colter also liked the fact that the video would be seen by the reporters and the world. It would be more proof that Solomon was a thinking ape, a sentient being.

He rose after the video ended. "Your Honor, I can have Doctor Philips testify as to Solomon's improved physical and emotional state after returning to his home and to the company of the other chimpanzees with whom he has close bonds. And she will testify that Solomon has undergone such stress—including anesthetic and being lost in the forest—that moving him again would not be advisable. And, in fact, that such a move might compromise his physical health, and thus his status as a source of a healthy heart . . . should it come to that."

Jenkins rose and regarded Abby for a moment, settling on his strategy. "All right, Your Honor. The defense will present Mr. Drake's updated security plan. And, we are willing to stipulate that this animal showed a preference for its original home. And even that it might not be advisable to move it. But I would remind the court again that a man's life is at stake. That consideration should weigh heavily in a decision."

"We agree," said Wainwright, and Colter glanced back to see worry cloud Abby's face. "Thus, pending the security report, the animal can remain in the care of Dr. Philips to ensure its well-being. However, I will give considerable weight to the advice of Mr. Drake's physicians that his health might require the tissue-engineering process to begin immediately. And, Dr. Philips must agree to relinquish the animal at the discretion of those physicians and the scientists involved, in order to have it available for the heart generation, should the court rule in the defense's favor." Abby leaned over to whisper urgently to Sarah, who placed a reassuring hand on her shoulder.

Jenkins nodded amiably. "So, to emphasize, Your Honor supports that Mr. Drake's physicians may, upon an assessment of their patient's medical need, require that the animal be prepared for harvesting."

"Precisely, Mr. Jenkins."

Wainwright drew the court session to a close, checked his schedule, and ordered the next session for Tuesday afternoon. Again, he threatened Colter with immediate incarceration should anything else happen to the animal, but Colter was only half-listening. He was furiously sorting through Jenkins' possible strategies in his mind, like a chess player tracing the outcomes of possible moves. Jenkins had agreed much too readily to Solomon being kept at the lab. The cunning lawyer had plotted a strategy that Colter couldn't yet fathom.

· · ·

The enclosure seemed smaller as Solomon ducked through the door from his cage into the sunlit yard surrounded by the deep moat and high wall. It held the same climbing tree with no leaves, the same large rocks, including the highest one that Solomon traditionally occupied. But after his freedom roaming the big open place and sleeping in the giant tree, this enclosure seemed somehow wrong.

Earle and Sandy were already out, and even though all the chimps had joined in great celebratory hoots of greeting when he first came back, they rushed to embrace him again, as if he had just arrived.

They hugged, kissed, and groomed each other, squatting and hooting softly in pleasure.

Jonathan emerged warily, hair slightly erect, unsure of how to treat the return of his rival. But Solomon approached him peaceably, and they sat near each other, exchanging only furtive glances, silently acknowledging their complex bond of brotherhood and rivalry.

When Bruno's door slid up, he rushed out with deep, resonant pant-hooting, pitching handfuls of grass and dirt into the air, bounding onto a rock, leaping at the tree, swinging from branch to branch and landing on the ground to lope toward Solomon. He circled Solomon as if to declare his complete alliance with the alpha chimp, and then danced sideways toward him, uttering happy grunts. Solomon play-cuffed the huge chimp, and the two embraced and wrestled with a noise and tumult meant both to signal their continuing friendship and their enduring physical prowess.

Once that display was finished, old Caliban limped over and sat near Solomon, regarding him with tired eyes as if to empathize with the hardships he must have endured. Wendy approached Solomon, carrying Wombat, and began to groom Solomon, while he tolerantly allowed Wombat to climb about him, play-bite his fingers, and generally pester the huge male as young ones do.

The keeper Ivy appeared on a platform that overlooked the chimps' outdoor enclosure and pitched down an afternoon treat—plastic gallon jugs of frozen fruit drink. The chimps grabbed them up and gnawed away at the tough plastic, chewing and licking at the icy sweetness, grouping and regrouping, sharing and stealing, grooming, and quarreling and gently reconciling.

When the sun sank low in the sky, casting cool shadows across the enclosure, Solomon climbed up on his high rock and surveyed the others. He remembered again the big place where he had been. He also remembered the other big cage with so many places to climb, all the strange people he had seen and the frightening explosions. But now he was back safe with the others, and he decided not to think any more about those experiences.

• • •

Digger stormed into Colter's office, spied Darrell Beckman sitting on the couch taking notes, flung a fistful of papers in his face, and hauled him up by his jacket lapels, flinging him like a rag doll against a bookcase.

"You little cocksucker!" he snarled, his sagging, florid, middle-aged face mere inches from Beckman's smooth-skinned young one. He yanked Beckman forward and slammed him against the bookcase again, dislodging two volumes of the California Penal Code. "I oughta take you outside so you won't bleed on the carpet and tear your fuckin' head off."

"Whoa, Digger!" Colter leaped, grabbing Digger's clenched fists, gently trying to separate them from Beckman's lapels. "Take it easy!"

Beckman allowed himself to be manhandled, but his face registered a dark hatred. "Get your hands off me, you goddamned drunk," he snapped. "What the hell's your problem?"

Digger gave him a last shove onto the couch and stalked back across the room, his hands clenching and unclenching, eager to do damage.

Sheba rushed in from the outer office, saying. "What is all this racket?"

"See all that?" Digger gestured at the scattered papers he'd flung at Beckman. "Phone records, bank deposit records, a surveillance report by a buddy of mine. These show that this little turd is the one who's behind the fuckin' kidnapping!"

"Darrell?" asked Colter incredulously. "What's this about?"

"C'mon, you believe this nut? Why would I do that?" Darrell's eyes darted from one suspicious face to the other, looking for support.

Digger grabbed one of the pages from the floor beside the couch. "Well, the fact that a retired buddy of mine who lives in the Caymans did a little under-the-table deal to trace that bank account back to you. And I just put my cop buddies onto phone records and receipts linking you to those four assholes they have in custody. One of them, in fact, was in law school with this little bastard."

Colter threw back his head and sighed in realization. The preppie. The shirt he wore was dark blue. Duke blue. A *Duke Law School* shirt.

Beckman scowled, his eyes shifting from person to person as a realization dawned that he wouldn't be able to talk his way out of his predicament. Digger perched his rotund frame on the arm of one of the large leather armchairs, looming over Beckman.

"Look. . . I had debts. I . . . I did what I needed to." Beckman straightened his jacket and smoothed back his hair. "I don't owe any of you a damned thing." He moved toward the door but found his way blocked by a determined Sheba.

Colter grabbed Darrell by the shoulder and spun him around. "Darrell, I just don't understand. How could you do this?"

"Oh, the story gets much better," growled Digger. "He had himself a really sweet deal. I found one of Drake's guards who don't like Drake very much. He said they fed this little shit inside stuff on security at the estate. Even helped with the kidnapping."

"You lost me, Digger," said Colter. "Why would Drake want the animal kidnapped?"

"He ain't a billionaire because he's simple," said Digger. "The idea was to link you to the theft, you're screwed, and the judge is more likely to decide the case his way. It was worth fifty million to him. But when you and the monkey got away, you messed up their plans good."

Colter shook his head sadly and, in a low voice, merely said, "Get out, Darrell. Just walk the hell out, and don't come back. I'm sure you'll see the inside of a jail cell soon enough."

"Bobby, you'd have done the same thing."

"Maybe. . . at one time. . . but I just found out I wouldn't anymore," said Colter. "And actually, I feel pretty good about that."

Beckman's face reddened, and he left under the fierce gaze of Sheba, who, Colter had no doubt, would make sure that he departed without taking as much as a Post-it note.

"So, what're you going to do now?" asked Digger.

"That depends on you, Digger." Colter sat down on the sofa near the old cop, peering up at him with tired eyes.

"Well, I'm with you, boyo." Digger clapped him on the shoulder, squeezing with his large ham-hand.

"I know that. That's why I need to find out whether you—and my dad's reputation—are going to go down with this case."

"Your dad? What do you mean?"

"I mean the Vasquez bust."

The name caused Digger to sag into the armchair, seeming to age him years in an instant. "Awww, shit," he muttered.

"Did you and Dad take money?"

"You got to understand, Bobby, It—"

"Goddamnit, Digger, did you and Dad take money?"

Digger stared at the floor for a while and then looked up with tears filling his old eyes, wetting the large bags beneath them. "Yeah, well, I did. Your dad didn't know anything about it. After the bust, he was busy hauling out the perp, and I stood there in that fuckin' room lookin' at a table full of money, and I thought, 'Why the fuck not?' So, I bagged a bunch that wouldn't be missed and stashed it where I could come back for it."

"But my law school tuition? Dad paid that."

"Hell, I told him I had an uncle who left me some. He was desperate about being able to pay your first tuition, and I said it was a gift from me, as your godfather. I had to beg the old fart to let me give it to him. He was too proud to even tell you."

"Damn," breathed Colter, lowering his head into his hands. "Damn. How did Drake find out?"

"Oh, it was probably that shit, Jimmy Tate. He was the property clerk then, and I always thought he'd come out with it someday, if somebody offered him the right money. Look, don't let this stop you. I've known you a long time, and I know when something really matters to you. Last time I saw you like this, it was when your mom died and you decided to become a lawyer. You really wanted it. And you want this. Bobby, this case, those two women, they're changing you. I think it's good, and I want you to go ahead. Don't stop just because some old has-been like me fucked up."

"They'll prosecute. They'll put you in jail."

"Nah, I'll have you as my lawyer." Digger put a meaty arm around him. "First offense . . . an old man like me . . . I won't do no time."

"They'll stop your pension."

"I'll mooch off you. Bobby, you go get that fuckin' monkey off."

CHAPTER 25

Monday evening

"It's the monkey lawyer! And the monkey woman!" The cry from the squat, disheveled man whose fat, sweaty neck supported garlands of cameras brought four other paparazzi sprinting down the sidewalk. They joined him to trigger a barrage of camera-flashes that strobed Colter and the glass-and-stone front of the restaurant. Colter ducked slightly, weathering the lightning of notoriety as he stood waiting for Abby to climb out of the car. Digger bolted from the driver's side and interposed himself between the photographers and Colter and Abby, ignoring their curses at him for spoiling their shots.

"Get out of the way, old man," commanded a paparazzo from behind his camera. "Hey, monkey lawyer, let's see you two together. Hey, give us a smile, hug each other. You two a couple?"

Colter clasped his hand on Digger's shoulder. "We'll be fine inside. They've got their own security. Come in and eat with us."

"Hell no," harrumphed Digger. "I don't eat fish bait. I'll go down to that sandwich place. Get a roast beef sandwich."

Colter turned to follow Abby toward the large oak door, reaching out to open it for her. "After you, monkey lady."

She smiled slightly, but her eyes showed an anxiety at the photographers' assault and the reminder it represented of her unwanted fame. As she slipped through the door, Colter was struck at how different she looked tonight, with her fine hair swept up, revealing a delicate neck, and wearing a light-blue silk pants suit that hinted at the curves of her body. He smiled at the contrast between her elegant look tonight and that of the slightly deranged jeans-clad woman curled up on the straw floor of the cage the night she had trapped them both there.

They were led by the maitre d' into the softly lighted room with walnut-paneled walls displaying exquisitely rendered calligraphy scrolls and furniture with the spare, clean lines of classic Japanese design. They settled into an intimate table within sight of the sushi bar and the white-hatted sushi chefs, whose intent, stoic expressions and graceful flourishes with their knives hinted at the artistic creations to come.

"Daiginjo saké," Colter said to the waiter, a balding white-coated little man, who bowed and left. He leaned toward her. "Okay, you said you ate nothing with a face. Fish don't have faces, right? They say fish is sort of midway between a meat and a vegetable."

"A compromise?" She smiled wryly, making a teasing face at him. "You lawyers are pretty good at that."

"If it means getting something we want." He matched her tease for tease. "And I want you . . . to enjoy a nice dinner with me. By the way, you look terrific."

"Well, I'm not a fanatic vegetarian. And I do like sushi. Haven't had it in a place like this before."

The waiter arrived with a chilled bottle of saké, pouring it into small cedar boxes near to the brim. "Kampai," toasted Colter, and they gingerly sipped the cold liquor, enjoying the smooth fruity taste, feeling the warmth of the alcohol suffuse their bodies, softening the evening. Colter told the waiter that they would have the chef's choice of sashimi and sushi.

"I figured we'd have the best chance of not being bothered here," he said. "You'll see producers, movie stars. They come here for refuge." He noticed, however, that knowing glances were being discreetly cast their way by the men in expensive suits and the women in elegant designer dresses. He had thought he'd detected a slight uptick in the buzz of conversation as they entered.

"Solomon has changed you. You're not as cocky," she said abruptly, the jarring change in topic perhaps signaling the effects of the saké.

He considered whether to admit it and decided he needed to be straightforward with this woman who was capable of bending ferocious chimpanzees to her will. She would not tolerate oblique banter.

"Yes, he has changed me. When we were in the forest, there was a moment. You were on the phone with me. It was when he stepped over me. I just felt something happen."

"There was a communication, right? A connection. That happens to a lot of people who begin working with them. Suddenly, one day, they do something incredible, or there's an understanding, and, from then on, you can't just think of them as just another animal." She took another sip of saké, as the waiter delivered small china plates of lustrous slices of pinkish-apricot-hued fish draped over opalescent rice.

"Toro," pronounced the waiter.

"Ah," murmured Colter. "Domo arigato deshita." Then, to Abby: "The chef likes us. If he doesn't like you, he won't give you toro. It's the best tuna."

The waiter bent down conspiratorially. "The chef ask, you want fugu? Don't worry. Chef know how to make with no poison."

Colter leaned over to Abby, passing on the conspiratorial tone. "You know fugu? Blowfish? Prepared wrong it can kill you, but it's incredible. Almost worth dying for."

"I lived through Africa—I can live through dinner," she said.

Colter nodded, and the waiter vanished with a satisfied smile. They brushed each slice of fish with a dollop of soy sauce and bit into the cool, velvety flesh, savoring its delicate taste. The waiter followed with morsels of mackerel sashimi, freshwater eel, and sea-urchin roe.

"Solomon," intoned Colter between bites, as if reciting a mantra. "Yeah, he did change me. It's as if I've reached into a part of me I didn't know existed. They have this . . . well . . . this presence."

"You're not usually so introspective, are you? The chimps will do that to you. Make you start thinking about what you are, anyway."

"May I ask you an impertinent question?"

"That's what you do for a living, isn't it? Ask impertinent questions?"

"Are you in a relationship?" He gave her that straight-on gaze that tended to discomfit people.

"Well . . ." She paused, regarding him just as forthrightly, weighing her answer. "I'm in a bunch of relationships. Just got into another."

"Full dance card, eh? Oh, well . . ." The spell was broken. Colter sipped his saké to hide his disappointment and bit luxuriously into another piece of sushi.

"The latest is a big hairy guy. Name's Lucky."

"Oh, you mean the chimps. C'mon, you know what I mean. A relationship with somebody on your branch of the family tree." Colter realized that he'd been so preoccupied with the woman sitting across the table that he was missing obvious jokes.

"This is delicious," said Abby choosing another piece of pink sushi, slowly nibbling it. "Very sensuous. This how you begin a seduction?"

Before Colter could restore his composure and consider a comeback, the waiter arrived with plates of thinly sliced fugu, garnished with sprigs of tiny white flowers.

"Usually, I just take first dates for hamburgers. I don't like to invest too much in a relationship early on." He used chopsticks to grasp a pearlescent slice of fish, deftly transferring it to his mouth and savoring the complex taste.

"This looks like you're pretty sure of yourself." She sampled the fugu, letting her lips toy with the glistening flesh before drawing it in.

"Answer the question."

"There is a man I've been seeing. But he's in Africa. We decided he should go to Africa, but I couldn't."

"I admire his dedication. I mean I *really* admire his dedication. I hope he keeps that dedication for a *long* time."

But she would not be wooed so easily. Her expression switched abruptly to dead-serious, and she launched a line of questioning that seemed well rehearsed. "Tell me about the MacIntire case. What did you do that's gotten you into trouble? They said bribing a witness. They said the family paid you to get your client convicted."

"It's a long story."

"Then you better hurry before the fish kills us." As if on cue, the waiter arrived with plates of silvery fugu skin embedded in cubes of clear golden-brown aspic, and they began to pursue the quivering morsels with their chopsticks, manipulating them precariously into their mouths. They savored the pungent taste of the bits of skin immersed in the smooth, cool aspic.

Colter decided again that this woman would tolerate no evasion. "I had this client named MacIntire."

"Well, okay, that explains the whole thing."

"I am going to tell you the whole story. Just eat your poison fish." He took another bite to give himself courage. "The guy was basically the lowest scum of the earth, but he happened to be from a wealthy family."

"So the money got you on the case."

"Yeah, that and the fact that he happened to be innocent of this particular crime. He'd been accused of molesting this little girl. Somebody raped her and left her in a coma."

Colter was acutely aware that he might be breaking a romantic mood that he liked to establish with a beautiful woman. But this was a different kind of woman. He continued.

"This guy had a record of doing that kind of thing before, he lived in the neighborhood, and forensics found evidence that he'd been in the house. Well, he had a friend who was his alibi. The friend was ready to testify that they were hanging out at the friend's house when the little girl was attacked. And MacIntire said he'd been in the girl's house on another occasion, so the forensic evidence was suspect, anyway."

"But the girl's family got to you? Paid you off?"

"That's what they're saying, but it's bullshit. It's a story Drake put out. What really happened was . . . well . . . I just did what I had to do."

"And what did you have to do?"

"Well, I was in the middle of trying the case, and this other guy calls me . . . a *really* close friend of MacIntire, if you know what I mean . . . somebody who did this sick stuff with him. And this guy, Burke, tells me that MacIntire had in fact killed another little girl, whose body had never been found. They'd done it together, and Burke was there when MacIntire killed her. He even showed me photos he'd taken. I'd never had evidence make me physically ill before, but those pictures did. So, here I was with a client who was about to get off, but who I knew really was a sicko, killing girls. And he'd do it again, no doubt."

"So, why didn't you just get this guy Burke to tell his story to the district attorney?"

"He disappeared. Vanished completely. I've never been sure whether MacIntire killed him, or he got cold feet, or maybe MacIntire's family bribed him. I had a feeling it was Burke who really killed the second little girl, and he figured if MacIntire got off, they'd be looking at other suspects, namely him. So, he wanted to get MacIntire convicted, and he didn't care for which crime."

"Then you were left with nothing?"

"All I had was the photos. It wouldn't have made any kind of case."

"So, you used the pictures?"

"I met with MacIntire's alibi witness and told him the story. I showed him the pictures. He got sick, too. I gave him enough money to live on for a while, and he took off. MacIntire's alibi evaporated, and he got convicted. He's serving a life sentence, and he's probably not very popular—child molesters usually are considered the lowest kind of humans by inmates. So, yes, I did tamper with a witness, and I did give him money. And, yes, I'd do it again."

She stared silently at him for a long while, studying his face as if she hadn't seen it before. The waiter arrived with slices of golden-brown fugu liver, sprinkling the plate lightly with tiny flecks of gold leaf.

"Best part of the fish. You really will like," he announced, trying to re-establish the mood.

She remained pensive as they ate the richly flavored liver and finished with a dessert saké, leaving the restaurant on the luxuriant cloud of elegant food, alcohol, and a warming relationship. Digger had the car waiting out front and escorted them to it, inflicting only minimal damage on the paparazzi. He drove the broad, traffic-ridden

Los Angeles boulevards down to the campus area, where he pulled up in front of Abby's condominium, a gracefully aging collection of 1960s-modern buildings set amidst lush, overgrown foliage. Colter and Abby strolled away down the walk, Colter waving Digger back with a "give-me-a-break" gesture. Digger held up his cell phone in a silent gesture that Colter knew meant Digger was calling another bodyguard to spend the night outside her condominium. He nodded at that.

They reached her door. He moved closer, wrapped his arms around her, and gently kissed her. He was surprised at the readiness with which her soft lips searched out his.

"Have you ever done that to a client?" she whispered.

"Solomon's my client, and I guarantee I won't do that to him."

"I've got two things to say to you."

"Are they complicated? Should I take notes?"

"Real simple. First, I'm pretty good in bed."

He chuckled. "I'll be the judge of that."

"No, you won't. That's the second thing. Even though I'm starting to have some significant feelings for you, it ain't going to happen right now."

"If it's Digger, he's gone. And the new guy will stay out front."

"It's not Digger."

He kissed her smooth, milk-white neck, something he'd been wanting to do all evening. The flesh was as soft and warm as he'd imagined. "Look, I don't really want to admit it, but I think I'm . . . well . . . I have feelings for you, too. If you don't trust me, then I'll do what's necessary to get trusted."

"Yeah, well, maybe trust is still a little bit of a problem. But mainly it's that I can't handle both a thing with us and what could happen to Solomon, too. I'm sorry, but there's room only for him right now."

"I've never had a rival who was such a swinger. Never been as jealous, either."

She backed away, opened the door, cocked her head, and raised her eyebrows in a matter-of-fact way. "It's just as well, you know. Frankly, if we'd gone to bed together, it would be so great, you wouldn't be able to handle your case on Monday."

Colter laughed and kissed her on the cheek. She quickly retreated behind the door—he'd hoped because he was on the verge of winning out for her affections over his muscular simian competitor. Her absence in the quiet night brought the fact of his situation back to him—reminded him that the evening had been only a refuge for the two of them. A brief refuge from dangers that could devastate both of them.

CHAPTER 26

Monday night

Abby let her hair down, brushed it out, and padded barefoot down the hall, past the collection of carved African ceremonial masks grimacing at her from the wall. She entered her small bedroom, moving a pile of scientific-paper reprints out of the way with her foot, and sat down on the edge of the bed, frowning. Some vague unease nagged at her. Even after drinking considerable saké and enjoying a lovely romantic interlude with a man who attracted her very strongly, she felt a dark, unresolved aura about the evening. She pulled the last raspberry Pop Tart out of its package on her bedside table and began to nibble reflectively. She and Solomon had shared Pop Tarts when she was a child, and she'd fallen into an almost eucharistic habit of eating one before bed each night. It was almost a way of confirming the continuing bond between them.

As she ate the crumbly pastry, the nagging feeling told her not to change into the worn cotton nightgown she slept in just yet, not to begin the ritual tooth-brushing, face-washing preamble to sleep. She'd had these premonitions before. She insisted to herself that they were either her subconscious playing psychological tricks or just her rational self, integrating sensory inputs to arrive at a logical conclusion. Ah, yes, that was the more satisfying scientific explanation.

"One call," she promised herself upon finishing the last morsel of Pop Tart. "I should check on Lucky. Yeah, and see if Solly's settled in. He's been restless, poor old thing."

Her reasoning seemed convincing, so she dug her land-line phone out of a pile of books and papers on the large work table that she used to remedy the chronic lack of flat-surface for her bedtime-reading materials.

She punched in the lab number and waited as it rang. No answer. Ivy should be there in the office, working on the animals' progress reports. Maybe Ivy had gone down the hall to check on the chimps. But they should be settled in for the night. Ivy would have texted her or called if something had happened. So, something must have *just* happened. The lab's voice mail answered with the message that began with a cacophony of chimp-hooting. She left a message for Ivy to call her back. But she wouldn't wait. The dark aura tugged at her.

"Twenty minutes to get there, I'll check things out, then twenty minutes back," she told herself. She slipped out of the pants suit, stealing a glimpse of herself in the mirror to remind herself how great the light blue looked against her fair skin. She raised one approving eyebrow. Bobby Colter never had a chance. She pulled on a pair of jeans and slipped on a t-shirt, digging socks and sneakers out of her closet. She peeked through the front blinds of her apartment to see whether the new guard had arrived yet, as Bobby had said. The lawn chair beside her front walk was empty. She opened the door and walked out, looking up and down the dark sidewalk. Seeing no sign of the guard, she scribbled a note that she had gone to the lab, left it on the chair, and went out the back way into the one-car garage that was attached to her unit.

"Safety first," she reminded herself, climbing into the Subaru Outback and raising the windows and locking the doors before pressing the remote for the garage door opener. Once the door opened fully, she backed down the incline and into the small parking lot behind the condos, swinging the small car out into the alley that led onto the main street. Traffic was light, and, within ten minutes, she had turned onto the winding mountain road leading to the research forest and the lab. The aura she was feeling now had an edge of urgency about it, as her mind became crowded with visions of all the possible bad things that could happen.

Her preoccupation and the winding curves at first caused her not to notice that a car was following her, until suddenly it had drawn close enough to be taking the curves right behind her. She stole glances at the bright headlights as best she could, given the need to pay attention to negotiating the sharp turns. This road led to very little except for the research forest, so she felt a knot of fear grow in her stomach. This car was following *her*, not on some mission of its own. Her fear rising, she pressed down the accelerator, taking the dark curves as fast as she could, with the remnant effects of the saké giving her a bit more courage than usual. The car drew even closer, and now it flashed its high beams.

"You want me to stop?" she mumbled to herself. "No damn way, whoever you are."

She sped up even more, steering into a wide left curve over a steep canyon about half a mile from the lab. A loud bang exploded from the vicinity of the front right tire. They had shot at her! She yelped in surprise as the Subaru canted over and careened wildly to the right. She reacted instantly, wrenching the steering wheel to the left, but the flat right tire and the Subaru's momentum sent the vehicle into a skid toward the canyon precipice.

"GOD! OH, JESUS!" she exclaimed, slamming on the brakes but failing to halt the inevitable skid toward the canyon and its rocky bottom.

But the other car whipped around to her right, sideswiping hers and driving it away from the cliff.

"What the hell—" she stopped, stunned as she glimpsed the driver of the car, which sideswiped hers again, with the screech of sheet metal on sheet metal. Digger was driving the car! He sped up, bringing the nose of the silver Mercedes sedan just ahead of the Subaru's and expertly swerving the Mercedes into the Subaru. He managed to jam her car against the dirt wall on the left of the road, scraping it along until it came to a final halt.

Digger backed the Mercedes off, but Abby found herself trapped in the Subaru, the driver's side door wedged against the dirt and the smashed passenger-side door jammed shut.

Digger's middle-aged face appeared at the shattered side window.

"YOU TRYING TO KILL ME?" she screamed, her rage boiling over. She twisted around and raised her legs, lashing out at him through the window. He managed to duck out of sight, and when she drew back for another thrust, his face was replaced with Colter's.

"Digger saved your life!" he exclaimed.

Abby's mouth dropped open. "My God! What? What's going on here?"

"Let's get you out first."

She wriggled through the side window and stood up beside her wrecked car, clinging to the broken side mirror for support. Colter wrapped his arms around her, and they held each other tightly, gaining strength from each other's embrace.

"Digger didn't try to kill me?" she asked.

"I wouldn't do anything like that, sweetheart," said Digger, who had returned from a search down the road from where they had come. He held up a small cell phone and a separate tube with wires jutting from it. "This little bastard did." He held the pieces in front of the Mercedes' lit headlights.

"What is it?" asked Colter.

"It's nearly the perfect murder weapon," said Digger. "Earlier, my guy saw somebody break into your garage with something in his hand and come out without it. We figured it might be a gadget like this. But you took off before we could check it." He held up the tube. "I read about this damn thing in *Soldier of Fortune*. It's got a blank shotgun shell in it, and it fires a bolt into the tire at just the right moment. Triggered by this cell phone. It blows itself off the car, so it looks like old debris on the road. All any witnesses see is a blowout and the car going over a cliff. The bad guys don't need to use another car, leaving tire marks and paint scrapings. You lose control real easy when you lose a tire. They had this all figured out."

Abby peered into the darkness. "So, they're around here. They watched me go into that turn?"

"Well, with the cell phone trigger, they could have been just about any place in LA." Digger rummaged in the Mercedes' trunk, coming out with a Phillips-head screwdriver, which he used to open the cylinder, revealing an integrated circuit board attached to a detonator for the spent shotgun shell. "This is a GPS chip. A Global Positioning System receiver. They just sat in a van somewhere and tracked you. And when they saw that you were at just the right place on this road, they sent a command over the cell phone—and, blooey!"

"It has to be Drake who's behind it. Perfect crime, those bastards," said Colter.

"Not exactly perfect." Digger grinned knowingly. "To make it perfect, if there's no fire, they've got to make sure you're dead. I'm sure the plan is to show up real fast to check. And if anybody sees them, well, they're just Good Samaritans who happened on the scene. So, the goddamned Good Samaritan ought to be along any minute."

"So, we've got to give them an accident scene?" asked Colter.

Digger merely raised his eyebrows in a questioning look at Abby.

The implication dawned on her. "Not my car! It's not even paid for!"

"Sarah will spring for a new one, I'm sure," said Colter.

After a few moments, Abby finally sighed in resignation and shrugged, quickly retrieving an armload of her paraphernalia from the car, dumping it into Colter's battered Mercedes. As Digger maneuvered the Mercedes into place behind the Subaru, she and Colter guided the crippled vehicle to the edge of the cliff, standing back as Digger precisely gunned the Mercedes to give the Subaru one last shove over the cliff.

Abby winced with each crash echoing from below as the tumbling car tore itself to pieces in its plunge into the darkness. Abby and Colter nestled themselves into a clump of roadside bushes down the road, and Digger raced the Mercedes around the curve and out of sight.

"How did you know this was going to happen?" she whispered to Colter, as she sat down in the dirt, leaning back on a large rock.

"We didn't. Just after we left the restaurant, one of Digger's guys called and told him a blue Mercedes like the one Lunt drives had left the estate really fast. Digger said something didn't smell right. We figured Drake was getting desperate. Beckman was useless, and Drake couldn't get me thrown off the case. You were the logical next target. With you dead . . . of an accident, of course . . . the case would've really fallen apart. Even Sarah would have given up."

Digger appeared behind them, squatting down behind the bush. "Yeah, and I also got a call from a source who told me the guy who was supposed to be watching you overnight made a real big bank deposit three days ago. We made it back just in time to see you leave for the lab, so we followed you."

"And why the hell didn't you two think to tell me this? Or, why didn't you call the cops?"

"I didn't know how leaky your lab was," said Digger. "They got to Beckman. How was I to know they hadn't gotten to one of your people? Hell, maybe they'd even gotten to you. We didn't know why you were going to the lab, anyway. And as for calling the cops." Digger grunted disgustedly. "They got this really annoying policy of not doing anything until a crime has been committed." A faint buzz prompted Digger to draw out his cell phone, answer the call, listen for a moment, thank the caller, and hang up. "My guy found Ivy and the campus cop who was watching your lab. They're okay. Ivy said she heard a noise outside, and, when she went out, somebody chloroformed her and tied her up, as well as the cop. Ivy says your monkeys are all okay."

A faint glow lit the gloom of the curve, signaling the approach of a car.

"It's our damned Samaritan," said Digger, scrunching down as low as his belly would allow him.

The headlights swept past their position as the car rounded the turn and slowed, as if the occupants were scanning for the spot at which the Subaru had gone over. The car stopped, and the passenger-side door opened, a faint crunching sound telling the three that a man was walking across the narrow shoulder toward the edge of the canyon.

"Yeah, here," said the man's voice.

"Then go down," said a voice from inside the car. "Use the rope."

"Aw, shit. It's way down there."

"Then use *all* the rope, damnit. C'mon! And check the body."

Abby shivered, realizing that they were talking about her. She wanted to jump up and curse the men at the top of her lungs, flinging rocks at them, but Colter laid a hand on her shoulder, patting it to tell her to remain calm. Digger held up an index finger to indicate that the time for their surprise assault was near.

They watched the beam of a flashlight dance about the dark roadside and listened to the flapping sounds of a rope being unfurled and tied around a tree, and of someone lowering themselves down it. Abruptly Digger stood up and drew his Glock pistol, slogging over to the car window.

"How fucking unimaginative," he growled. "It's Fred Lunt himself. You dumb mother—"

But Lunt had already slapped the car into reverse and slammed the accelerator to the floor, launching it hurtling backwards down the road in a swirl of dust. Digger brought up the pistol and let loose several rounds at the car, the explosions reverberating into the night. Lunt whipped the car around and accelerated away around the curve.

"Well, I made enough holes so the cops can trace it," said Digger, holstering his pistol. "He's not very loyal to his underlings, is he?" quipped Digger, as the three of them stepped to the ledge, where the taut rope indicated a man hanging his full weight on it.

Abby signaled that she wanted to handle this one. "Say, *you* down there. Giacomo, is that you?"

"Aw, shit," came filtering up from the depths of the canyon.

"Giacomo, you're kind of screwed, aren't you? Digger's got your little toy. Your boss took off. Come on up, and take it like a man."

Silence settled on the canyon for a full minute, no doubt while Giacomo assessed his situation. Then the rope abruptly went slack and the still canyon yielded the sound of a large body crashing its way through brush, into the distance.

Digger shrugged, "I guess he prefers to take his chances with rattlers and cliffs, rather than face us." He took out his cell phone and called the police. "Now they've got a crime, and with a little luck, they'll net at least one of the criminals."

Colter put his arm around Abby, and they stood together, waiting for the police. They said nothing, but their silence spoke of the evaporation of any doubts about their mission and the crystallization of a grim, hardened determination.

Chapter 27

Tuesday afternoon

At one p.m. Colter sat in the courtroom amidst the preparatory bustle and edgy chatter of reporters and spectators, waiting for Wainwright to appear for the afternoon session. He tried to focus on the structure of his legal arguments, but the clouds of memory kept intruding. The intimate dinner with Abby but, most of all, the attempt on her life, which, to his surprise, had shaken him to the bone. He had faced his mirror that night a changed man. Cindy and Rachael had called, and he tried dutifully to banter with them. But they seemed people from another life. This new Colter found himself inevitably and, in fact, disturbingly, falling in . . . damnit . . . love.

His concentration had also been rattled by the media. Colter, Abby, and Sarah had arrived at the courthouse to find a mass of reporters and cameras that had swollen to evolve into a life of its own—a huge, perpetually hungry amoeba that enveloped them in an insatiable search for facts, quotes, rumors, background . . . any morsel of information. The reporters had surrounded the three of them outside the courtroom, interviewing and videotaping him as their spokesman. He tried to say as little as possible but to sound meaningful and above all, confident. Once satisfied that they'd extracted all the information possible, the reporters went off to regurgitate it over the Internet and satellite dishes back to their employers. The hunger was made all the more urgent, because the facts of Friday's court session had already been digested over the weekend, as editors editorialized and commentators commented.

The newspaper editorial pages and bloggers expended vast expanses of text analyzing the case from every angle. And the issue had filled the weekend political talk shows, thankfully with Childs and other PMAT advocates forcefully asserting his side. The very idea of a chimpanzee having legal rights offered a juicy debate topic that attracted a pack of other experts proclaiming their opinions—lawyers, politicians, priests, philosophers, biologists, psychologists and anthropologists.

They pronounced Colter, Abby, and Sarah the most exalted of saints and the basest of sinners. They were labeled fools and sages, publicity hounds and selfless crusaders. The intense media spotlight had also made them eminently marketable. So Colter's phone messages included—besides the usual interview requests, "fuck-yous", "damn-you-to-hells" and "bless-yous"—at least a dozen offers for book deals, TV movie deals, feature film deals, TV series deals, and even a pitch for a Solomon doll. Sheba had laughed and cracked "Yeah, wind *that* doll up and it ruins your life," when she handed him that message.

He remembered ironically a time when he'd craved such attention, lusted after celebrity so badly he was even willing to settle for notoriety. But, now, when it had engulfed him and he sat preparing himself for this very public reckoning, he felt that the carefully constructed identity of R. William Colter had been tattered into bits, only to be reconstructed as they saw fit by the media, the police, Jenkins, Drake, even by Abby and Sarah. He had become a Frankenstein's monster, his persona assembled from the disparate body parts of others' expectations and perceptions.

As he sat waiting the last few minutes for the court proceedings to begin, again the cloud of memory rolled in of the previous night. After the attack on Abby, he had felt incapable of getting her out of his thoughts. He'd begun the morning by dutifully immersing himself in preparing his arguments. But the instant he paused, he felt himself drawn to call her. His pretext was a need to spend just a little more time with the chimps, but it also allowed him the excuse to speed to the lab, to sit beside her on the observation platform overlooking the outdoor enclosure.

Interrupted only by the occasional roar of a news helicopter, which set the chimps to irate screaming, they talked over the case, watching the chimps go about their morning socializing. He ostensibly reviewed his arguments and talked about the police investigation into the attack and the continuing search for both Lunt and Giacomo. But their conversation was like a carrier wave, with the real information superimposed subtly as modulation over the mere words. They both sent unspoken signals conveying deepening feelings for each other.

As Colter sat watching the graceful, emphatic motion of her hands as she talked, the intense expression on her face, his profound attraction, enriched by admiration, was absolutely nothing he had ever expected. Until now, his days and nights had been happily satisfied by spectacular, golden women who seemed to skim across life, borne on their beauty. This serious woman, Abby, had none of their flash but rather the fire of a dedication that gave her a deeply luminous quality, one that would grace her even after her smooth, young face had weathered with age and ordeal.

Colter returned his attention abruptly to the courtroom as the leonine Jenkins appeared with a pride of young, confident assistants. He stood at the defense table, turning his silver-maned head slowly to regard Colter with the superior tolerance one would display toward a not-too-bright underling. He smiled slightly and nodded his head in acknowledgment, with perhaps an infinitesimal raise of the eyebrow in surprise that Colter had even shown up. Colter felt the flush of anger rise through his body in a hot wave. "Thanks, you arrogant son-of-a-bitch," he thought. That smirk helped focus his attention on his ultimate goal: to defeat this alpha male. Colter was tempted to bellow a chimpanzee-like pant-hoot, ending in a glorious bellowing scream. The act would have felt eminently and viscerally satisfying.

The bailiff announced Wainwright's appearance, and they rose as he swept in wearing his black robe and an expression somewhere between scowl and smirk. He settled in his chair, smacked his gavel, and announced,

"It's time to get this over with. Mr. Jenkins. Could you please begin?"

Jenkins sat with his head bowed for a long moment, gathering his exalted thoughts, then rose.

"Your Honor, I will not take too much of your time, for I think the arguments I made previously still carry the same inevitable logic. First, that this is clearly a matter of property. Mr. Colter has already stipulated to the validity of the contract. And more generally, as I have said, the concept still holds of *hominum causa omne jus constitutum*—that 'all laws were made for man's sake.' So has said the *Bible* in the Tenth Commandment, which holds that one should not covet thy neighbor's ox or ass or any other such *property*. Clearly, the *Bible* held that animals are property, and so has the common law that we inherited from England. And so has confirmed the Supreme Court in Geer versus Connecticut." Jenkins' voice rose a notch, signaling a ratcheting up of the drama of his argument.

"Mr. Colter and his clients, who may not appreciate the depth of our most sacred beliefs, are asking us to cross wide gulfs. A profound gulf between species, and a vast gulf between what our laws have long held and some alien new world where cherished values and beliefs mean nothing."

Jenkins stepped out from behind the table clasping his hands together as if in prayer, his sonorous voice filling the courtroom.

"We have evolved beyond our base animal origins. Our intelligence has made us the dominant species on earth. We certainly have a responsibility to the creatures of this planet. But we should not lower ourselves to bring these lesser species into our society as equals. This animal Solomon is not intelligent like humans. He does not have that God-given self-awareness that is the glory of humankind. It is unfortunate that his life must be taken, but we have a higher moral responsibility to preserve a human life."

Now Jenkins threw his hands apart in puzzlement.

"Where will this end? Where will you draw the line? If you give legal rights to an ape, next will come monkeys, then cats, then snakes, then spiders. Your Honor, if you allow this animal to have guardianship and legal personhood, will you someday have before you a lawsuit in which a bacterium sues a drug company whose antibiotics have endangered its life!"

The derisive laughter rolled across the courtroom, as Jenkins had clearly expected, and he sat down to Wainwright's tolerant rapping of the gavel for order. Colter thought he detected a satisfied twinkle in Wainwright's eye as the judge turned to invite Colter to begin his argument. Colter needed anger here. He needed fire. He pictured Solomon sitting with such dignity, playing with his friends, ambling through the forest, tearing through a loaf of bread. He pictured

Solomon dead, spread out across an operating table, his heart removed, his body to be discarded. Anger filled him, its pressure goading him to rise and launch his arguments.

"First, Your Honor, I would like to settle this business about Mr. Drake having some contractual right to kill Solomon. Mr. Jenkins argues that a man's life is at stake, that Mr. Drake needs Solomon's heart to live. True, Mr. Drake's life is in peril, but I would argue that his decision to use Solomon to briefly extend his life is completely irrelevant to this case. As Mr. Jenkins so clearly emphasized, this is a case about contracts. And the contract that both Mr. Drake and Dr. Philips agreed to does *not* explicitly state that Mr. Drake has the right to use Solomon for a particular purpose. It only states that Mr. Drake made a contribution to Dr. Philips' research in return for rights to Solomon. He obtained only the right to care for Solomon without liability. Thus, Mr. Drake does not have the right under this particular contract to use this near-human known as Solomon like some laboratory rat, discarding his life. Thus, I ask Your Honor to make his decision based on Solomon's rights, not some nonexistent contractual right that Mr. Jenkins claims under this contract."

Colter paused. He was an inch away from asserting that it was surely wrong to kill a virtuous animal like Solomon to give a bastard like Drake a few years of life. But he took another breath and steered away from that treacherous shoal.

"Now, with regard to Solomon's legal rights—how can Mr. Jenkins claim that an intelligent creature like Solomon should have no legal rights, when an unformed human infant does? You have heard testimony that the difference in intelligence between the most intelligent human and the least intelligent is far greater than between human and ape. Logic tells us that one cannot own an intelligent, feeling animal like one owns a piece of furniture. There is a moral responsibility here. And once you have a moral responsibility, you should have a legal responsibility."

Colter moved to stand closer to Jenkins' table to tower over him—an act he had learned from Solomon, as the ape had towered over him to assert his dominance.

"And even if you do accept, wrongly, Mr. Jenkins' false assertion that Solomon is less intelligent than any human, the law says that doesn't matter. Yes, Your Honor, in 1992, the Massachusetts Supreme Judicial Court in the case The Care and Protection of Beth, held that a child in a vegetative state still had legal rights. That case held, quote, cognitive ability is not a prerequisite for enjoying basic liberties. End quote. Our brains are bigger, but does that make our moral or even legal standing higher?"

He moved to stand directly before Wainwright. Now he would have to question the *Bible*, which required him to show a fair sense of moral outrage. Colter worked himself up again by picturing Solomon dead.

"Mr. Jenkins also says that the Tenth Commandment prohibits coveting a neighbor's animals, but it also prohibits coveting a man's wife, servant or handmaid, or anything that was his. Now, the Ten Commandments are certainly a compelling moral guide, but they are no legal guide. They must be reinterpreted in light of new wisdom. We have realized the error of this early thinking in our legal system and corrected it."

Colter shivered inside. He could see the headlines. "Ape Lawyer Denounces Ten Commandments." He moved to his table, glancing at Abby and Sarah, who had assumed the attitude of rapt attention he had coached them on. He flipped through his brief.

"Not that our legal system has been perfect, by any means. I note that in 1854, the California Supreme Court barred Chinese from appearing as witnesses in proceedings involving a white person because they were believed to be an inferior race. And in 1857, the U.S. Supreme Court held that African-Americans were not citizens, and were seen as, quote, beings of an inferior order that had no rights which the white man was bound to respect. End quote.

"And even more recently, women were not allowed to vote, because we relegated them to a lesser status. And gays were not allowed to marry, because their love was considered unnatural. We have now reconsidered all these misguided legal principles, discarded them as being tragically and profoundly wrong. Just as our moral concepts evolved then, we must allow them to evolve now. We have now entered a new era of scientific understanding, which reveals that the great apes have the moral capacity to deserve a standing that they have not had before. The ancient rules, the ancient cosmologies that allow such injustice, no longer make sense in the light of new knowledge. We must change them. I ask Your Honor to have the courage to take the next logical step."

Again Colter opened his notebook, reading from a new authority he hoped would supersede the old.

"The lawyer Steven M. Wise—considered the most eminent authority on rights for non-human primates—has written so aptly that, when judges today rule on human and non-human legal rights, they base their opinions on ancient, outmoded moral law that has been superseded. Wise writes that, quote, By mechanically citing to earlier cases and other sources of law that cite to still earlier cases and sources, and so on to the ancients, judges have no way to realize that the foundations have rotted away. End quote.

"Your Honor, I ask you to recognize the rot in those legal foundations, to construct a new scientifically firm foundation. It may seem a daring step, but only because it has not been taken before. Once, other disenfranchised groups were considered only *things*. Once they were freed from this thinghood, they became part of us. And Solomon is part of us." Colter closed his book and riveted his gaze on the judge. "These animals have natures and interests fundamentally like ours. This means they also deserve basic rights of bodily integrity and bodily liberty. It is arbitrary and a breach of the fundamental principle of equality to deny them these rights merely because they are not human beings."

Scattered applause, boos, and cheers echoed around the courtroom, and Wainwright gaveled them down, allowing a silence to descend. Colter sensed it was a silence of tacit disapproval. Wainwright leaned forward, returning Colter's gaze.

"Do they have souls?" he asked in a gravelly voice.

Startled, Colter found himself unable to gather his answer, and Wainwright repeated his question.

"Sir, do these animals have a soul? When this animal Solomon dies, will its soul depart for heaven?"

"Uh. . . Your Honor, a soul is a religious concept, not a legal one."

"Bailiff, hold up the *Bible*," commanded Wainwright, and the large black leather bound book was held high for all to see. "We swear on that holy book, don't we? That means something, doesn't it?"

Wainwright was a fundamentalist! Colter felt as if a searchlight had clicked on in his head, illuminating a fact he had been too stupid to see before. Why hadn't he had Digger do more background work on the old man's religious beliefs! He desperately searched for a reply.

"Your Honor . . ." He stopped. Nothing came. The court's silence seemed to smother him, bringing a dread of impending failure.

"Mr. Colter, please do go on. The court is waiting," said Wainwright. Colter felt as if he were squeezing his mind like a sponge. An answer dawned!

"Your Honor, there is no dispute between religion and this case. To me, the *Bible* is a guiding light not just for the head but also for the heart. We are meant to interpret its wisdom with our hearts open to new understanding . . . in fact, understanding from *knowledge gained by the very mind that God gave us.* That new understanding told us that human slavery was evil. That we had done grave injustices to many other minorities. And now it tells us that we must forge a new bond with the creatures of our planet. We do, indeed, have dominion over Earth and its creatures, and with that dominion comes responsibility. I am asking us to assume a new form of responsibility for these creatures, our closest relatives."

Wainwright stared at Colter in contemplative silence and then bowed his head and stared down at his hands. Was he praying? Colter sensed that he had touched a nerve in the old man. The judge raised his head and asked, "But the soul, Mr. Colter. I ask again, what about the soul?"

Before Colter could answer, Jenkins rose and said, "Your Honor, may I be allowed to answer that?" Wainwright nodded benignly to give him the floor. "Of course, the soul is a theological concept, but it is part of the moral underpinning of our law. And, as such, it must be considered. Clearly, you could say that, in a religious sense, Solomon has no soul. But you could also extend that into the moral sphere and say he has no sense of right and wrong."

Colter glimpsed an opening, a chance for recovery. "Ah, but he does have a sense of right and wrong, and of justice. In fact, Solomon, of all apes, is perhaps most qualified to express his sense of right and wrong. Doctor Philips has trained him in a computer-assisted verbal-language system that allows him to address such issues. Solomon could tell you that he and his fellow apes have a sense of morality. And he could tell you that depriving apes of their rights to liberty and bodily integrity is wrong and cruel."

From the instant Jenkins cleared his throat, Colter knew he had allowed himself to fall into a trap. "Your Honor, then I would demand that we examine Solomon directly as a witness, to determine whether this sense of justice, or right and wrong, actually exists."

"But your honor already has scientific papers and affidavits to that effect in our submitted material," protested Colter. "And bringing Solomon here would present enormous problems of transport, of housing. We would have—"

"Your Honor, Mr. Colter can't have it both ways. Either Solomon is an animal that can't understand being brought here as a witness, or he is a sentient being that can understand what is happening. If he stipulates that the animal can be examined as a witness, as would a human, than the defense would require that he should be treated like a witness and be called to appear in court."

Wainwright paused, peering back and forth at the two lawyers. "I have heard in these proceedings that this animal has been transported thither and yon with little problem and no ill effects. I'm not ruling whether he will be a witness or an exhibit. But you *will* have the animal in this courtroom tomorrow morning."

The courtroom erupted in a chatter of excited voices, punctuated by Wainwright's gavel, as Colter sat heavily down at the table, trying to figure out what to do next. Abby leaned over, clutching his arm in a desperate grip.

"Bobby, this is a disaster. You bring Solomon here in a cage, and you're making their case. The judge will see him as a caged animal. He'll go nuts at all the people. After all, he is a chimp. He acts like a chimp. God, Bobby, what're we going to do?"

"Hell if I know," muttered Colter. "I've never prepped an ape for court before."

. . .

Colter's office was a tomb for hope after the session, as they merely stared at one another in a depressed silence that seemed to smother thought and action. Sarah sat imperiously in one of the big chairs, as if attempting to will a solution to their problem. Her assistant Emma sat near her on the couch, waiting patiently for a direction . . . any direction. Sheba occupied the other end of the couch, shaking her head silently, and Abby had sunk dejectedly into the other chair, with Colter pacing in front of his desk.

"Nobody's ever done it . . ." said Abby, finally, from the depths of her chair. ". . . bringing a caged adult chimp into a courtroom full of people and expecting him to behave naturally. We can't sedate him. He has to function. But he won't stand being cooped up in that cage. I doubt he'd even be willing to answer questions for me, and he loves me."

"I will not accept this," said Sarah. "I simply will not accept that there's no way to accomplish this. We will demand that the courtroom be cleared."

"No way that'll happen," said Colter. "Wainwright wants this. I know that now. He wants this image of Solomon going crazy in a cage to be the last thing people see before he renders his judgment. He wants public opinion on his side when he kills Solomon."

"I can guarantee they'll see Solomon go bonkers," said Abby. "When a chimp is especially intimidated, he displays his genitals in assertion. I predict the world will get a good look at Solomon's when he—"

"Whoa," said Sheba, holding up a hand glittering with rings. "What if he doesn't see any people?" She stood up and walked to the bookcase, running one finger along the row of richly bound law journals, shaking the other hand as if to scold a reluctant idea into revealing itself. "What if he doesn't see anybody but Abby? What if he's not in a cage?"

"Impossible!" Abby waved her hands in dismissal. "He's got to be in a cage. He's a big, strong guy. He can also be a very dangerous guy."

Sheba merely grinned, stopping at one volume on the shelf, sliding it out, and thumbing through it. She found a page and looked triumphantly at Colter, her wagging finger having goaded her memory into complying. She said only, "The State of California versus Theodore Burns."

CHAPTER 28

Wednesday morning

Remnants of Wainwright's vitriolic fury from the previous evening seemed etched into new lines on the old man's face as he entered the courtroom for what he hoped would be his last session of this damnable case. He paused to glare at the offending structure that Colter had caused to be installed overnight in his courtroom, his sanctorum. It was a large, blue-curtained rectangular enclosure that reached almost to the ceiling, and the judge hated it. When Colter had called him away from his dinner the night before, Wainwright had railed angrily against the idea, declaring that such an installation would transform his courtroom into a sideshow. He asked, "Why not simply transport the animal in a cage?"

Colter had cited the precedent of *The State of California versus Theodore Burns.* In that case, a judge had allowed such a structure to be installed so that the defendant, a dangerous psychotic, would not have to appear in restraints, prejudicing the judge against him. A cage would create the same prejudice against Solomon. In fact, noted Colter, the county already possessed such a courtroom enclosure, in storage, for just such a use.

Wainwright had been adamant, saying, "Mr. Colter, I think I can resist the temptation to be swayed simply because the animal is locked in a cage."

Unable to budge the crusty barrister with other arguments about the effects on public opinion of the sight of a caged Solomon, Colter and Abby raised the ante. They stubbornly insisted that, without such an isolated enclosure, they could legally refuse to allow Solomon in the courtroom, on the grounds that it would be cruel and dangerous to his well-being to be exposed to people. Wainwright loosed a succession of grumps—the rusty sounds of his neural gears shifting—but he finally yielded in sour surrender. He contacted Jenkins, who reluctantly agreed,

So that night, the Lexan enclosure had been brought out of storage and only a few hours later replaced the jury box in the courtroom, with curtains hung around it. Beside the box sat a computer on a table, and above the computer a large video screen. Wainwright, determined that the world should have a clear look at this travesty, readily agreed to have the court video camera mounted on the other wall to give an optimum view of the curtained monolith.

Now, Abby stood bleary-eyed at the plaintiff's table, only half an hour after having awakened next to the large box, on the cot on which she had spent only two hours sleeping after a full night of work. Inside that box had rested Solomon, whom she had made sure was calm after having been transported in by cage in the early-morning hours. She made sure he had his favorite bedding, had accustomed himself to the new enclosure, and had been fed his favorite foods.

Colter sat waiting for the session to begin, his troubled gaze moving from the haggard young woman, to the curtained box, to the sullen judge. He decided to reconsider his abandonment of religion at age eleven. He silently beseeched whatever saint, if any, watched over lawyers to protect this precarious adventure from utter, life-ruining catastrophe.

Collective gasps and murmurs from the courtroom gallery interrupted Colter's beseeching. Entering the courtroom was Walter Drake himself—ashen-faced and slumping weakly in his wheelchair, an oxygen tube beneath his nose. He was being wheeled slowly down the aisle by Clair. Following them were Kane, Jenkins, and Drake's cardiologist, Kevin Rehnquist.

Colter busied himself arranging papers to disguise his nervousness. Jenkins wouldn't even have to call the man in the wheelchair as a witness. Drake's appearance as a husk of a man testified unequivocally that he was dying. Jenkins had skillfully orchestrated the appearance so that, when the world and Wainwright compared the enfeebled Drake with the healthy Solomon, they would undoubtedly decide that it was only humane that the animal should be sacrificed to save this tragically ill man.

Colter could almost palpably feel the audience's sympathies shift, like a subtle change in the air, signaling a storm. The odds against him and his client had suddenly become astronomical.

When Sarah realized that her son had entered the courtroom, she halted a conversation with Abby to stare straight ahead, absolutely refusing even to look at Drake. For his part, Drake glanced in her direction but settled into his own illness as if it were a rebuke against her. It was so ironic, thought Colter, that their lack of communication carried so much information about the pain between them.

"My apologies for being late," said Jenkins, as he and Rehnquist elaborately busied themselves taking care that Drake's chair was positioned behind the defense table, the brake set, his comfort attended to. Only when his client was settled did Jenkins peer disapprovingly at the blue-curtained enclosure, most certainly calculating how it would affect his courtroom strategy.

"Not to worry, Mr. Jenkins," said Wainwright, after a long pause, during which he had watched Drake with evident concern. "I have not yet called the court to order, but I do so now." He tapped the gavel and directed his attention to Colter. "Sir, I believe you have been directed to produce the animal Solomon for examination."

"Yes, Your Honor, I call Dr. Abigail Philips as an accompanying expert witness and who will interview Solomon."

Abby took the oath, swearing on the *Bible* that had been so prominently displayed the day before. Colter stationed himself at the enclosure, to support her with his closeness.

"Dr. Philips, could you tell the court how Solomon will respond to your questions?"

With her best professorial demeanor, Abby explained how Solomon had been taught to use a computer touch-screen to choose symbols, which the computer translated into spoken words.

"Is the computer putting words in Solomon's mouth?" asked Colter.

"It's the same as when deaf people use sign language. If you translated directly the words that they signed, it would come across as quite crude, quite inarticulate. When we interpret their words, we assume the grammar. Similarly, since we're trying to get at the thought behind Solomon's words, we've programmed the computer to add the grammar. It's nothing but rules, after all."

"I see. So, the words we hear will accurately reflect Solomon's thoughts, with the grammar added as a convenience."

"Yes, as a convenience."

"And Solomon has a large vocabulary?"

"Some fifteen thousand words that he understands as concepts."

"What do you mean by 'understands'?"

"Our studies show that he has a mental map of the word meanings as concepts. He integrates them with his life and with the world around him. He uses them in his daily communications with humans."

"That's about as much as any of us can hope for ourselves. Is he unusual?"

"Well, yes and no. He is very bright, but not what you'd call a genius. What's unprecedented in this field of research is that he has been intensively taught over nearly his entire life to use these symbols to communicate. My father began teaching him when he was an infant. In a sense, he is an ambassador, an interpreter for his species."

"Your Honor, we stipulate that Solomon is a quite remarkable animal," said Jenkins. "But we object to the term 'ambassador.' He is not an ambassador in the human sense."

"Sustained," said Wainwright. "Let's move to the demonstration."

"Very well," said Colter. "Dr. Philips, may we see Solomon?" Colter smiled to reassure her, as she visibly tensed against the moment of Solomon's appearance.

"Of course," said Abby, nodding at the courtroom gallery, from where Sheba stepped to begin drawing the cord to open the curtain surrounding the monolith.

"Your Honor, may I request that the lights in the courtroom be lowered, for reasons I will explain?" asked Colter.

Jenkins rose, cocking his head suspiciously. "I am assuming that they will be legitimate reasons and not mere showmanship."

"The court agrees. This is necessary, eh, Mr. Colter?" Wainwright gave Colter a wry, questioning look but waved a hand at the bailiff to lower the lights, and the courtroom darkened.

"Solomon is a very sensitive animal, like others of his kind," said Colter as the curtain slowly withdrew, and the people in the gallery craned their necks to see what lay behind it. "He is fearful of strangers. So that he would not be frightened, we have asked that he give his testimony in this manner. This testimony will show that he does have a sense of morality, a sense of himself, proving that depriving him of his life is so wrong as to be illegal."

Colter's last words were drowned out by an eruption of babbling wonder from the spectators, as the curtain completed its journey to reveal the huge, dark ape pacing slowly back and forth inside a room-sized chamber of thick Lexan that had been coated with a tinted film. The darkened courtroom and the lighted chamber focused attention on the massive animal as if he were an animate sculpture on display. He climbed with prodigious animal grace onto a platform, sitting and slowly rocking his large body back and forth. Every inch of him emanated power—his great head with its broad simian face and brooding brow; his piercing amber eyes; his thick, muscled arms and legs, and his large, leathery hands that casually scratched his gray facial hair.

Wainwright seemed transfixed for a moment before recovering himself and gaveling the court into silence.

"He can't see us or hear us," said Abby. "The chamber is sound-proof, and we added a tinted film so that he cannot see out into a darkened room. Also, it was necessary that he become comfortable with the chamber, so he was brought early this morning, and I spent those hours with him."

"But we can talk to him?" asked Colter.

Abby stepped from the witness stand and sat down at the computer next to the chamber wall, beside a small section of the wall that had remained curtained. She reached up and swept aside the curtain to reveal a clear window three feet wide on a side facing the opposite blank wall. Solomon reacted instantly, scrambling off the platform and excitedly rapping the window where he could see Abby.

"From his angle, he can see only me," said Abby, switching on the microphone. "Solly? Solly? How are you doing, buddy?"

Solomon answered with a pant-hooting that burst from the speaker on Abby's computer table. The chimpanzee squatted at a touch screen on his own side, impatiently tapping it with the back of his sausage-sized index finger.

"You want to talk? Sure, we can talk. I'm turning on the screen."

Solomon turned his attention to the computer, as the courtroom's large video screen glowed to life for Wainwright and the rest of the court to see. Its display was covered with a multitude of colorful symbols—stick figures, stars, dots, clouds, lightning, various human and ape figures, cans, bottles and numbers. Several symbols scattered about the screen lit up as Solomon tapped them.

"I want some candy," issued from the speaker in Abby's voice, slightly disjointed as the computer pieced the sentence together from her recorded words.

"What kind?" asked Abby into the microphone.

"Chocolate. Now. Now. Please."

"I'll give you a chocolate now, Solly." Abby held up a Hershey's Kiss for the court to see, unwrapped it, and pushed it through a small hole in the window. Solomon deftly retrieved it and popped it into his mouth.

"Thank you. Give me more candy."

"If you keep talking, Solly."

"I see me."

"You see yourself in the wall?" She flicked off the microphone and turned to Wainwright. "From his side, the walls of the chamber appear mirrored. Apes like to look at themselves in the mirror, so he's in heaven. Only a few animals. . . elephants, dolphins, apes, and humans. . . recognize their reflections as themselves."

Colter stepped up next to the Lexan wall, careful not to let Solomon see him. This was good legal theater, and both Abby and Solomon were performing well. Abby had made a telling point with the comment about apes and mirrors. "Dr. Philips, could you demonstrate his level of understanding?" Abby nodded and turned back to the clear window.

"Solomon, what do the things on the screen mean to you?"

"Different words."

"What kinds of words?"

"You taught me the kinds. Words for things, emotions, ideas, actions."

"Dr. Philips, ask him how he feels about being here?"

Abby flicked the microphone on. "Solly, do you like it here?"

Solomon set to work tapping the screen, and the projection video showed a series of symbols lighting up as he touched them. "No. I want to go home. I want to see Sandy, Earle, Bruno."

"Answer some questions, and we will try to get you home."

Colter instructed, "Ask him whether he understands the difference between him and us."

Abby asked, "Solomon, are you an ape or a human?"

"I am an ape."

"And how are you are different from humans?"

"I am pretty." Laughter rolled across the courtroom as more symbols lit up on the large screen. "I am stronger. I have a lot of hair."

"What else?" asked Abby.

"You talk with your mouth. I cannot talk with my mouth. I want a candy."

Abby slipped Solomon a candy, and Jenkins rose. "Your Honor, if I may, I would like to examine the animal to determine its thinking ability, if any." Wainwright agreed, and Jenkins thought for a moment, and then instructed Abby, "Ask him if he understands this case."

"I can't," replied Abby. "He doesn't understand the concept of a court case."

"Ah, well, that's a significant shortcoming, isn't it? Then just see if you can possibly explain the issue to him."

Abby leaned into the microphone, her brow furrowed. "Solly, do you remember the man in the chair with wheels?"

"I want to go home."

"I know you do. Do you remember the man in the chair with the wheels?"

"Sad man."

"Yes, Solly. He is sick."

"Sick man."

"Solly, do you remember the big cage you were put in; the cage beside the house where the sick man lived?"

"Yes."

Jenkins asked, "Does he understand death?"

Abby replied, "Oh, yes. We talked about the concept when his mother died. He really understands death."

Jenkins instructed, "Then tell him about his heart being harvested."

Abby pushed away from the computer, her face clouding with anger. "That's cruel! I can't do that! It would frighten him terribly!"

"Would it, really?" asked Jenkins. "That's really what we're here to find out. That would be a sign of intelligence." Jenkins appealed to Wainwright, who instructed Abby to do as the lawyer had asked.

Abby took a breath, lowered her head, and paused. Finally, gathering herself, she leaned into the microphone. "Solly, the sick man wants to take your heart. He needs it to get well."

"My hard?"

"No, Solly, your heart. In your chest. You know about your heart. When it stops, you die."

"Heart." Solomon tapped his chest with his large hand. "I will die?"

Jenkins instructed, "Ask him what he thinks about that. Does he think it's right or wrong?"

Abby paused again, tears glistening her eyes. She took a deep breath to steady herself. "Solomon, what do you think about the sick man taking your heart?"

Solomon rocked back and forth for a long moment and then tapped several symbols. Abby jerked back in her chair as a menu of words she hadn't seen before popped up on the screen.

"Fuck you, asshole," emanated from the speaker in Colter's voice. "Son of a bitch, sick bastard."

A roar of amazed laughter erupted in the courtroom, so loud that Solomon heard it through the microphone. Startled, he leaped away from the computer, launching his mass in a frenzy against the Lexan wall with a boom, screeching loud enough to be heard even over the uproar. The courtroom laughter abruptly stopped as Solomon continued his screaming tirade, lips curled back to reveal his frightening set of canines. He pounded against the wall, the thick plastic shuddering with the assault, producing startled gasps and some shouts from the gallery. Abby flicked off the microphone and glared at Jenkins.

Even as Solomon's assaults on the wall increased, Wainwright slammed the gavel for order and pointed it at Abby. "I will not have obscenities in my court, even from an animal! And I will not have such violent outbursts . . . even from an animal. Bring up the lights. This demonstration is over."

Colter stepped forward as the courtroom lights rose. "Your Honor, you can't do that. It would—"

He was interrupted by a loud scream from Solomon. With the lights up, the chimpanzee could see out into the courtroom, and he displayed his pink genitals, producing another round of gasps and shouts of "Oh, my God!" from the gallery.

"There will be no such further experiments in my courtroom," declared Wainwright. "Dr. Philips, you will—"

A thunderous boom interrupted him, as Solomon leaped to the opposite wall of his chamber and threw himself with his full force against the Lexan, slamming it with his powerful legs.

"Calm that animal!" demanded Wainwright, but the last word was drowned out by another boom from Solomon's impact. Wainwright pounded his gavel, but it was a puny grace note compared to the two more thundering booms wrought by the powerful chimp. A few people in the gallery stood up, uncertain whether to flee the chimp's attack or stay to watch the spectacle. Their decision was made for them, when on the next impact, a corner of the chamber ripped apart with a sharp crack. With his next impact, Solomon widened the split and, discovering the potential exit from his prison, forced his fingers through the opening and heaved the two walls even farther apart.

Screams and shouts of panic erupted in the courtroom, as spectators began to flee.

"You will stop this right now!" shouted Wainwright, although it wasn't clear who he meant.

"Solly, stop it!" shouted Abby, but Solomon was intent on his task, now forcing his head and chest through the slit, triggering the crowd to launch an even more panicked headlong rush for the exits.

Colter stood his ground, telling himself that he had to remain by his client, despite the fact that the client was causing such havoc. Clair and the cardiologist Rehnquist grabbed Drake's wheelchair and forced their way through the fleeing crowd.

Now Solomon freed himself completely from the chamber, leaped to the floor, and stalked across it, stiff legged, jaw jutting out, hair fully erect. With a mere swat of his arm, he upended the oak defense table, driving Colter away from it, leaping over the railing and into the now-deserted gallery. Spying Wainwright's high bench, Solomon bounded to it and hauled himself on top, looming over the judge, who backed against the wall, his face a mask of fury and fear.

"BAILIFF, YOU WILL SHOOT THIS ANIMAL! Now!" bellowed Wainwright, still flattened against the wall, clutching his gavel.

"No!" shouted Colter and Abby in unison, but the beefy bailiff came shoving his way through the crowd, drawing his pistol.

Solomon stalked across the judge's bench, climbed down and leaped up to grab the video screen bracket, hauling his bulk up and tearing it down. He used the bracket as a launch point to vault himself over to grab the massive wrought iron chandelier, swinging up to grasp it with his foot and pulling himself up, where he sat panting with the exertion, hooting at the people below as the chandelier swung back and forth above the courtroom.

"I SAID SHOOT THE ANIMAL!" bellowed Wainwright again over the screams of the last people to flee the courtroom.

"Yes, *sir!*" answered the bailiff, aiming the pistol, beginning to track Solomon on the swinging chandelier.

"You can't do this, Your Honor!" shouted Colter. "This animal is no threat!" He began to scramble over the gallery benches toward the bailiff, who by now had Solomon squarely in his sights. Colter saw the tendons in the man's hand tighten as he began to squeeze the trigger. He wasn't going to make it in time! He tripped on a bench, falling over its back, but pulled himself up, fully prepared for the explosive blast of the pistol, the death-scream of Solomon, his falling body, his blood spreading across the floor.

But a breathy explosive *whoosh* erupted behind Colter, and the guard yelped in pain, brought down the pistol, and clutched his leg, which had now sprouted the red puff-ball marking a tranquilizer dart. Colter whirled to see Abby standing just behind him, aiming the tranquilizer pistol. He turned back to see the guard crumple slowly to the floor, his eyes roll back, and finally sprawl unconscious.

"JUST WHAT THE HELL DO YOU THINK YOU ARE DOING!" Wainwright shouted, descending from behind his bench. Her jaw clenched in fury, Abby ignored him, bending to the task of pumping another dart up to pressure, loading the tranquilizer pistol and pressurizing it with a larger hand-cranked pump. Wainwright reached her and, although he was about her height seemed to loom over her. "Doctor Philips, I will see that you are charged with assault with intent to—"

"Your Honor," interrupted Colter. "Doctor Philips would like to apologize for the *accident* in which the tranquilizer gun *accidentally* discharged while she was attempting to subdue the chimpanzee." He moved between Abby and Wainwright. "I witnessed this *accident*, and I will testify to it." Wainwright stiffened, seeming about to strike Colter, but Abby ignored them, moving into the gallery, and peering up at the softly hooting chimp, who rolled back his lips to reveal his large teeth.

"Solly, it's all over. Let's go home. Do you hear me? Home. Come down, now." Abby held out her arms, the tranquilizer pistol still in her hand.

Solomon allowed himself two more swings atop the chandelier and, after more coaxing by Abby, swung down to hang by one hand from the chandelier, then dropped with a thump to the floor. Abby moved to him, squatting down and taking him in her embrace, talking softly to him.

"Now Solly, go over there, and show me your butt. I've got to dart you." Whimpering softly, Solly moved off and stood on all fours, his back to Abby. She took aim with the pistol and fired, and Solomon flinched at the impact of the dart. At Abby's command, he pulled the dart from his rump and brought it to her, sitting quietly beside her until he slowly collapsed into unconsciousness, his breathing coming in slow puffs, the tongue lolling from his mouth.

Only then did they become aware of Jenkins, who had returned to the courtroom to stand just behind the gallery railing.

"Your Honor, it is time," he said.

"What do you mean, Mr. Jenkins?" asked Wainwright, his face red with anger.

"Mr. Drake's physician has informed me that this shock has caused Mr. Drake's condition to deteriorate such that we must ask that the animal be transported to the laboratory and prepared for organ harvest, in the event that the decision is in our favor. Given the time it will require to grow the new heart from the extracellular matrix, every minute counts now."

"So ordered," said Wainwright, turning to leave.

Colter spread his hands in disbelief. "But this hearing isn't over. This animal still deserves—"

Wainwright stopped at the entrance to his chambers and turned back. "Mr. Colter, I have ordered that this animal be removed to the laboratory. Carry out that order. *Now!*"

Abby looked desperately at Colter, who shook his head in resignation.

"When will you render your decision?" Colter asked.

"The court will take a recess while the animal is removed. I will prepare my decision and present it at four o'clock." Reporters began to crowd into the courtroom, shooting video of the unconscious Solomon and the bailiff, peppering the air with shouted questions.

Sheba also appeared and hurried over to Colter, who ordered, "You stay with Solomon!" he shouted over the rising babble. "You get Digger, and the two of you make damned sure they don't harm him."

"Don't you worry. Nothing's going to happen to that poor thing," she declared, whirling around and heading for the door, shoving her way through the crowd, sending an unfortunate photographer blocking her way staggering back against the courtroom railing.

As cameras continued to crowd around, Abby sat down next to Solomon, cradling his large head in her lap, stroking it gently. Their lights casting a merciless glare on the scene, the cameras zoomed in for a close-up of a glistening trail of tears rolling down her determinedly stoical face.

CHAPTER 29

Wednesday noon

"Ten million dollars," whispered Drake so weakly that the cardiologist Rehnquist had to lean down and ask him to repeat it. Drake clutched the physician's white coat with a skeletal hand with an IV tube attached that ran to a bag of clear liquid suspended above his head. Behind him, the lawyer Albert Kane closed the door of the hospital room.

"I will give you ten million dollars to tell the surgical team that they need to go ahead with the harvest and begin the organ-generation process before the decision. Same for James and for the other scientists. I will write the checks now. Just do what your oath requires. Save a human life."

Rehnquist abruptly straightened up and shot a disbelieving look at Kane, who nodded in confirmation. "I have the money transfer ready," said Kane. "I have contracts drawn up that make it clear that you and the chief surgeon and all the others are receiving these fees for services rendered."

"But this is not legal. The hearing—"

"Who would convict you of saving a life?" Clair's voice quavered, as she stepped forward and took Drake's hand. "For God's sake, it's just an animal!"

Kane brandished the contracts, a sheaf of densely printed pages, each in a blue folder. "These also commit us to paying any and all legal fees, including providing the services of Michael Jenkins, should any legal complications result."

"Does that include the hearing before the state medical board that'll cost me my license?" asked Rehnquist.

Kane extracted another document from his briefcase, handing it to Rehnquist. "We already asked Mr. Jenkins to prepare a brief on the applicable statutes. There's nothing really on point. It's not considered a breach of medical ethics to perform an operation on an animal, especially one that clearly saves a human life. The worst legal problem you might have is contempt of court. And I'm betting Wainwright plans to rule in our favor, anyway."

"Then why not just wait until the decision?"

"I don't gamble on my life," said Drake. "It's worth the money for me to make it a sure thing. If he rules against me, then your hands are tied. But right now, there's room for you to do this and argue it was necessary. Once it's done, it can't be undone. The heart-generation process might as well proceed."

"I've got to talk to my colleagues."

"Do it fast."

Rehnquist left the hospital room and after a quick trip pushed through the doors of the laboratory's surgical suite. There, Solomon lay sprawled on his back, his limbs strapped down, an oxygen tube inserted into his throat, an anesthesiologist monitoring his vital signs. An operating room technician was shaving his chest. The ape, so powerful when Rehnquist had last seen him, looked so utterly helpless now. His chest, sagging with the fleshiness of age, rose and fell as the technician shaved it. The faint rasp of his breathing whispered through the room.

Rehnquist caught the attention of a tall, slim, thin-faced man in green operating-room scrubs, who was conferring with an operating room nurse.

· · ·

"What the hell did you do?" shouted Abby. Her eyes wide with fury, she drew back her hand and slapped Colter as hard as she could. His cheek reddening, he drew away to avoid another blow. But she was done—done with striking him, but also done with him. She retreated to the corner of his office, hanging her head, sobbing softly, supporting herself on the book case.

"Look, I'm sorry," said Colter, holding his hands wide in supplication. "Solomon calmed down when he asked me to teach him those words. It was a way to get to him. To learn more about him. I had no idea it would—"

"No, Mr. Colter, you clearly had no idea," said Sarah. "You apparently had no idea then, and you have no idea now."

"Save him, damnit!" Abby turned and thrust her face right into Colter's, now searching for help, her anger now colored with utter despair. Her hands were clenched fists, clearly an attempt to avoid attacking him again. "You just can't let this happen! Look, just do it! I'm going to him. They're going to do something to him—I know it."

Colter grabbed her by the shoulders. "No, you have to stay with me in court. Please. I'll need you to help save him. Sheba and Digger will take care of Solomon."

"So, do you have any kind of plan?" demanded Sarah. "Any strategy at all?"

"I'll have one." Colter's voice choked. His back was against the wall as it never had been before. "You two just go somewhere and rest, calm down, prepare yourself for what we'll have to do. Leave me here. We've got until four o'clock. I'll meet you in the courtroom."

"Goddamnit, I want to do something!" exclaimed Abby. "I feel like I'm failing him." Sarah put a motherly arm around Abby and walked her to Colter's office door.

Before leaving, Sarah turned. "They said you were a clever son-of-a-bitch. I hope this case doesn't lose you the first part of your reputation."

Once alone, Colter hauled out all the briefs on the case and spread them on his desk, as if exposing them to light would cause a legal strategy to emanate from one of them like a revelatory vapor. He sat down and began to pore over the documents, scanning them desperately, taking notes on a yellow legal pad. Colter knew he had almost certainly lost the argument for legal rights for Solomon as an ape. The old judge saw Solomon only as an animal, thanks in part to Solomon's violent outburst. Colter shook his head and ran his fingers through his hair, smacking the desk in frustration. Damn! No matter what arguments he could give, the old judge saw Solomon only as an animal.

If only Solomon hadn't reacted so violently to the idea that he would be sacrificed to save Drake. As he thought back to the wild scene, however, the sliver of a legal argument formed itself, one small puzzle piece not yet benefiting from the existence of any other fitting pieces. Solomon had reacted. He had reacted like any human would to the thought of his execution.

Elements of his argument began to click into place, creating a triumphant whole, until he bellowed "HAH!" and sprung up to pace the floor, clutching the yellow pad and fervently scribbling on it. To have incredible brainstorms like this was the closest to snorting cocaine that practicing law ever came, a disbarred friend once told him.

"I AM, INDEED, A *CLEVER* SON-OF-A-BITCH!" he exclaimed to the empty room. He threw on his coat and ran for the door, headed for Wainwright's courtroom.

. . .

Sheba glared suspiciously at Digger, whose single raised eyebrow told her he was hatching a not-quite-legal plan. "You want to use his Porsche and his Corvette?"

Attempting to follow the van containing Solomon, they had just been barred from Drake's laboratory complex by a phalanx of armed guards. Now they sat in Digger's aged Chevy Caprice on the side of the road within sight of the gate. They had no legal right to access Solomon unless Abby was with them. And she was many miles away, in court.

"We've got to get in there. God knows what they're doing to the monkey. Just tell me where the keys are. I know you have sets in your office."

"What the hell—"

"Look, Sheba, this is desperation time."

Sheba continued to scowl but gave him the information he needed.

"Okay," said Digger, chuckling at whatever he was dreaming up. "I just have to make some calls. Stuff you shouldn't hear," he said, hauling his hefty body out of the car and walking around to the back to make cell phone calls.

"What're you doing?" asked Sheba as he crawled back in. "What do we do now?"

"Wait," said Digger, ratcheting back his seat and closing his eyes for a nap.

Forty-five minutes later, a series of loud crashes down the road roused him and caused Sheba to utter a shocked *"What the hell!?"*

Colter's Porsche and his Corvette roared past them, sideswiping one another, leaving a trail of auto trim parts. Now grinning, Digger, started up the car and accelerated slowly to follow them.

"Jesus Christ, Digger, they're destroying his cars! What is all this?"

"Called some retired cops I know. Asked them to raise some hell for us. And when I told them they'd be totaling Bobby Colter's cars in the process, I got *lots* of volunteers."

They reached the gate to the laboratory complex to see that the two battered sports cars had veered off the road and plowed into the chain-link fence a hundred feet east of the gate. Four hefty middle-aged men had leaped out of the cars and were seeming to slug away at each other in an uncontrolled brawl.

The action drew all the guards off the gate, as they attempted to separate the fighting men. And other guards had streamed out of the laboratory and through the gate to join them.

In the melee, they didn't see Digger ease his car through the gate and up to the building's main door.

He and Sheba leaped out and burst through the doors into the building's foyer. They met a burly man in a white laboratory coat.

"Where's the operating room?" demanded Sheba. The man advanced toward her, but Digger pulled his pistol, aiming it at the ceiling. The man turned pale and rattled off directions. "Third floor, east wing, follow the signs." Sheba and Digger ran off down the hall just as two guards slammed the front door open and gave chase.

On the third floor, Digger bolted from the elevator like a bull from a chute. They ran down a stark white corridor lined with scientific posters depicting research projects and past an orderly pushing an empty cage. They turned right, following signs until they found the door they wanted. Sheba took the lead, shoving through the door into the scrub room. Digger followed, brushing aside a protesting woman scientist. They entered the operating room to see Solomon on the table, with sterile plastic sheeting encasing his shaved chest, which was orange with Betadine disinfectant. The tall, thin-faced surgeon, a scalpel in his hand, stood talking to a shorter, slim man, who bent over Solomon. He slowly squeezed a bag attached to the oxygen tube. A cardiac monitor traced a strong, steady heartbeat across its screen, but beside the operating table rested the large jar filled with milky liquid that would hold Solomon's heart.

But not if Sheba could help it. "Wait one damn minute!" she commanded.

"Get the hell out of here!" shouted the tall surgeon. "This is a sterile operating room!"

"What if you don't operate?" asked Sheba, cocking her head quizzically. "Can you still call it an operating room?"

"Call security!" shouted the surgeon through his mask.

"This is what's called an imbalance of force capability," said Digger, coming up behind Sheba. "See, doc, all you got is that little scalpel. And I've got this big damn pistol." He pulled his black Glock semi-automatic from its shoulder holster, leveling it at the surgeon.

The surgeon froze, raising the scalpel in mid-air, staring wide-eyed down the barrel of the pistol. But after a moment, he straightened perceptibly, stealing a glance at something over Digger's shoulder. The click of a pistol cocking registered above the hum of the operating room.

"Drop your weapon," said a tension-husky male voice behind Digger.

"Who is it, Sheba?" asked Digger without taking his aim from the surgeon.

The man answered for Sheba. "Security. I have a pistol trained on your back, and I will use it. Drop your weapon, or I will shoot."

"He *does* have a gun, Digger," said Sheba. *"Big damn gun."*

"Sheba, sweetheart, think you could make a call for old Digger?" asked Digger, keeping his pistol aimed and using his other hand to ever-so-slowly pull out his smartphone.

CHAPTER 30

Wednesday afternoon

"I've decided to put you back on the stand," Colter told Abby, as he strode down the hall toward the courtroom, his smartphone to his ear. "Send me images," he said into the phone, pocketing it.

"This is our last chance. Sheba says they have Solomon on the operating table, and it looks as if they've decided to go ahead with the organ removal."

"God, no!" exclaimed Abby.

Sarah picked up her phone. "One call, and I can have a dozen security people at the laboratory."

"They wouldn't make it," said Colter. "Drake's security people are there, and if they get Digger and Sheba out of there for a minute, they can crack Solomon's chest and start to remove his heart, and nobody in their right mind would try to stop it. He'll be brain-dead, anyway. Drake is a clever son-of-a-bitch, too. Our best chance is to get a decision and communicate it to the lab before that happens. That way, they know they're violating the law. Now, they can claim they just bent the rules to save a patient. When you're on the stand, just answer the questions I put to you."

They pushed their way through the crowd of reporters and into the courtroom, where the tension seemed to have thickened even beyond what it had been that morning. The shattered, empty chamber that had held Solomon seemed irrefutable evidence that he would be considered a wild animal, whose life could be readily sacrificed to save a human. Jenkins already sat at his table, along with his assistants.

At precisely four o'clock, Wainwright entered and crisply began the session. "Now that arguments are complete, I will give my opinion. In the matter of Solomon versus Drake—"

"Your Honor," interrupted Colter. "May I present one additional argument in this case?"

"Mr. Colter, I've had about all of your arguments I can take," snapped Wainwright. "I have made my decision on the matter of a guardian in this case."

"I know, Your Honor, but this argument is on an important and different point that I think will profoundly impact your decision in this case."

Jenkins had been smiling pleasantly, anticipating a decision in his favor. But now he rose with all the weight of his indignation. "This is nonsense, Your Honor. I have a dying client, who as we speak is in dire need of the animal's heart. Nothing Mr. Colter could say about supposed legal rights will add to this case."

Colter waved his yellow pad. "As I said, this is a different argument. I'm sure Your Honor would not feel this case had been completely explored if all the critical arguments had not been presented."

"Fifteen minutes, Mr. Colter. No more." Wainwright leaned back, his expression implacable, as if he anticipated allowing the argument to wash past him with little effect.

Colter called Abby to the stand, and she sat in the witness chair, anguish on her face.

"Dr. Philips, we saw Solomon express himself. . . well. . . forcefully when he learned of his fate. In your expert opinion as a primatologist and one who has known Solomon his entire life, what did that reaction represent."

"Well. . ." Abby's voice thickened with emotion. "He was angry, but he was desperately fearful. The language, the baring of the teeth, the effort to escape. . . that's a fear reaction."

"When Mr. Jenkins. . ." Colter turned to face Jenkins to make it clear who had instigated the reaction ". . . *demanded*. . ." Colter paused and repeated the word. ". . . *demanded* that Solomon be brought into court to testify and *demanded* that you tell Solomon he would die, did you expect that reaction?"

"Yes. I expected abject fear. Solomon was in a frightening environment that could provoke panic. And he knows what death is, because he saw his mother die in the cage near him."

"So, would you say these were cruel things to do—bring him here and to tell him of his death?"

"Yes, absolutely."

"So, Mr. Drake's lawyer forced a situation that he *knew* could cause Solomon anguish. And forced you to give Solomon information that terrorized him. These acts violated the contract with Mr. Drake stipulating that Solomon not be subject to cruelty." Colter waved the contract, emphatically reciting the page and paragraph containing the relevant language.

Sensing a turning tide, Jenkins rose to his feet. "Your Honor, bringing him here was perfectly in order. And as for his reaction, what we saw was pure animal fury. This creature was running wild. If you were to bring the animal back here—"

"Actually, Your Honor . . ." Colter took a step toward Wainwright ". . . such a return would not be possible." Now, thought Colter, for the final move to checkmate. If Wainwright was even slightly inclined to rule for Drake, revealing the next fact—which Jenkins probably didn't even know—would likely push the judge's well-known anger button and win the case.

Colter's tone rose to urgency. "*Solomon is currently in no position to be brought back. He has been placed under anesthesia on an operating table and is about to have his heart removed, against the will of this court.*"

"WHAT!" bellowed Wainwright, forgetting his judicial decorum. "WHAT DO YOU MEAN?"

"Just that, Your Honor. My investigator called me from the laboratory. My investigator is in the operating room right now, preventing the operation. But he won't be able to for long. I have images of the scene. May I?"

Wainwright nodded, and Colter handed the bailiff an iPad, which he passed to Wainwright. The judge scrolled through images showing Solomon splayed out on the operating table, an oxygen tube down his throat, the surgeon poised over his chest with a scalpel. Anger rose on the judge's face. He abruptly stood bolt upright, careening his chair backward and leaning toward Jenkins, his jaw thrust out in fury. "Mr. Jenkins, did you allow this to happen?"

"No . . . uh . . . Your Honor, I was completely unaware—"

"Sir, you were apparently unaware of many things, including the decisions of the U.S. Supreme Court about the consequences of seeking to circumvent a judicial ruling."

"My apologies to the court if I—"

"ENOUGH, MR. JENKINS!" In the shocked silence that blanketed the courtroom, Wainwright pulled his chair back up and sat down, clutching his gavel high above him like a sword. Anger choking his voice, he continued. "I have decided not to rule on the issue of whether this ape deserves the legal right of a guardian. However, I do find compelling the argument that the animal known as Solomon does have sufficient awareness of the implications of his death that informing him was a cruel act. Since the contract with Mr. Drake does stipulate cruelty as a reason to void the agreement, it is clear to me that the contract is void. The chimpanzee is now the sole possession of Dr. Philips."

An exultant shout exploded from the spectators, a whirling pandemonium of exultation, triumph, anger, shock and utter surprise. Colter's hand shook as he punched Digger's number into his smartphone. With Abby clutching one arm and Sarah the other, his emotions teetered between joy and anguish. He could barely hear the faint sound of Digger's voice. This was no time for decorum. He shouted into the phone at the top of his lungs over and over "SOLOMON IS OURS!" and "THEY HAVE NO LEGAL RIGHT!" And finally "IS HE ALIVE? IS HE OKAY?"

He stopped and listened intently to the faint sounds that were nearly drowned out by the bedlam in the courtroom, punctuated by the steady pounding of Wainwright's gavel. He physically shoved a reporter back, clamping the phone to his ear so hard it hurt. Finally, he heard the answer. He dropped the phone to his side and let the sounds of the courtroom envelope him. He turned to a trembling Abby and to Sarah, who both had tears in their eyes.

He knew he could not talk, or he would cry, too, which was not appropriate for a hard-assed, money-grubbing lawyer. He just nodded and smiled.

CHAPTER 31

Wednesday evening

Abby and Colter burst through the operating-room double doors to find Digger and Sheba perched on matching stools, protectively flanking the operating table that held the dark, unconscious form of Solomon. Digger had holstered his pistol but left his jacket pulled back to show it, as a reminder that it could be easily brought out again, should the occasion warrant. A glowering, uniformed laboratory guard stood beside the door, arms folded, alongside the head researcher, James, in his white coat.

"Solly," breathed Abby urgently, hurrying to his side and proceeding to check his respiration and pulse. "God, no breath! No breath!"

"We didn't know what to do," said Sheba, backing away, rubbing her hands in anxiety. "The doctor, the anesthesiologist, they—"

"They left?" demanded Colter, moving to the other side of the table, laying one hand on the animal's shoulder, feeling the long, coarse hair, the warm skin, and the thick muscle beneath. With his other hand, he clasped Solomon's thick, leathery fingers, feeling no response. The chimp's broad, whiskered simian face sagged in leaden unconsciousness, his eyes closed, his mouth gaping open, with the oxygen tube inserted down his throat.

Colter felt a smothering fear clutch his chest, the same helpless fear he had felt waiting sorrowfully at the bedside of his dying mother, and later his father. He recovered himself. He was not helpless.

"Digger, go down and make sure we've got a clear shot to the ambulance loading dock. We're taking him out of here. There're reporters all over hell down there." Digger hurried out, intent on his new mission.

"An ambu bag! I need an ambu bag!" exclaimed Abby. She cast about, found the translucent plastic bag, attached it to Solomon's oxygen tube, and began to squeeze it rhythmically, pumping air into his lungs. She turned the task over to Sheba, found a stethoscope, tore away the plastic surgical covering on Solomon's chest, and placed the metal disk on the shaved, betadine-painted flesh, listening intently.

"Heart rate's depressed. Too slow. God, too slow! They didn't care about him living. They just wanted the heart slowed."

James stepped forward. "The court judgment means that the animal is your property, so we aren't responsible."

"*Want to bet*?" asked Colter, his hand firmly on Solomon, as if he could somehow transmit his resolve to the animal. "*Where are we, Dr. James?*" asked Colter. He circled the table to confront the little man, advancing on him and causing him to back toward the guard.

"I beg your pardon?"

"Oh, God, Solly!" exclaimed Abby, leaning over the chimp. "Can you hear me, Solly? Don't go away! Please don't go away!"

"Goddamnit, I asked you where are we, dr. James?" thundered Colter. "We're in your laboratory, aren't we?"

"Well, yes, of course, but what—"

Now Colter assumed his best lawyer's threatening voice. "And since you are responsible for everything that goes on in your laboratory, in your operating room, you had damned well better get a doctor and an anesthesiologist back in here to make sure this animal safely comes out of this anesthesia. You've got mighty deep pockets. My clients are perfectly willing to see how empty they can make them."

"Indeed, that is so," came the stern voice of Sarah Huntington, who had just entered the operating room. "Mr. Colter would have my full support in such a legal action. And I'm sure my many friends would take a considerable interest in your role in this process, as well."

James glanced from Sarah to Colter and back, his eyes widening. Without another word, he hurried from the room. Colter returned to his place beside Solomon.

Sarah stepped over to Abby, placing her small hand on the young woman's shoulder. "How is he?" she asked. "We're not too late, are we?"

"Don't know," said Abby. "He's not a young animal. He could easily go into arrest. His heart could just give up." She turned back to Solomon and began to talk to him, stroking his face, gently slapping his hand. "Solly, Solly, please don't give up, old fella. Please come out of it."

The tall surgeon and the anesthesiologist appeared, followed by a nurse, their faces taut with grim anger. Abby, Colter, and Sheba backed away to give them room. Without a word, they bent over the immobile chimpanzee. Working quickly, the surgeon reattached electrocardiogram leads to electrodes taped to Solomon's chest. A slow, steady blip on the monitor replaced the straight line that it had traced before. The anesthesiologist called for the nurse to cover Solomon with a heating pad, took over squeezing the bag, and increased the oxygen flow. A reassuring hiss arose from the flowing gas.

James reappeared, his brow knitted. "We'll do our best," he said with almost a whine.

"It had better be enough," warned Colter. He glanced over at the guard. "And get him out of here." James dismissed the guard, who slammed the swinging doors with the flat of his hand, launching them open, and left.

Long minutes crept past, each person in the room frozen in place, held by thick tension, except for the surgeon, who called for an injection of a drug to reverse the anesthesia, with great effort struggling to insert the needle into Solomon's thickly muscled arm. The injection accomplished, he straightened up, staring intently at the monitor, his jaw muscle tight. More long minutes seemed to pass like hours. The anesthesiologist briefly stopped squeezing the bag and listened.

"*No breath*," whispered Abby urgently, moving up to grasp Solomon's hand, tears streaming down her face. "*Still no breath.*"

Long minutes went by. Finally, the anesthesiologist announced, "Breathing on his own. Heart rate's coming up."

"Oh, dear God!" breathed Abby. The anxiety seemed to evaporate from the room, relieving a pressure. The light suddenly seemed brighter.

Abby and Colter found each other's embrace, and the comforting warmth seemed to give each strength for anything that was to come.

Carefully, the anesthesiologist extracted the breathing tube, placing his ear close to Solomon's mouth. "Still breathing on his own," he said. He also removed the iv needle and taped a bandage to Solomon's arm.

"He'll come out of it fine," said the surgeon tersely and turned and left the room with the anesthesiologist and the nurse.

As if to confirm the prognosis, Solomon abruptly took a deep breath and let out a long deep sigh. His mouth closed and then opened, with a lip-smacking, and his head rolled to one side, his pink tongue lolling out one side.

Abby smiled and petted his great head, scratching behind his ears. "Yeah, we're relieved, too, old buddy." She allowed herself only a brief chance to enjoy the moment, before gathering herself and organizing the effort to heft Solomon onto a gurney, securing his limbs. Digger returned, calling in the surly guard to help.

With Abby and Colter pushing the gurney and Digger clearing the way, the group rolled Solomon down the hallway. Following them was Sarah, with James solicitously tagging along beside her. They took the elevator to the ground floor and out to an ambulance loading dock, where sat the primate center van. Beyond the dock and behind the fence, a sea of reporters and cameras waited. The clicking of still cameras erupted like the chattering of a horde of locusts, nearly drowned out by the demanding clamor of shouted questions from the jostling reporters. Many hands helped load Solomon into the van, with Abby jumping in the back with him. The van doors slammed shut, and the vehicle moved away slowly, out the gate and through the crowd, like a ship easing from the dock through a thick, roiling sea.

Colter stood watching the van depart, feeling a hand clasp his arm. He turned to see Sarah looking up at him, her face uncharacteristically pale, her expression troubled. With a gentle tug, she urged him away from the reporters and back through the laboratory doors to a quiet stretch of the hallway.

She paused, her brow knitted, and then managed to regain her strength and straightened to her accustomed commanding posture. "My son is weak. I should go see him. I want you to come."

He nodded, and they rode in silence to the hospital, finding Drake in a large suite crammed with monitoring equipment, intravenous bags, and people—the cardiologist Rehnquist, Kane, Jenkins, and three nurses. All the people, all the equipment, centered their electronic and human attention on the frail body of Walter Drake.

When they entered, Drake was staring at the ceiling with glazed eyes, mouth slightly open, an oxygen line looped beneath his nose. Perhaps he noticed the movement, or perhaps it was instinct, but when Sarah and Colter entered, he turned his head to fix his gaze dully on them, his eyes like dark marbles, their shine etched away.

"Son," said Sarah, the word carrying more weight than Colter knew the word ever could.

Drake worked his mouth open and shut a few times, as if trying to remember how to speak. "You've killed me, mother."

Any of the sturdy resolve Sarah Huntington had managed to preserve disappeared, and her small body slumped so markedly over the bed that Colter stepped forward to support her. He turned to the others in the room. "Could you let them talk alone?"

They looked to Drake, who with a weak wave of his hand dismissed them. Colter gently released Sarah and turned to leave as well, but with a surprisingly firm hand, she took his arm in an unspoken plea that he remain.

"Walter, I'm so sorry," she said. "God, how could it have all come to this. Son, I am so sorry. What did I do?"

"You've killed me. At least in a few weeks." Drake tried to shift his body to turn it toward her but failed. He mustered what was left of his strength. "Are you happy now?"

The question didn't have the demoralizing effect Drake had hoped. Rather, it seemed to trigger something in Sarah—some small seed-crystal of remaining spirit. She straightened and looked up at Colter, a familiar expression of determination returning to her face.

"You know, Walter, actually I am happy. After all you've done, I know I'm not the one who killed you. You did it yourself. Even on your deathbed, you're a son-of-a-bitch."

"And that makes you—"

"I'm quite aware of what that makes me, Walter. I accepted that part of me a long time ago. I changed. I got better. But you didn't. I remember all the heartache and pain and tragedy you have caused. And, son, now that I've seen you, I remember . . . and I'm glad . . . that

I prevented you from causing one last tragedy. Can you understand, even now, what you have been? What you have done?"

Drake began to speak but returned his gaze to the ceiling, the rise and fall of his chest nearly imperceptible. A blanketing quiet settled over the room. Colter moved to put his arm around Sarah, a move she did not resist.

A wetness glistened in Drake's nearly closed eyes and, after a moment, grew to give birth to a tear, which traced a shiny trail down his ashen face. He whispered something, his voice a feeble, breathy rattle.

"What?" demanded Sarah. "What did you say, Walter?"

But try as he could, the man was too weak to speak louder. Sarah leaned over her son for a long moment, turning her small ear to his mouth.

She stood up, and from where he stood, Colter could see her shoulders begin to shake in the spasms of sobs. He moved forward and once more put his arm around her small frame, and she slumped against him.

"What did he say?" asked Colter.

"He . . . he . . ." Sarah Huntington tried twice before she was able to get the words past the thickness of emotion clutching at her throat. "He said 'I'm sorry.'"

CHAPTER 32

Saturday morning

The steel door slid up, and Solomon wobbled slowly into the daylight. Moving sluggishly, eyes slightly glazed, the old chimp was still groggy from the anesthetic even days later. The other chimps greeted him with hooting and dancing about as they had before, grooming him and making play-faces. Abby and Colter sat on the edge of the wooden observation platform overlooking the enclosure, their feet dangling over the side. They'd been silent for a long while, letting the delicious triumph of the moment soak in, washing away the troubles of the last week. Colter put his arm around Abby, and she leaned close, learning to allow herself the warm luxury of another's support.

He finally broke the silence. "Sarah went in to see him. They talked. I didn't tell you right away. I had to think about it a while. He said he was sorry."

Abby turned to gaze into his eyes, searching for his feelings. "Do you think she felt guilty about contributing to what might be his death?" asked Abby.

"No. Do you feel guilty?" asked Colter.

"I wondered if I would. But I don't. Even now that I know he said he was sorry. Maybe it was real. Maybe it was a ploy."

"Maybe if Walter Drake had been a good man," said Colter. "But I expected I'd have a problem advocating sacrificing a bad human for a good animal. I guess I was surprised I didn't. Besides, he still has time. His people still have time to find another way."

They watched Solomon slowly leave the others and make his way up ponderously to his favorite rock, settling onto it and sleepily soaking in the warmth of the late morning sun.

"You shouldn't have been surprised at your reaction," said Colter. "You know Solomon. You know him as a . . . well . . . thinking being."

She sat up and shifted around to face him questioningly. "The bribery case against you. MacIntire. You never told me what happened."

Colter smiled and rested his chin on the bottom railing, watching Earle groom Lucky. The maltreated chimp was recovering his health, if not his spirit under the ministrations of Earle, who'd adopted him as a friend.

"It was a very peculiar thing. Yesterday, I got a call from the district attorney's office. It seems that an envelope mysteriously showed up with a sworn, notarized affidavit from the MacIntire witness testifying that I had nothing to do with his decision to disappear. He said he left because he'd lied when he alibied MacIntire, and he was ashamed."

"Where did the envelope come from?"

"Kane, maybe. Jenkins might have had something to do with it. I'm sure he didn't like what Drake had done to him."

"And Digger? Is he in trouble over the stolen money?"

261

"You kidding? Digger's an old-line cop with lots of friends. Yesterday he called to tell me that the records of that drug bust just up and disappeared. And once Drake gave up, the property clerk's amnesia came back. Digger's in Palm Springs now. I think he's keeping company with a divorcee who he helped become a wealthy divorcee by getting dirt on her husband. Before he left, he checked on the search for Lunt and Giacomo. They still haven't been found, but it's just a matter of time, even though they probably have a good deal of traveling money."

Colter's expression changed to a knowing grin at Abby. "I take it your money problems are over, too."

She smiled back, a quiet happiness in her eyes he'd never seen before. "Yup, no money problems at all. That agent you got for me says I'm going to need smelling salts when I see the figures on the book and movie contracts. He says my speaking fees will run into the six figures. And Sarah has committed to endowing the lab. The department chairman called this morning. He says he and the university administration are extremely pleased to offer me tenure and a permanent commitment to the lab as part of the academic structure. By the way, the agent said you're going to do great, too."

"Yeah, well, I thought I'd never say this, but the money's not as important any more. I'm getting calls from clients who think I can walk on water, not to mention change it into vintage wine. They figure if I can save Solomon, I can get them off."

Below, in the enclosure, the other chimps began, one by one, visiting Solomon on his rock, to groom, to kiss, or just to sit near him for a moment, expressing kinship before moving off.

Watching the procession, Abby's expression grew pensive. "I wish we could have gotten him legal rights," said Abby. "I wish we could have established that for all the apes."

Colter shrugged. "I had a choice. Lawyers face choices like that. Did I want to save a client or make a point? Actually, I did make a point."

"But all you could argue was that giving him knowledge of his death was cruel, and that violated the contract."

Colter grinned slyly. "That's right. *Knowledge*. That implies *intelligence*. That opens a big wide legal door for arguing legal rights. Wainwright was so ticked off, I think he overlooked that implication when he ruled for us. That's a precedent. It establishes conscious intent. It's a good start. Now, thanks to Wainwright, there exists a formal ruling in a court case that holds that apes aren't mindless creatures. They have conscious intent."

She took his arm and leaned against him. "Look, I'm sorry I slapped you."

"Not the first time it's happened. And you had good reason."

"Well, I think I know a way to make it up to you." She reached into the back pocket of her jeans and pulled out a brochure. "I made a reservation at this very nice villa overlooking the ocean down in Cabo San Lucas. A week." A sly, faint smile rose on her face. "I figure that's enough time for us to explore one of the most important differences between humans and apes . . . our capacity for perpetual sex."

Colter nodded, assuming a mock-serious expression. "Indeed, I am beginning to appreciate the science of primatology more and more." He stroked her hair, smoothing it back from her face. "So, now you think you could add another primate to your relationships?"

"A primate that has no hair and talks for a living? I think so. Oh, and, of course, Mr. Colter, we will spend a lot of time talking about the next case you're going to bring for apes' legal rights."

"I figured as much, Dr. Philips. It's going to get tougher now, really political. It's going to mean making entirely new law, so I've got to figure something out."

"What's that?"

"Whether Solomon would vote Republican or Democrat," he said, leaning over to kiss lips that at first failed to fully engage because they were widened in a laugh.

Read on for an exciting preview of
Dennis Meredith's new novel

The Cerulean's Secret

For more information, go to
www.CeruleansSecret.com

CHAPTER 1

I lay there in the dark like a dead man, still paralyzed under the weight of heavy sleep, as the horrifying realization began to seep into my groggy brain. I couldn't hear the cat *anywhere*! Jesus, it might be gone! The realization struck like a punch in the face, because, if I lost that cat, I really would become a dead man!

I jumped off the couch, whacking the coffee table with my shins, sending empty cans rolling, clinking across the floor. I held my breath, sifting through the faint night sounds for the low growling in his throat he'd been doing constantly since the dye job. Or, for a meow, a purr, even the delicate crackle of food wrappings being stealthily nosed. But I heard nothing catlike and no feeling, either, of the cat rubbing against my leg in the darkness to say he forgave me. I couldn't really blame him for being ticked, after the gray dye job I'd given him. He'd probably just decided for spite to retreat to a corner and do private cat-things, ignoring me, like cats will do. I rubbed my eyes and tried to shake my head clear of cottony sleep-stuffing. I'd really gone down hard after a week of running and hiding and then wrestling with a big, all-muscle, ticked-off cat. I hadn't meant to fall asleep but just to rest a little before working on some plan of action.

The torn window shade flapped in a puff of wind, making me jump. That sound must've been what woke me in the first place. Outside, the rain still fell steadily, leaden and liquid, as it had when I'd passed out from exhaustion. But now a wind had risen, occasionally gusting through a broken pane, injecting a cool dampness into the musty, still room. Fully awake, heart pumping, I held my breath and listened hard again. The old apartment house produced only a few distant creaks at this hour from my fellow anonymous tenants moving around. No more muffled hollering and explosions from the viddie next door, since the guy had finished watching his movie and gone to bed. But also no cat sounds.

Enough listening; I needed to start looking. I bumped around the table, tramping through the fast-food sacks scattered on the floor, flattening a spare hamburger in one, and felt my way around the room, fumbling on lamp switches. I'd need as much light as I could get. He was dyed dull gray now, not being his natural genetically pumped iridescent blue, so he could hide in any shadow. I made a quick, hopeful scan of the living area—torn couch, battered chest of drawers, water-stained walls—and didn't see him. The hard little knot of fear in my gut grew to a big rocklike chunk of panic. I realized it was a pretty useless exercise, searching an apartment that was only the one bedroom, a prefab plastic kitchen wall unit and a tiny old bathroom. I found the bathroom empty of cat, too, but still showing the gray spatters marking our struggles; still smelling of pungent hair dye. I even checked in the cracked plastic tub, where I'm sure he thought I'd tried to drown him. It still held six inches of scummy, gray water but no cat.

As if the disappearance hadn't buzz-freaked me enough, another jolt struck when I passed the bathroom mirror and saw the puffy secondskin face and brown-dyed hair of a stranger. My translucent secondskin disguise had sagged a bit off my left cheek, and the right jawline had curled up at the edges. This was my last set from Rudy the makeup guy, so I smeared a little more glue from the tube under the loose flaps and, with careful little fingertip-pokes, smoothed them back into place. I experimentally frowned and smiled and screwed around my mouth and cheeks, to make certain a piece of jaw or a nose wouldn't drop off in public, showing part of my real framed-for-murder face.

Repairing my disguise gave me a chance to calm down, to think a little. Cats could curl up in the smallest space, so I needed to search every little hidey-hole. I flopped down onto the scarred wooden floor and scootched around, peering into the shadows behind and under the couch, the chest of drawers, and the cabinet that held the decrepit early '40s plasma TV. No cat—just dust balls and random gobs of grunge that I didn't want to know any more about. As the very last thing, I looked into the opening in the cat's old cardboard box. Maybe I saved the box for last, so I could savor the anticipated relief when I found him curled up there, staring at me with accusing slitted eyes. Or maybe I wanted to put off the disappointment when he wasn't. But the box was empty except for the rumpled piece of old quilt, smelling cat-musky, with a few shiny blue hairs marking where he had slept.

Down low where I crouched, I could see smudgy paw prints and drips on the floor, and even up the wall, where the dye-soaked cat had literally gone ballistic before I caught him and wrapped him in the towel. Boy, had he zanked out, bouncing like a superball from wall to door to window, yowling and cursing me! But still, no cat.

The poor cat. He really was a great cat, an amazing cat, in fact. He had a presence, a power, as if the scientist who made him had condensed all nine of his cat lives into one intense cat—like squeezing a bunch of plain old light into an ultrabrilliant laser beam.

He'd saved my life a couple of times, and we'd become friends, even though I was this young, dumb guy who'd kidnapped him, or catnapped him . . . or whatever. In fact, I'd really gotten attached to the big genetically engineered cat with amazing cerulean fur that made people treat him like a god, calling him the most beautiful cat in history. I felt like some sadist the whole time I was dyeing him, like a guy slopping house paint all over the Mona Lisa. But it was the only thing I could figure to save his life and mine. Basically, I guess I was just too stupid to come up with a better plan.

Also, I must have missed a way he could get out! My multi-stupidity brought me to a boil against myself. "You syntho-brain!" I cursed myself, sitting up and looking around. "You canky worthless spit-bubble! Think!" Calling myself names pumped me up, focused my thinking. The broken window, of course! When we'd arrived, the wind hadn't been blowing, and I hadn't thought to check for a broken pane. I dragged a flickering floor lamp over to see better and yanked the grease-stained window shade, letting it clatter up. In the yellow light, the dark mirrored surface of the glass showed smeared paw prints below the hole, which was at the top of the window. He was some really smart cat to figure out how to get up on the chair and wait for the shade to blow out, so he could then launch himself from the chairback and pull himself through. I stared, puzzled, at the chair, the rickety collaborator in his escape. It had been by the door before, I was almost sure. Obviously chairs don't move themselves. Had the cat actually moved it? Nah, I decided. I must have done it in my stupor; cats don't move furniture.

I took a deep, shaky breath and stared at the battered wooden door to the hallway and the rest of the world. I knew I had to find the guts to open it to search for the cat somewhere in the murky rainy night in a dangerous Seattle slum. Could I do it, knowing the cops might be out there with their guns and their Cop Network cameras? I'd make good viddie going down in a hail of bullets, leaving a glorious multi-punctured corpse for the virtie-viddie vampires to feast on.

Could I do it, knowing that out there might be the killer, Julio Miravelle, sleek and dangerous, aiming his black pistol at the door, waiting?

Or, could I face . . . I fought a wave of fear-nausea . . . a Big Nasty programmed on my scent, ready to rip out my chest in one swipe of his taloned claw? I'd never really known what evil was until I encountered the genetically concocted killing machine I'd dubbed a Big Nasty.

I could open that door. Of *course,* I could open that door. I stood up and took a few deep breaths. Sure I could. After all, I'm the gopher. That's what my dad nicknamed me when I was a scrawny little kid and I'd come home around supper time covered with layers of grime from running wild in the North Carolina woods all day, building earthbases, battling evil aliens. He'd smile tolerantly, shake his head, and go back to watching the news, and Mom would make tutting noises, guide me upstairs with a single finger in my back and make me skin my dirt-stained clothes off to soak clean in the bath. She always threatened to burn the clothes but never did. I wouldn't have had any clothes left after a week.

Sure, I could open that door. The gopher would do just about anything, even go out that door and look for a cat. Especially a cat that was my only guide to getting me out of this mess and to finding two people I loved, Lulu and Callie. Somewhere, Miravelle held them hostage, and the cat was both bargaining chip and clue. I ached over the plight of the beautiful, bright-eyed Lulu, who made me even more goofily infatuated every time I looked at her. And over her mom

Callie, my greatest friend, who'd saved my life, even though she'd never even met me before this all began.

I'd survive only if I figured out what the cat knew and what secrets lay in the tangle of its stitched-together genes. And I'd figure out the cat only if I found the cat . . . out that door.

CHAPTER 2

I'd stalled long enough. I unlocked the door and eased it open, eyeball peering through the crack, ears listening for raspy animal-breathing or the cocking of guns. The hall was dirty, dim, and quiet. No cameras, no guns, no six-inch claws; only the stained, peeling wallpaper whose dark blotches had been bright little flowers a hundred years ago. No cat, either, so I slipped out, down the hall, out the front door and across the porch into the street.

I took a deep breath of damp night air and tensed, waiting. No bullets, no claws here, either. The chill rain on my head washed away the last tattered remnants of my grogginess. The cold water also shocked me into some realistic thinking. Standing out in the muddy gutter, I realized I knew absolutely nil, nada, nothing about where the cat had gone. And I didn't even know how to call it. If I yelled "Cerulean!" some mindslug holed up behind one of these dark windows would surely figure out the famous cat was here and call the cops or maybe the company that built it, Animata, for the reward.

So, as my shirt wetted down into a soggy, cold, clinging shroud, I experimented with a loud, whispered "kitty-kitty-kitty," and began to circle the old apartment house. I kitty-kitty-kittied up the narrow, gloomy alley, peering into the garbage cans and crouching down to look down the steps of the basement side entrance. No shining cat eyes. I kitty-kitty-kittied over to the next block, where more cars splashed along and an occasional person walked, hunkering down against the rain. I trotted a ways down it, past other paint-challenged apartment houses, still finding no cat. The exercise didn't much warm me up from the rain dribbling down my neck, cold and slithery snakelike. The water loosened the secondskin even more, and I poked it back into place, feeling it squish beneath my fingers. All I needed was for my face to start coming apart. I squeezed a clump of hair and held my fingers up to a streetlight. I thought I saw a little brown dye, and if mine was coming off in the rain, so would the cat's.

I approached the nearest person, a bent old guy wearing a rain slicker, limping across the street from a hole-in-the-wall bar. He kept his head down and pulled back like a turtle's inside the hood, maybe to keep the rain out of his face, maybe to avoid dealing with me.

"Sir? Sir? You seen a cat?"

"Seen lots of cats." He squinted at me suspiciously as he limped faster, pegging me no doubt for some wimpy cat lover who'd lost his precious puss. Well, okay, maybe I was a cat lover. So what? I'd really started to like that cat.

I kept up with him. "A gray cat. Big."

"Looking for a gray cat at night?" He wheezed a kind of wet gurgly chuckle. "They's all gray at night, boy." He shook his head inside the plastic hood and hurried away.

"Well, if you see him . . ." but the old man was gone. I knew if I'd mentioned the Cerulean, he'd have whipped back like a yo yo.

I decided the best way to look was to take a quick run around as large an area as possible, so I took off slogging down the sidewalk, my sneakers splatting on the water-skinned concrete. I circled the block trying to look like a regular jogger-guy just out for his routine nightly run on this cold, wet mess of a night. Yeah, right, a routine jog wearing soggy jeans and a t-shirt.

I slowed, wiping the rain out of my eyes to get a better look at the alleys, the building entrances, the porches. I reached a main street of darkened shops and food joints, where whispering electrics and an occasional gas car sped past, splashing through rain-filled potholes with rattling thuds. In the flash of passing headlights, I caught sight of a crumpled gray form on the street, and the panic-rock in my gut seemed to heat up. Panting hard, I jogged closer and peered down. Just a greasy rag! I blew a puff of relief and ran on, circling and circling blocks and blocks, going farther and farther away from the apartment house. I passed a striped cat sitting in a house window, and a yellow one slinking away down an alley. But no big gray with that odd searching look it always had on its face.

I hoped its dye hadn't washed out. I hoped I really wouldn't see him dead in the street. I hoped I wouldn't hear a growl from the shadow of a dark alley that told me a Big Nasty had me cold. The thought dredged up the agonizing memory of torn-apart flesh and staring open eyes of dead men, sending shivers through me that had nothing to do with the cold rain. I ran harder to escape the image, to work it out of me.

After a few miles of running, I finally just lost my steam and bent over gasping with hands on rubbery knees. I waited until I got my breath and my bearings and trudged back to the apartment house. I stumbled up the apartment-house steps and back into my rented room. I stripped off the soggy clothes, ran a towel over myself, patted the lifting secondskin back on my face, and pulled on dry jeans and a shirt. The gray towel showed some brown dye from my head, but the mirror reflected a fully brown-haired guy, so I was okay in the hair area. Probably, the cat was, too—a little good news.

Since I only had the one pair of sneakers, I put them in the microwave on low. I unwrapped some of the fish I'd brought him from the Seattle waterfront market and plopped it into his red bowl. I wrapped the musty blanket from the bed around me and went back out in my sock feet onto the front porch. With the bowl as my lure, I'd sit there a while on the rusty metal chair under the light and wait. When I got back my wind and my legs, I'd find a raincoat or something to keep me dry so I didn't get pneumonia, and I'd spend the night running, looking. I convinced myself it was okay to allow myself to rest on the front porch. He was about as likely to come back here as anywhere.

And, I convinced myself I was safe here at the apartment for the time being. I'd taken it as Nick Adams, not Timothy Boatright. And I'd paid with a non-traceable cashcard, which the old lady who ran the place scanned with the little scanner pulled out of her baggy housedress. She looked at me—standing there fidgeting and holding my cardboard box full of hidden cat—with narrowed, suspicious eyes, but accepted the money and gave me the room.

As I sat hopefully on the porch, the rain drummed steadily on the roof, reminding me of the winters back home when a rolling storm would sweep across the sky from the mountains. I'd sit warm in my room and watch the quicksilver sheets of rain sweep across the bare gray woods around my house. I missed those woods. I missed home. I forced myself back to my predicament.

I knew I needed the cat, and I also absolutely knew that somewhere in the history of this unholy mess lay clues that would get Lulu, Callie, and me out of it. I had to go over everything about how I got here, chasing a genetically engineered cat and being chased . . . by just about everybody.

Chapter 3

It all started on a day I drove my cab like always, and New York stunk the way I liked New York to stink, with the sharp tangy aroma of electrics, the fumes from the gas cars, the aromas of sidewalk food, and just the general rich organic funk of people and the city. As it got hotter, all the great smells just sort of cooked themselves together like a steamy bubbling stew. Everybody immersed in the stew busied themselves acting the way only New Yorkers do. The drivers inched along in bumper-to-bumper Manhattan traffic, cabbies cussing and big traffic-scarred trucks double-parked, with everybody trying to squeeze in on everybody else.

The sidewalks could barely hold all the people: salaries in suits, slickies in their randomweave hemp jackets, funkies in trashwear, shifty peddlers selling junk, sex-joint hustlers passing out wiggly-naked-woman electroholograms, and tough, pretty New York girls, proud and knowing, wearing just about anything. As usual, the crowd included Helpers, striding along with the purpose their owners had given them, on some errand or another. The mechie Helpers looked like the robots they were with metal arms and heads all clinky and clanky. The humanalogs, however, with their electrogel flesh and secondskin covering, were being built to look more and more like people every day. Except the humies were smart enough or polite enough not to walk in front of cabs. All the people and Helpers flowed and swirled along in the city canyons like the rapids boiling over and around rocks in the mountain gorges back home in North Carolina.

Through my cab windshield, I could pick out all kinds of interesting people from the flow. I saw a terrific long-haired funky-guy striding along wearing a long shimmery trashwear coat woven of plastic strands from six-pack holders. He wore shoes made from milk jugs and a vest from stitched-together flattened beer cans.

I saw a salary-guy wearing a conservative blue suit and dark tie stuffing a sexy holo from a hustler into his pocket. Tonight, I'd bet he'd postpone dinner with the wife and kids to sit in a squirt-strip joint trying to spray a naked dancing girl with a water pistol to make her naughty chem-tattoos show up.

I saw a pretty, long-legged girl shimmering along in an electrofilm dress with constantly changing, swirling rainbow colors. She walked arm-in-arm with a slickie in a light gray randomweave suit, his own electrofilm tie showing alternating Picasso images.

When there wasn't much to see on the particular street I drove down, I could watch my fares in the rear-view mirror and talk to them if they were willing. I enjoyed talking to a family of tourists I took from the Waldorf over to the Met. They chattered so much about all the things they planned to do, I could barely hear the central cab computer report the route with the lightest traffic. They were the kinds of folks who were friendly enough that we could swap stories. They said they were the Newcrofts from Pennsylvania and they'd come to the city because Mr. Newcroft had business he couldn't do virtual-reality in the Mirror, so they all came along. Marie, the mother, designed data-sites in the Mirror for small businesses, and the two girls went to grade school, both real and virtie. The parents believed in real school, not just virtie.

I tried not to stare at the two girls, but I was trying to figure whether they were twins or clones. Probably clones, maybe of the mother. They had her straight little nose, and matching mouths with cute little short upper lips. But I didn't say anything, because it wasn't polite. Clones had enough problems as it was.

They said I was one of the few native-born Americans they'd seen driving a cab. I told them how I'm going to be a writer, and how, after I got my degree in English from the University of North Carolina at Asheville, I decided that coming to New York was the best way to do that. Actually, my degree should have read American Literature, I said, or even more specifically Hemingway. Once I started reading Hemingway, I realized I had to be a writer. He wrote about this guy, Nick Adams, who got into all kinds of adventures, and Nick Adams was really him, but he was me, too. I held up the copy of *For Whom the Bell Tolls* I keep on the front seat.

One daughter asked why I had a paper book and didn't just use an e-reader or download it and read it on my viddie-googles. I told her I preferred printed paper books; they had a kind of literary feel to them you didn't get with a book on disk or downloaded. And besides, I said, the cops ticket cabbies for even having googles in their cars. And passengers didn't trust pavement pilots who might have just come off their breaks buzzbombed from using the virtual reality glasses to immerse in some virtie role-playing game or do something weird in some Mirror sex-joint.

Anyway, just when we reached the Met, I'd gotten around to telling them I came to New York to learn about an entirely new place and to get into the publishing industry. But they had to go before

SOLOMON'S FREEDOM

I finished, so we said goodbye, and they cashcarded the fare with a nice twenty-dollar tip.

After taking a salary in a suit to Battery Park, I got a slim older woman in an expensive red pantsuit, who held some kind of furry animal in her arms. I didn't get a good look at it, but I think it was one of those genetic cat-dog combinations. It made a kind of mewy barking sound once, so it probably was a dat or a cog. She wanted to go to Madison Square Garden, which I should have figured. When I'd taken a fare by there the day before, the screen out front showed a big sign advertising a cat show, with animated images of herds of cats running around. As I think back on it, the screen did advertise a special appearance by an amazing cat, which I guess meant the Cerulean.

After the traffic computer reported I'd get there fastest on Hudson to Eighth up to the Garden, I asked the lady about her animal, but she just made a little polite noise like people do when they don't want to talk. She was too busy looking at some booklet.

It surprised me that she didn't want to talk about her pet. Most of the time, people who buy expensive genetically engineered animals are only too happy to give you the whole story. They take their animals on talk-show programs and rattle on about what it's like to live with a bear-dog or a lion-lamb combination. Or, if it's a really cool animal, they get it a big contract to advertise for a soap or something. My favorite ad animal was the feather boa . . . an honest-to-god snake with feathers. It slithered around in its feathers in some kind of perfume ad.

Or, people take their animals around and exhibit them for fifty bucks a look. I'd seen a hard-shelled, snake-necked snurtle and a furry, winged hamakeet up close at the state fair. The animals had gotten to be a zillion-dollar business. Dad said he thought it was pretty interesting, but Mom and the ladies at the church agreed with all the protesters who picketed the company and tried to get their Congressmen to pass laws against the animals.

Anyway, I didn't get to talk to the lady about any of that, because she really concentrated on the booklet, which I think was a cat-show program. Of course, now I know that the Cerulean's premier appearance was probably why she was so intent.

She and her animal and her program made me particularly primed to pay attention to animals in my back seat. I let her off and had just started to pull away from the curb when somebody pounded really hard on the side of the cab. Scared the biscuits out of me! I thought I'd hit somebody! I stopped, and, as I turned around, the back door whipped open, and this guy piled in with some kind of box covered with his raincoat. He was a thin, bald guy, with beads of perspiration popping out all over his expansive forehead. I asked him where he wanted to go, and he just sat there breathing hard and swallowing. I heard a shuffling sound inside the box. He peered out the window like he was expecting somebody to join him and then told me to take him to the Castle Hotel. I repeated "Castle Hotel" into the microphone, and my traffic computer took a second to find out from central control about open routes. It told me how to get there, but added an ominous "level 4" notification. That's cabbie code for a dangerous area, meaning that we can refuse service if things don't feel right. It didn't bother me, though, because I live in one of the most dangerous parts of the city, and it was broad daylight, so I didn't even flick on the cab's external navcams, which I really should have, it turned out.

I swerved into traffic, cutting off a honking truck, and my passenger put on his googles. I couldn't see his eyes, but I could see that he had this little birdbill of a nose that came to a downward point, with a tip that looked like something was dripping off it. I heard more shifting sounds from inside the box. He mumbled something into the googles . . . a number I guess . . . calling somebody up.

"Where the hell were you, you dumb bastard?" the bird-guy shouted into the mike on his googles.

I knew he wasn't talking to me, but I flinched all the same.

He kept hollering at the dumb bastard. "I don't care! I don't care! Shit, I don't care!" He was really ticked off! "You almost screwed the whole thing up. We got maybe ten minutes before. . ." He glanced up, remembering that I was there. ". . . look, I'll be where we said. You damn well be there!"

I got a stop light and tried as casually as I could to adjust the mirror to get a better view of what he was carrying. His raincoat had slipped a bit, and I could see that his box looked like an animal carrying case, which he'd wrapped his arm around tightly like he was afraid it would get away. More muffled thumping sounds of movement came from inside.

He finished his conversation and perched the googles up on his bald head and again twisted around to look out the back window. He moved like a bird, too, with quick darts of his head, as he checked the scene outside the windows. Finally, my curiosity about him got the better of me.

"So, you been at the cat show?"

"No . . . yes. I . . . uh . . . I had a cat in it."

"That the cat?"

He cackled a triumphant laugh, but sarcastic, like a squirt of acid. "Well, not this one. Another one." Then his face clouded up again. "Just drive, okay . . . Boatright?" He'd checked my name on my cabbie picture ID on the back of the seat.

"Sure, fine, sir."

He twisted around again to look out the side and back windows, and, while he was concentrating elsewhere, I adjusted the mirror again to get a better look at him. He had little ears and a fringe of stubble around his bald head. He had on a dark green shirt with a small anteater logo.

Traffic was light, so we got into upper Manhattan pretty fast. The buildings were old and canky, the newest being mid-twentieth century. Tired, tattered people slumped on the worn stoops and watched the cab go by with blank, bored expressions. A skinny, squirrelly looking guy on the corner stopped in the middle of selling a small white box to a fat guy. He waited until I passed in case I had my cameras on. The cops could use the images as evidence.

"Hereherehere!" The bird-guy said as I neared the hotel, to my surprise stuffing an actual hundred-dollar bill in my money tray. He quickly shoved the door open, and I twisted around really quick, like I was only grabbing the bill, but really so I could look straight-on at him as he got out. That's when I saw it!

The raincoat had slipped even more as he dragged the case out, and a furry, puffy tip of a tail poked itself out of one of the case's little side windows and wiggled back and forth. The tip was colored this shining, glowing blue, like the blue poof-ball from a Roman candle arcing into the night sky. It shimmered when it caught a little sliver of sunlight, mesmerizing me even though I didn't know what it was then.

In an instant, the tail withdrew, and the bird-guy saw the coat had slipped and yanked it back in place. He glared at me for a moment to see if I'd noticed anything. I remember those nasty little brown eyes looking at me and a whole collection of perspiration drops glistening on his forehead. Even though I was sure he hadn't caught me seeing the blue tail, I made it a point to grin innocently back at him and say "Have a great day, sir!"

He slammed the door, and I stayed put, pretending like I was talking to the trip computer, so I could see where he went. Hefting the box at his side, he hurried right past the hotel entrance, to the end of the block, and disappeared around the corner.

And that was how it all started.

www.ingramcontent.com/pod-product-compliance
Lightning Source LLC
Chambersburg PA
CBHW020234260626
47156CB00002B/674